Heir Untamed

Danielle Bourdon

For my grandma Pauline
Thanks for a lifetime of love and laughter

Chapter One

Chey stared at the pink eviction notice on her apartment door with a heavy heart. Setting the bag containing her camera equipment by her feet, she pushed up her sunglasses to read the fine print: *This is your final notice. Pay delinquent rent or face eviction on October First.*

"I know, I *know*. I can't pull money out of thin air." Chey peeled the paper off her door and fished her keys from a pocket. Letting herself inside, she set the camera case by the wall and put her purse down precisely in line with the edge of the couch.

Exhaling a long breath, she placed the eviction notice on a side table, using her fingers to align it exactly with the edge. Turned down for two jobs *and* getting threatened with eviction in one day was a little more than she could handle. Three weeks after losing her regular day job, she was still looking for work. The remaining prospects were grim.

Hands on her hips, she scanned the interior of the apartment with a critical eye. The couches, white with a soft floral pattern, had belonged to her parents. Chey inherited them along with the end tables, a hutch and kitchen table when they perished in a car accident eight months past. A coat rack, fake ficus tree and various antique odds and ends she had picked up at the local flea market. It wasn't much, but it was hers.

Where she would move it, she wasn't sure. What landlord would take her in with no job? Never mind she didn't have first and last—she didn't even have this month's rent. Walking to a calendar hanging on the wall just inside the kitchen, she glanced at the date. *September Thirteenth*. She had roughly two weeks to come up with this month and next month's rent.

Running her fingers over the close up shot of wildflowers on the calendar, Chey appraised her work. When she wasn't employed at a portrait studio, she made calendars and prints to sell through various outlets online. She'd been hoping to pull in supplemental revenue but sales had been disappointingly slow after the last holiday rush.

Flipping the calendar to the next month, she eyed the landscape of poppies. It was a good, clear shot. Somewhat whimsical. The problem was the other million or so photographers trying to make a living the very same way. Getting seen was the hard part. Maybe today someone had purchased a hundred coffee cups with hydrangea or calendars with spectacular sunsets.

Heading into her bedroom, Chey picked her laptop up off her nightstand and sat with her legs folded beneath her on the bed. Opening the cover, the machine sprang to life from sleep mode. Rubbing her palms together, sending up a silent prayer, Chey got her fingers on the keys and accessed her seller account.

She needed sales. Desperately.

With hope in her eyes, she watched the correct screen pop up.

Nothing. Not even one sale.

She checked the account on another site. Just in case.

Nothing there, either.

Bringing up the local newspaper, she surfed to the classifieds and scanned the possibilities. She really wanted to stay within her chosen field—photography—but anything that would pay the bills would suit at this point.

"Day care, fast food, fast food, coffee cafe—all part time." Part time didn't cover her rent and utilities, much less leave enough for groceries. The rent on her apartment, located in a slightly upscale neighborhood with good security in Seattle, was steep. Before the death of her parents, when she'd worked as an assistant to a prominent, private photographer, things had been much better. Since then, everything had taken a nose dive, including losing her beloved job when the photographer moved out of state.

"Convenience store. Full time, benefits in three months. But the pay..." Chey shuddered. It just wasn't enough.

Propping her elbows on her thighs, she brought her fingers to her temple and rubbed. She could hear her mother now, rattling on about stretching the skin around her eyes. Did she want premature wrinkles?

Chey rubbed anyway. It helped with the massive headache about to obliterate her world.

Maybe alcohol was in order.

A hard series of knocks on her front door startled Chey out of her descent into self pity. The manager of the complex wouldn't send people to kick her out early, would he?

Gripped by sudden anxiety, Chey set the laptop aside and climbed off the bed. Smoothing her hands down the burgundy, long sleeved sweater she wore over black slacks, she made her way to the door. When she peered out the peephole, she had a view of a man in a strict, very expensive looking suit.

Oh *no.*

Swallowing a knot of worry, she unbolted the lock and swung open the door.

Two men, hands clasped before them, eyes hidden behind sunglasses, stood waiting. One looked like he could have walked off a runway: dark hair, square jaw, straight nose. He wore a fine layer of short whiskers trimmed just so. His shoulders filled out the black suit perfectly. He held a briefcase in one hand.

The other...was frightening. Lighter haired, face craggy with a long scar slanting across one cheek, mouth a hard line. He was an inch or two taller than his companion, with broader shoulders and a thicker frame. Not fat, she could easily see, just more muscle mass.

These men had nothing to do with the apartment complex. Their clothes were too fine, their demeanor too strict.

"You're not the angels of death, are you? Because that would *really* round out my day," she said.

The dark haired man laughed while the one with the scar cut a vicious looking smile.

"Madam, no. We're not the angels of death. I'm Allar and this is Hendrik," the dark haired man said.

He had a smooth accent Chey found difficult to place. Instead of giving her name, she said, "Yes? What can I do for you."

Just because they looked like a million bucks didn't mean they were on the up and up.

"We are here on behalf of the Ahtissari family," he replied with an expectant pause, as if Chey should know who they were.

She arched her brows, searching her memory for the name. Had these been former clients? It didn't sound familiar. "I don't think I know anyone with that last name. I'm sorry —is this to do with a former shoot?"

"Not a former shoot," Allar said. "New clients, should you agree to come photograph the family and their estate. Is there a coffee shop or somewhere we might sit and discuss business, Miss Sinclair?"

Chey, surprised that he knew her last name, held up a hand. "Excuse me a moment. How do you know who I am?"

Allar opened the briefcase and pulled out one of her latest calendars. The one of old structures at sunrise around Seattle.

"You *are* the Chey Sinclair who shot the photos for this, yes?" Allar asked.

"I'm...well yes, that's my calendar. Who did you say you're working for again?" Chey glanced between men. She wished she could see their eyes behind the shades.

"The Ahtissari family, Madam." Allar slid the calendar into the case and withdrew a business card that he extended between two fingers.

Chey accepted it and glanced down. The royal blue card sported a family crest—two rearing lions back to back surrounded by ivy—and neat silver script: *Allar Kusta. Security.*

Security?

Hendrik also produced a card from an inner coat pocket. He handed it over.

Chey accepted it, noting it was the same crisp color and design. *Hendrik Vello. Security.* Both cards had nothing on the back. They also had no phone numbers or other identifying marks.

"Let me grab my purse and we'll go down to the clubhouse here. It should suit for discussing business. All right?" Chey slid both cards together and glanced at the men. She couldn't afford not to at least listen to their proposal.

"At your leisure, Madam." Allar bowed his head.

Chey eased the door closed, pushed the cards into the slim pocket on her slacks, and bent down to pick her purse up off the floor. Slinging the strap over her shoulder, she plucked her keys off the table and stepped out. Locking the door behind her, she led the men down a flight of stairs and across a cobbled courtyard to a set of french double doors. Here she depressed a code into the keypad specifically issued to residents. Hendrik opened one door before she could reach for it.

Murmuring her thanks, she led them into the main part of the clubhouse. A stone fireplace took up half of one wall, while a kitchen and several conference rooms took up another. Under a vaulted ceiling with heavy beams meeting in the middle sat an array of couches, four overstuffed chairs and a coffee table.

Perching on a chair, she set her purse at her feet and addressed the men as they smoothed their ties and sat down.

"All right then. What are the details of the job?" Chey wasn't surprised when neither man removed his glasses. Allar was the one who replied after balancing the briefcase next to his polished shoe.

"A liaison for the Ahtissari's discovered

your work during a search, presented it to the family, and they narrowed down their choice to you. It's a rather intensive offer, Miss Sinclair. They will request your presence at their estate for the next four months. You will photograph the family in various settings, at various times, along with an extensive portfolio of the house and grounds. They're looking for fine detail, unique perspective and imagination."

Chey twitched in surprise. "Four months? Why so long?"

"They would like snaps of the seasons, Miss Sinclair, and the family engaged in activities suitable to fall and winter. You will need to be there as the foliage turns and the snows set in. I daresay, after viewing your work, that it's right up your alley." Allar smiled.

Four months sounded like an eternity. That was an enormous commitment she wasn't sure she could make. Living on site would prevent her from finding another job in the meantime. As if he read her mind by watching her expression, Allar spoke up before she could.

"They are willing to pay you thirty-five thousand dollars, Miss Sinclair. Half now, and half when you're through. They expect all rights to the photos, as well, just so you're aware."

Chey's mouth fell open. Thirty-five thousand dollars? Stunned into silence, she stared at the two men. That would easily salvage her apartment and allow her to sock a good sized chunk away for savings. She could return in four months and have the luxury of finding a job at will rather than rush to take whatever she had to.

Maybe fast food wasn't in her immediate future after all.

"I'm—wow. That's a very generous offer. I have no problem giving them the rights to the photos." It wasn't standard practice, but for that price, Chey was more than willing to make an exception.

"So you're considering it, then? They're also paying for all travel expenses and any new equipment you might need."

"Travel expenses. I see. Where, exactly are we traveling to?" Chey wondered if the family lived in an exclusive neighboring city. They had money, there was no doubt about that.

"To Latvala, Miss Sinclair. You will be photographing the Royal Family."

"...excuse me?" Chey wasn't at all familiar with the country. She knew it was small and in Europe. That was about it. And what was this about Royals?

Allar's lips ticked like he was fighting off a smile. "The King and Queen? You will be staying at the castle, in your own quarters. Very nice accommodation, I might add. Not every guest is allowed to actually stay in residence with the Royalty."

It all felt like a surreal dream. The Royal family wanted *her* to take their pictures? What might that do for her career?

Light it on fire, an inner voice insisted. What an incredible addition to her resume. She might even be able to go into business for herself when she returned with that kind of experience in her background.

Four months suddenly sounded terribly exciting. "Yes. I accept."

Allar smiled. Reaching down into the briefcase, he withdrew a packet and extended it to her. "This is the contract and confidentiality agreement. All it really says is that you agree to give up rights to the photos and that you will not discuss anything you see or hear with outsiders regarding the family. Obviously, taking 'extra' photos to sell to anyone else, such as a rag, is off limits."

"A rag?"

"Tabloids, Miss Sinclair."

Chey took the envelope. "Oh, of course. No, I wouldn't dream of it. When do we leave? I have a few affairs to get in order."

"As soon as possible. The family is offering a five thousand dollar bonus if we depart within twenty-four hours. When you've signed the contract, I'll issue you your first check. If you need a passport, we'll expedite one. The private jet is waiting at a local airstrip." Allar and Hendrik stood at the same time.

Chey, clutching the packet and her purse, rose as well. When Allar extended his hand for a shake, Chey slipped hers into his and sealed the deal. For an extra five thousand dollars, she would have had everything ready to go by dinner if she had to.

"It shouldn't take me longer than twenty-four hours to get everything in order," she said, releasing his hand. Hendrik didn't offer his, and she didn't push it. Chey had the idea he was the actual security rather than security-negotiator.

"We have your cell phone number, Miss Sinclair. We'll be in touch in the morning." Allar, briefcase secure in his grip, departed the clubhouse with Hendrik on his heels.

Chey bid them farewell, watching until they were gone.

Excited, nervous, and still shocked, she left the clubhouse for her apartment. Royalty, castles, foreign countries oh *my*.

She hoped her life had just taken an abrupt turn for the better.

. . .

The private jet was the most luxurious thing Chey had seen in a long time. White leather seats and sofas trimmed in gold sat in a spacious layout which included a television, a wet bar and a kitchen further back near the bathroom. Opulence reigned, from the fine carpet to the sleek color scheme to the little luxuries such as fine chocolate, wine and the plush make of the furniture.

They had been in the air for eight hours already, the plane cutting through a dark sky with impressive speed. Before leaving Seattle, she had deposited the first check in the bank, pre-paid her rent for six months, and arranged for her neighbor to collect her mail.

As promised, Allar had a passport waiting when they arrived in a sedan to pick her up. Contracts signed, the only thing left to do was travel.

After an hour layover to refuel, they were back in the air. The stewardess, attired in a neat, dark blue suit, served her an early breakfast of fruit and toast at her request. Chey didn't want anything heavy sitting on her stomach when they landed. While she ate, she lamented that she hadn't had any time in Seattle to do research on the Royals. She wondered what they were like, and how many of them there were. Just how big was the castle?

Despite herself, intrigue crept in. She was going to be photographing Royalty. Rulers of a kingdom. Would they speak to her, or would they simply pose as she instructed and ignore her?

What a surreal turn of events.

Out the small oval window next to her seat, Chey watched the sun breech the horizon. At least they would be landing in daylight. She didn't want to arrive in the dark, when the impact of the country and the castle would be diminished.

An hour later, the captain announced their imminent arrival. Handing over her empty bottle and her plate to the stewardess, she buckled up and awaited landing. She caught glimpses of Latvala bathed in colors of the sunrise. It was difficult to tell any detail from this height, but she made out patches of farmland and a snaking river with ease.

The smooth transition from air to ground happened in a matter of minutes. After landing, taxiing and disembarking, Allar and Hendrik showed her to a waiting limousine. Painted a deep, royal blue, the vehicle sported silver accents which carried over to the plush interior.

Luggage stowed in the back, Chey watched the private landing strip fall away in favor of pristine, wild landscape that stretched as far as the eye could see. Chey likened the view to something primordial, lost to time, something one might find if they'd inhabited Earth a half million years ago. Broad meadows, mist clinging to the tops of the grass, were flanked by the distant outline of trees. The forest sprawled for miles, promising abundant wildlife and more importantly, privacy.

To her right, after a stand of Spruce fell away that had been choking the side of the road, the terrain gave way to the sea. Waves crashed hard on a shore with stretches of creamy looking sand interrupted by collections of boulders thrusting up from the ground. It was primal, beautiful, undisturbed by the advance of man.

Chey wanted to get out and start

photographing immediately.

"We're here," Allar said from the seat across. He gestured to the left.

Chey switched her attention from one window to another, gasping in shock as the Ahtissari family seat came into view.

Nestled in broad swathes of open land sat a castle worthy of fairy tales. It had everything a castle should: incredible architecture, turrets with spires, an iron toothed gate and the family standard flying high.

The only thing missing was a moat.

After passing through an initial checkpoint, they approached the iron gate. It cranked up a foot at a time as a guard, dressed in a dove gray uniform with silver trim, stepped out of the guardhouse to greet them. Exchanging brief words with the guard, the driver cruised through a fifty foot long tunnel that emerged into an immense courtyard. A fountain stood in the middle, carved of back-to-back lions standing on their hind legs, front claws raking the air.

Supported by eight columns, a porch ran the length of the main entrance, offset by enormous archways and broad, flat steps leading to a set of carved double doors.

The effect was imposing, stunning.

Chey could only gawk at the grandeur and the sense of history that emanated from every stone. She hadn't been able to appreciate the sheer enormity of what she was getting into until now.

When the car came to a stop, the driver got out and opened her door. Allar and Hendrik disembarked, standing aside to wait.

Following them out of the limousine, she shielded her eyes and swept a look all the way up the facade of the castle, awed by the size and scope. It was one thing to look at it out the tinted window of a car, and another to actually stand before it, feeling as impotent as a speck of dust on the pavement.

Relieved that she'd had the foresight to wear a business suit instead of something more casual, she smoothed a palm down the pale pink pencil skirt and straightened her matching short coat with a tug. The collar of a crisp white shirt showed beneath. On her feet, a pair of taupe heels added a modest three inches to her five-nine height.

More guards in military uniforms flanked the front doors.

"We'll be meeting with the liaison first thing," Allar said, escorting her to the steps. Someone else obtained her luggage from the trunk and toted it behind.

"The liaison?" Chey parroted, falling in at Allar's flank. Hendrik, she noted, hovered in periphery.

"Yes. He is who you will report to, work through. When the family wants pictures, he is the one that will relay all pertinent information." Allar preceded her through the front doors that one of the guards opened.

Chey sucked in a breath as she crossed the

threshold in his wake. A foyer with a domed ceiling opened off the entrance, stunning with its arching beams and sparkling chandelier the size of a small car. Gray stone blended into cream walls and gold gilded baroque molding. A round table in the center held a floral display so colorful and striking that it nearly dominated the entire room. Shafts of sunlight spilling in tall windows illuminated two Great Halls that stretched to either side of the foyer, the décor a study in antiques and rich fabrics that probably cost more than she made in a year.

It was the most striking interior Chey had ever seen. Paintings from the hand of masters lined the walls and statuettes in marble stood near potted plants that added a touch of greenery to the austere décor. A double set of stairs swerved from the foyer to the first of several floors, ending in a long landing that seemed perfect for a Royal family to stand and look down at visitors from behind a banister carved in white.

"Miss Sinclair?"

Chey realized she was standing there gawking like a schoolgirl. "Yes?"

"This way, please." Allar waited between the staircase in another hallway leading deeper into the castle.

"Of course." Chey fell into step behind Allar. He led her past smaller rooms set off that main artery in the castle toward a smaller archway to the left. Here, doors to libraries, parlors and other formal gathering places opened off each side. So many that Chey wasn't sure how anyone didn't get lost on a regular basis.

Allar took a sharp turn through an open doorway toward the end of the hall.

Chey discovered a great room—great by her standards, at least—with a high ceiling, ancestral paintings in gilt frames and lavishly appointed furniture situated near a fireplace a grown man could walk into. Persian rugs decorated the floor and floor to ceiling windows at one end threw early morning light through the entire space.

"This is where the first photos will take place," Allar explained, gesturing to the collection of divans and settees gathered at one end.

"It's certainly a beautiful room." Chey had a difficult time dragging her attention off the splendor long enough to concentrated on work related things.

A man, perhaps six foot in height, with salt and pepper hair combed carefully away from his face swept into the room. He wore a strict suit in navy with a white shirt and tie.

"Miss Sinclair, I imagine," he said, approaching with an appraising once over.

"Hello, yes." She glanced away from Allar to the man she suspected to be the liaison.

He extended a well manicured hand once he reached her, a vague smile on his lips. "I'm Mister Urmas, your liaison to the Royal family."

Chey shook his hand and released. "Allar mentioned that. My pleasure, Mister Urmas."

"Likewise. I realize you have just arrived, but the first photos are scheduled for just after lunch in this room. That leaves you roughly three to four hours to set up your equipment and plan your poses. I'll have your regular luggage taken to your room and have the rest brought here, if that suits you?" He arched a brow, one hand smoothing down the front of his tie.

"I...yes. Of course." This was what she'd come here to do, after all. Work. If she could just ignore her surroundings, it would make things a lot easier. "How many family members will I be photographing this afternoon?"

"The King, the Queen, two of their four sons and their significant others, along with their daughter. Seven altogether. A few things," Urmas said, meeting her eyes as if to indicate the importance of what he was about to say. "There is standard protocol when dealing with the Royal family. Do not speak unless spoken to, try not to gawk and fawn, hm? They expect professionalism. Certainly do not ask if you can take your photograph *with* them, and should you need to pose a hand or a body, it will be done with suggestion and not touch, understood?"

Chey listened to the instruction with a hundred questions crowding the end of her tongue. She wasn't sure if she was surprised at the sudden way Urmas put her in her place or not. The easiest thing to do, was agree. So she did.

"Of course."

"Excellent. I'll show you to your quarters once the first session is over. There are certain floors and rooms you are not allowed into, despite that you're here to capture the essence of the Royal family. I'll let you know which those are. Otherwise, the guards are aware you're here to photograph the castle, the gardens and the grounds. You may come and go as you wish in between sessions with the family. I should like to see daily updates and photos," he said, taking a sleek, black phone from his pocket. "Also. This is yours to use while here. It is a secure phone that I'll be contacting you on. My number, as well as Allar's and Hendrik's, are already in there. If you find yourself in trouble, or with questions, use this."

"I understand. Thank you." She accepted the phone, noting it was a make and model she'd never heard of.

"I'll leave you to your planning, Miss Sinclair. If you have need of anything, Allar will be close by." Urmas smiled, pivoted on a polished shoe, and departed the room.

Chey set the phone on a small round table just as several men carrying her equipment came in.

Time to get busy.

. . .

Once she delved into work, Chey became distracted with the details. It took her a half hour to set up her camera and tripod to best use the available light spilling in the windows. She knew this room had been chosen for the diffused glow casting it into shades of gold and meant to use it to her advantage.

Men and women came and went the entire time. Allar hovered near a wall, at the doorway itself, and back near a corner as she worked. Maids flitted in and out, taking care of last minute cleaning errands. They did not wear traditional little skirt uniforms, but athletic type pants in dove gray and white shirts with three quarter sleeves. Their pristine white tennis shoes squeaked on the floor where ever the Persian carpets gave way to marble or stone.

Once she was ready to go, Chey nudged the sofas and chairs into exactly the formation she wanted. She might change the arrangement at the last second depending on the people involved, but for now, this suited.

A half hour before the appointed time, Urmas made another appearance, thoroughly inspecting her equipment, the angle of the lighting and the furniture. He seemed pleased. Informing her time was short, he swept back out, shoes clicking smartly with his brisk stride.

20

Ten minutes before the arrival of the Royals, Chey checked her appearance in one of the overlarge, framed mirrors. She didn't want to present as scattered and harried. Chey preferred to look professional, in control and confident. The pink suit, a subdued color instead of a brash one, complimented her olive complexion. She also thought it went well with her dark hair. Worn half up and half down, the mass fell past her shoulders in soft, wavy layers. The make up she'd applied so many hours ago made her high cheekbones look sharper and accentuated the blue of her eyes. A dusky rose lip color had, alas, begun to wear off.

Smoothing her palms over the narrow indent of her waist, she turned away from the mirror just as eight men swarmed into the room. Imposing, dressed in black on black business suits, eyes covered by sunglasses, they could only be the next stage in security.

Four broke away from the group; two split off to check her equipment and two more approached her without smiles.

"Excuse us. We'll need to make sure you're not carrying anything, Madam," one said.

Chey, taken by surprise at the abrupt way they entered her personal space, had no time to protest. One man simply began patting her down while the other picked the phone Urmas had given her up off the table.

For the first time since her arrival, Chey wanted to scowl and slap at hands. The security guard never touched her inappropriately, yet he also did not miss any pertinent places she might be hiding camera phones, microphones or weapons. He was exceedingly thorough and seemingly indifferent to basically feeling her up.

It was over before she really got steamed, the phone returned to the table while the men retreated to stand at different points in the room.

Was this how it always was for Royalty, even in their private residence?

Or was it her presence among them that upped the security level?

Chey returned to her camera and equipment to double check that none of the security guards had accidentally messed with the settings. Everything was in place, exactly as she'd left it.

A flurry of movement outside the doors preceded the prowling entrance of a man with dark hair combed away from his face. Unlike the guards, this man wore a regal mantle like some men wore cologne, effortlessly and with devastating effect. He commanded attention by the sheer force of his magnetism, which filled the room to overflowing.

It was impossible, Chey thought, *not* to follow him with her eyes.

Allar appeared at her shoulder, head bent to murmur near her ear. "I know it's difficult, but try not to stare to the point of his discomfort, hm?"

Before Chey could think to shape an answer, the unnamed man pinned a look directly on her. He had eyes the color of coffee grounds, so dark she couldn't tell where the brown ended and the black of his pupil began. The way he assessed her felt like a shredding; her character, her morals, her soul. He cocked his chin a fraction and arched a brow.

"*Miss* Sinclair," Allar said, this time with more urgency.

Chey looked away from the dark haired man and fumbled with her camera. But she felt the lingering stare from across the room. He had to be Royalty.

Two women strode in next, both blonde, one natural and one born of a bottle. They were of a similar height and wore upscale, demure clothing that complimented their coloring. Neither so much as glanced Chey's way. The taller of the two paced her way toward the dark haired, dark eyed man like she owned him.

Indeed, perhaps she did. When she arrived at his side, she slithered a long fingered hand through the crook of his elbow and tilted a sleek hip against his. Whatever endearment rolled off her tongue was in a language Chey didn't understand.

The man smirked and looked out the window instead of at the blonde, replying in a voice too low to make out his words. The sound nevertheless resonated, a pleasant burr on the skin.

A third woman stalked in, heels clacking on the floor. Right off the bat, she had a petulant demand. "How long is this going to take?"

Beautiful by anyone's standards, the brown haired, blue eyed woman flounced herself into a lean against the side of a chair, exhaling in a very obvious display of being put upon. She caught sight of Chey and looked her up and down in a way that might have stripped other women to their core. Then, just as fast, she dismissed her.

"Only as long as it takes for everyone to arrive. I shouldn't imagine the actual picture taking will be an extended affair," Urmas replied as he entered from the hall.

On his heels, another man strode in, hair black as pitch, green eyes sweeping the room before landing on the natural blonde. He went straight to her and murmured in her ear.

Chey decided the dark haired men were the brothers Urmas mentioned, the women their wives or intended. The pairings made sense and the men weren't security, which left Royals.

The petulant woman must be the sister.

"Those two there by the window are Mattias and the woman he dates, Viia. Mattias is second in line to the throne behind his eldest brother, Dare," Allar murmured.

Chey now had a name to go with the man who exuded so much primal magnetism: Mattias. It suited him.

"The other male, with the green eyes, is

Paavo. Third in line to the throne. His fiance there is Aurora. And the little beauty who is impatient to start is Natalia. All we await now are the King and Queen, then we may begin." Allar straightened after he completed filling Chey in on who was who.

"Thank you," Chey said under her breath.

Mollified to know she'd at least guessed the status, if not the rank, Chey fixed her attention on the equipment. Although it was already set and ready, she went over it again. Just to keep her fingers and mind occupied. She wondered if this was the way it would be for every shoot, with the security heavy and the Royals staggering in at intervals.

"Oh, and because you're American, you're not expected to curtsy to Royalty, but it would be a mark in your favor if you learned and displayed your lesser rank at some point," Allar added.

Chey noted the men in the room had all at least bowed their heads in deference. She wasn't sure how she felt about curtsying to anyone, especially people who were not of her home country. Curtsying wasn't a custom anyway in America—why should she do it here?

When in Rome, do as the Romans do, she reminded herself. It sat ill with her, as well, hearing of her *lesser rank.* Mildly irked, she hid it behind a professional veneer.

"I'll take that into consideration." Chey kept her voice low, like she worried she might disturb the waiting Royals.

"Excellent." Clearly, Allar approved.

A disturbance in the hallway alerted Chey to the arrival of the King and Queen. They entered with a surprising air of normalcy. The King, a tall man with salt and pepper hair and a neat mustache-goatee combination, held himself with importance but also nonchalance. Dressed in a sharp suit of navy pin-stripes, he wore a draping mantle of fur around his shoulders, denoting his status and title. His wife appeared almost bored, but not rudely so, dark hair swept up into an intricate coif held with tiny pearl pins. Her eyes were the exact same color as Mattias's. She wore a dress in gray so light it was almost white. The beaded lapels matched the three inch cuffs.

Everyone in the room stopped what they were doing to either bow or curtsy.

Chey felt out of place and diverted her attention back to her camera. She didn't want to stare and be reprimanded nor did she feel comfortable attempting an awkward curtsy. She had trouble getting past the notion that these people ruled an entire country, had ruled it for generations. It was incomprehensible that someone had so much power and influence, even though the rational part of her mind understood that this was the way it had been in many countries for centuries.

The moment passed as quickly as it had arrived, much to her relief. She watched the pomp and circumstance, all the people coming and going that had some sort of duty to the Royals, with no small amount of subdued awe. One staff member approached the Queen carrying a pillow with a gilded staff nestled on top. The Queen picked it up with care and tucked it regally into the crook of her arm like a mother with a newborn baby.

"And *that,* of course, is King Aksel and Queen Helina. You will be doing several sittings with just them in the coming days," Allar explained in a low voice at her ear.

"I imagine so, considering their status," Chey whispered. After all, she was here to capture their likeness for the history books and future generations.

"How would you like your first pose?" Allar asked.

Chey didn't need to stop and contemplate. She pointed to chairs and sofas and added names to go along with them. Women in the front, Queen in the center, the men standing behind.

Allar stepped away and approached Urmas, relaying the information. Urmas, in turn, began gently suggesting seating, brisk and businesslike.

Chey stepped behind the camera to size up the scene. Maids hurried in to arrange the clothing just so, brush off shoulders and fix pieces of hair at the last second.

Queen Helina suddenly glanced to her left when Viia left Mattias's side and strode out into the hallway.

"What is she doing?" Helina inquired.

"Mother, she is not family--" Mattias began to explain, but Helina cut him off.

"She will be shortly. Bring her back in," she insisted.

"Nothing is set in stone. You should have asked me before you invited her," Mattias said, a muscle flexing in his jaw.

"Aurora is not technically family and she's in the photo," Paavo said. "Or is this your subtle way of saying she should go, too?"

"Try not to tax your brain too much, little brother. I care not if your *fiance* is in this picture. A woman I'm *dating* is much different." Mattias exchanged a dark look with Paavo.

After a glance between the Queen and the King, Aksel lifted a hand to gesture. "Bring Viia back in."

Mattias hissed and stared forward.

Viia re-entered the room with a haughty set to her shoulders. She acted as if this was her due, something she had already rightfully earned.

Chey paused, using the view finder of the camera to stare at the Royals in a way she could not otherwise. The tension in the room rose by leaps instead of fractions. She re-issued instructions to Urmas to fix the seating arrangements and prepared to get the session under way.

Soon, the Royals were situated, spines stiff,

shoulders square. Chey wanted to tell them to relax a little, to smile. They wanted to come off as more human, unless she missed her guess, and this wasn't exactly fitting the bill.

Taking the remote shutter in one hand, she straightened to view the group with the naked eye over the top of the camera. Right away her gaze locked onto Mattias's. Ensnared, Chey traded a look with him that left her a little light headed. Tearing her eyes from his face, she got back to business.

"Ready?" she asked the group. There was no way she was going to try and coordinate this part through third parties. The Royals would just have to deal with her personally. "On three, two, one..."

She squeezed the bulb in her palm. Not one of the Royals smiled. They wore stern expressions, thin mouths and an overall tense mantle that would carry over into the photo.

"Once more, please." Chey repeated the countdown, studiously refusing to meet Mattias's eyes again. She could feel him staring. Was he unhappy with her for putting Viia next to the Queen?

Settling into a routine, Chey organized—via Allar and Urmas—to take singles of the King and Queen, of the King with his two sons, and the Queen with her daughter.

The entire time she avoided making eye contact with Mattias, though she felt the weight of his attention often.

When she'd taken upwards of thirty photos,

she knew the Royals were at the limit of their patience and she was thoroughly done with organizing poses through Allar and Urmas.

She took down her equipment as the Royals filed out of the room, busying herself with her task. The security detail followed them out, leaving just a handful of liaisons and staff in their wake.

Relieved to have session one out of the way, Chey carried one bag while Allar carried the rest with Urmas in the lead for her private suite.

She couldn't wait to change, relax and investigate more of the castle on her own.

Chapter Two

Chey stood in the middle of her suite, trying to comprehend what she was seeing. Left alone at last, she turned a slow circle, eyes raking over the pristine walls in a color she could only describe as powder blue. Pale, subtle, offset by ivory colored crown molding. Gold accents—baroque shapes, tassels on pillows, a faint leaf design—added a regal flair to the décor.

This was the living area, separate than that of the bedroom. A collection of divans and wingback chairs, all keeping in the color scheme, bracketed a coffee table that looked direct from the renaissance age. Masterpiece paintings of foxhunts and beautiful landscapes covered the walls. More antique pieces of furniture sat in corners and stunning Persian rugs covered large swathes of floor.

She felt like she shouldn't touch anything. As if this was a space in a museum not made for actual living, just viewing.

Entering an archway, she found herself in the bedroom. The blue, white and gold theme existed here as well. The bed, a monstrosity that took up a good portion of one wall, sported a column at each corner with gauzy netting looping through gold painted iron scrollwork overhead. Whimsical bedding fit for a King looked plush, expensive and comfortable.

The bathroom, as large as her apartment back in Seattle, was a private affair with a huge walk in closet, shoe shelves and built in drawers that pulled out of the wall. A tub that looked more like a jacuzzi dominated the center, with a tall walk in shower, extensive cabinets and double sinks in marble adding to the appeal.

She wondered what in the world the King and Queen's bedrooms must look like if the guest suites were this lavish. Living here for the next four months would be no hardship.

Drawn to double french doors in the main room, she stepped out onto a private balcony overlooking the back bailey, another gate and the acreage beyond. It stretched as far as the eye could see.

More buildings and what had to be the stable sat off to the right past the bailey gate. Horses meandered in fenced pastures, though Chey saw no one riding. Just the stable hands grooming, walking and training.

Anxious to explore, she unpacked all her luggage and changed from the pink skirt suit into jeans, a thin sweater of turquoise with sleeves pushed to the elbow, and hiking style boots. Grabbing a smaller camera from her bag, she departed her room.

Urmas had been explicit in his instructions about where in the castle she was, and was not, allowed. The entire third floor was off limits. Home to the Royal family, only they, their staff and the guards had availability. Two different rooms on the main floor had been barred, as well as a walled garden and a specific dining room.

But the rest of the castle and the grounds she was free to roam. The guards all knew who she was, and what her purpose was, so she could expect to be given hassle free passage.

She spent an hour on the second floor, beginning to snap pictures of some of the fine detail. The corner of a painting with half the person in the portrait visible. A long shot down a hallway with light spilling in a round stained glass window.

There were literally thousands of shots to take like this.

What she tried to capture this time around were the vantages normal people might never see. Angles of Royalty, of the money and power that made the family who they were.

Walking backwards away from a doorway leading to a huge library, camera up at eye level, she bumped into a body behind her.

Startled, she stopped and whirled, an apology already on her lips. Expecting a guard, Chey found herself face to face with Mattias. Leaning against the wall, one ankle crossed over the other, still in his suit from the photo shoot, he smiled. It was a temperate smile, not unlike a wolf walking into a sheep's pen might wear.

"My apologies, I didn't--" she began, before Mattias cut her off.

"Why are you apologizing? I put myself in your path," he said, sliding his gaze down to her camera and back again. "I believe we have not been properly introduced. I'm Mattias Ahtissari."

Chey let the camera come to rest against her chest, confident the strap around her neck would hold. She searched his face, his eyes, unsure what to do, exactly. Her mind went on the fritz when the reality hit that she was sharing space with Royalty.

"You have no name?" Amusement flashed through his dark gaze. "Or has the cat got your tongue?"

"No, no—I mean yes, of course I have a name. Chey. I'm Chey Sinclair." Remembering about the curtsy, she performed an awkward one.

He laughed, brows arching when she dipped. "Well, Miss Sinclair. Someone has been giving you instruction. I didn't think Americans went for all that pomp and circumstance." He straightened from the wall and held out a well manicured, long fingered hand.

Licking her lips, she glanced down at his hand, then around at the hallway, positive it was a trick of some kind and the guards would rain hell down around her head for thinking to touch him.

34

He rumbled another laugh, still holding his hand out. "I don't bite, if that's what you're worried about. And if it's the guards—don't worry about that, either. I choose who I greet and who I do not."

Caught out, she looked back and slid her hand into his. Chey shook with meaning, with purpose, grip firm. "We usually don't. Well, *I* usually don't. It's nice to meet you."

Just when she would have pulled her hand free, he turned it over and brought it to his lips. There he brushed a kiss across her knuckles before releasing.

Chey, dumbfounded, stared like a green schoolgirl. Why was he kissing her hand? Was that another Royal custom? Why, oh why, was he even paying any attention to her? She was the lowly photographer, not worth his time. Right?

"The pleasure, Miss Sinclair, is mine." He retained strict eye contact while gesturing to the hall. "Walk with me?"

Unnerved by the weight of his attention, Chey inclined her head and turned to walk with him along the hall.

"I thought to take some pictures of the interior. There are so many unique ways to capture the essence of your home, it's hard to know where to start," she said, sticking to the safe subject of work.

"I suppose there are. It's a lot of ground to cover. But then, you will be here a while, which gives you plenty of time to be thorough." He clasped his hands behind him, pacing languid as a tiger beside her. His accent rolled smooth from his tongue, raspy and cultured.

"Almost four months. It's the longest I've ever been on assignment anywhere. I'm looking forward to finding the shots no one else has yet." She risked a glance aside. He was watching her instead of the hallway, pinning her with dark eyes that gleamed with intelligence and interest.

"Four months. A lot can happen in four months," he said in a musing tone. "What does your family think of you being gone that long?"

Chey felt a pang at the thought of her parents. "My parents perished in a car accident almost nine months ago. I have no siblings."

"I'm sorry to hear that. No husband, either?"

"No husband. Not even a boyfriend."

"I find that difficult to believe. Surely there is *someone* you hold even a small amount of affection for?"

"Not any longer. I broke that off when I caught him on a date with not one, but *two* other women." Chey snorted, forgetting herself. Covering the snort with a delicate cough, she brought a hand up to check the weight of the camera hanging around her neck. A distraction for herself if nothing else.

Mattias laughed. He had a deep, rich laugh

that shook his chest and shoulders. "Well. Then I suppose he deserves what he gets."

"What he got was a heck of a one night stand. Good riddance." Her candor showed through speaking of her past. Chey thought she should temper her sometimes bold tongue —and then decided not to. After all, what did it matter? She was here to work, not to impress a Prince. Especially one who was so obviously involved with someone.

Another laugh greeted her candid reply. "A kitten with claws. I would have never guessed."

"And yet your tone suggests that was *exactly* what you expected," she countered. Why was she calling him out? He was a Prince for crying out loud, and here she was, baiting him. Testing his penchant for truth.

Mattias stopped walking so quickly that Chey found herself five steps ahead before she realized he wasn't at her side any longer. Just that fast, she regretted her wayward tongue. She'd offended him by talking back, or challenging him. On his own turf, no less. Stifling a cringe, she turned back to see him regarding her in that intense way he had, eyes narrowed to slits.

Don't get yourself kicked off the assignment before it even gets started, idiot, she chided herself. She'd already spent a good portion of the initial payment on rent. Chey didn't have the luxury of being fired and having to pay the money back. Before an apology could tumble from her lips, he smiled. A subtle curve of his mouth that accentuated the cleft in his chin.

"I hadn't realized just *how* astute you are, Miss Sinclair. Well done. That, indeed, is precisely what I was thinking. Can you guess what else is on my mind?" he asked, resuming a slow walk. He didn't take his eyes from her, even when he drew abreast.

Chey broke eye contact, exhaling in relief. She hadn't offended him. Continuing their walk, she stared ahead at the upcoming juncture in the hallway. His loaded question gave her pause. It was the kind of question men who had been trading electric looks with a woman asks when he expects her to play coy and mention something about sex or bed.

"You're hoping I'll take a few extra pictures just for you." Because if not sex, what else would he have sought the photographer out for? Chey used deductive reasoning to come to her conclusion. It wasn't all that difficult to understand he wanted something from her. Princes probably didn't hobnob with the hired help. When he didn't immediately reply, Chey glanced aside.

He wore a devilish grin. "It's like you know my very mind. I'm impressed. I would like to request you snap some shots of Viia. By herself, if you can manage it, and when she's not aware you're doing so. Natural, candid pictures is what I'm after."

So that's what this was all about. Chey

checked a wry expression before it could take hold of her features. "Of course. It's why I'm here. Sooner than later I'll become familiar with the routine, which will give me a greater chance to catch her in unaware moments. Consider it done."

"Excellent." He stopped long enough at the juncture in the hallway to lay a warm hand on the back of her shoulder. "I'll check with you in a few days to see if I need to help set something up should you not be able to find her alone."

Chey paused when he did, half turning to face him. The weight of his hand was light, yet she felt the heat from his palm through her shirt with ease.

"That sounds fine. Have a good rest of the day." Chey decided she must be imagining the sparks between them. Except when she met his eyes, she found him watching her like he might devour her on the spot. They spent fifteen seconds searching each other's gazes before he pivoted and stalked away along the other corridor, heading god knew where.

Chey watched him go, the feel of his hand lingering long after he was gone.

It was high time to put some distance between herself and the castle. She headed for the stairs, trotting down to the lower level with the intent on finding the stables.

Perhaps a ride would clear her head.

. . .

A hundred and fifty photographs later, distracted by the beauty and serenity of the stables and horses, Chey finally decided to mount up and ride. She left her camera safely with the stable master, assured it would come to no harm. Swinging up over the back of a buckskin mare, she took hold of the reins and guided the equine toward a section of forest that the stable master suggested. He spoke of riding trails, a sparkling creek, stunning vistas and a small lake nestled in the greenery.

Leaving the stables at a trot, Chey allowed herself to enjoy an old hobby that had fallen by the wayside back in Seattle. She had ridden often before her parents passed, taking to winding trails through stunning scenery that never failed to calm her mind.

Here, too, was the promise of spectacular terrain. She found the trail easy enough, sinking from the first kiss of dusk into the dappled shadow of enormous trees. The branches and leaves tangled overhead, whispering and creaking in a gentle breeze. Slowing the mare to a brisk walk, Chey let her pick her way along the trail. One hand rested comfortably on her thigh.

She found the meandering creek and eventually, the lake. Already she mourned the loss of her camera and promised herself she would return the following day. Maybe in the morning to catch the sunrise and in the evening to take pictures as burnt orange rays slanted across the sparkling surface of the water. Astride, facing the lake, Chey breathed in the scent of bark, earth and damp foliage.

It really was a gorgeous spot. She loved how the trees crowded close to the lake on the far end, and how boulders the size of small cars took over half way around, lending rugged beauty to the scene. Out in the middle of the lake, several fish flopped and splashed.

"What do you think, girl, should we come back tomorrow?" Chey talked to the mare, rubbing a hand along the sleek neck under the mane. The horse nickered and bobbed her head, tail swishing against her flanks.

Just as Chey decided they better head back, before the sun slipped so low she lost enough light to see by, the mare twitched to attention, ears pricked forward. It was a marked change from the lazy stance of a moment before.

"What is it? A squirrel? Maybe a raccoon?"

A snap and crack of twigs jerked Chey's attention to the left, where a cluster of trees made the shadows a little darker than everywhere else. She let the mare stay put, waiting to see if a deer hopped into sight. That's what Chey thought it was—a deer. The snap of twigs had been too solid to be something as small as a squirrel or a raccoon.

Nothing appeared.

The deer probably caught her scent and was standing there frozen, afraid to move.

Chey reined the buckskin around, kneeing her into a walk for the trail. They had diverted off of it to get a better look at the lake. Ducking a few branches, Chey stroked her hand once more along the buckskin's neck, giving her a confident pat. The animal really was a joy to ride.

Reaching the trail, the mare instinctively wandered onto it and headed in the direction of the stables, as if she knew her rider was ready to return home.

Another snap of wood swerved Chey's attention over a shoulder. She was in time to see a shadowy figure slip between trees, on horseback no less, obviously following her.

If it were one of the guards, he would have just made himself known. The guards, she'd discovered even after this short of a time, had no problem announcing themselves.

So who could it be?

Unease trickled down Chey's spine.

Urging the mare into a canter, she thought to put some distance between the shady figure and herself. A stable hand would have called out. What if someone had managed to slip onto the property to do the Royals harm?

The sound of hoof beats on the path behind her whipped Chey's attention back. To her shock, the horse charged onto the same trail, its shadowy rider bent low and half obscured by a branch and leaves.

"Yah!" She dug her heels into the startled mare's side. The buckskin surged forward, ears pricked back. Chey guided the equine along the path, fear gripping her shoulders to the point they ached.

The sun inched lower, stealing even more light from the day. Now the trees aided the advance of shadow, dipping whole sections of the trail into a gray gloom.

To her horror, the hoof beats behind her grew louder. Closer. Someone was in open pursuit. Yet they didn't call out for her to stop, or halt, like a guard should have.

Veering swiftly off the main trail, Chey took the mare overland, between the tree trunks, desperate to lose their follower. It was treacherous business, with roots, rocks and other debris poised to trip the buckskin. Bring her down, and Chey along with her.

Twilight faded, gloom pervading the forest. Between one minute and the next, Chey found it harder to see. The mare, more sure footed than Chey gave her credit for, dashed around trees and over a fallen trunk. It was low, only a foot or so off the ground, but Chey was not an experienced rider in jumping and had to hang on with both hands.

In the next second, Chey found herself falling. Falling to the right, toward the ground, with a body impacting her from the left. A heavy, strong body that knocked the breath from her lungs when they landed. Grunting, she twisted beneath the weight of the attacker and jammed her heel against his shin. One fist swung out with the intent of cracking him

—or her—on the jaw.

She landed both blows, for all the good it did her. The feel of short whiskers against her knuckles let her know it was a man that she'd struck. His head snapped to the side while his body sprawled, pinning her shoulders like a wrestler might.

"Get off me!" she shouted. She knew she was too far from the stables, from help, for her yelling to do any good.

A resonant voice thick with a Latvala accent sounded above her. "Hold still. Who are you and why are you riding unaccompanied through the woods?"

"I was told I could ride this trail, if you don't mind!" Chey stilled, breathing hard. The scent of both fresh and dried leaves beneath her vied with the masculine scent of leather, oil and a light, spicy musk she would have found pleasing any other time. Finally, she got a good look at her attacker as they both stopped struggling.

Glittery blue eyes the color of a clear sky glared down at her from a face shaped by a straight nose, defined cheek bones and a chiseled jaw. Hair so light brown it was nearly blonde, cut through with golden streaks from time in the sun, hung to the top of his shoulders. Half the front had been scraped back into a tiny ponytail that somehow made him seem all the more male. He wore a navy, thin ribbed sweater that outlined the hard muscles of his shoulders and chest.

Chey rarely thought of men as beautiful—but this one was.

He got up and pulled her with him, hardly out of breath for the chase and tumble to the ground.

"By who? Start talking before I arrest you and haul you to jail." He didn't bother to brush clinging bits of debris from his navy dockers. Putting his hands on his narrow hips, he glared down at her from a height of at least six-three.

Shaking with anger, Chey acted before she thought. As if her hand had a mind of its own, she cracked her palm against his face. "I'm a *guest* of the Royal family, you ass. No one mentioned any escort when they said I was allowed to use the stables!"

His head barely twitched for the slap. Absorbing the impact, he narrowed his eyes and took a threatening step closer. "*Visitors* don't roam the lands without escort. I think I know the rules."

Chey held her ground, chest rising and falling rapidly. How dare he. "Then I guess you need to check in with your superiors more often. Because I was given leeway to ride and explore as I please."

"And just which member of the family are you a guest of?" he asked in a silky voice, like he didn't believe her. "Viia? Aurora? Can't be Natalia."

"They flew me here from the United States to take pictures of the family and the grounds.

I'm a *guest* here for the next four months," she spat, wiping the side of her wrist against her mouth.

The rude man barked a laugh. "Is that so? A photographer, eh? What's the old man trying to do, capture the 'essence' of the Royal family and their holdings?"

Taken aback by his sarcasm, Chey narrowed her eyes. "Are you always this cynical about your employer?"

He pulled a cell phone from the front pocket of his trousers and took a few steps back. The man had the gall to smirk. "Sweetheart, if I find out you're the paparazzi, you're going to have a lot more to worry about than how cynical I am."

"I'm telling you, I'm their guest--"

"So you've said. We'll find out soon enough, hm?" He pressed his thumb over the screen of his phone and put it to his ear. A rapid stream of his mother tongue hit the air, none of which Chey understood.

In between his conversation, he whistled toward the horses, both which stood nearby between two trees. The creatures wandered back, hooves clopping over leaves and other debris.

As full dark descended, Chey fretted about finding her way back to the stables. The last thing she wanted to do was ask this man for anything, directions included.

Lowering the phone, he slid it into his pocket. "Chey Sinclair, photographer for hire.

Looks like your story pans out. Next time you go riding, do so before dark and stay out of the woods."

"But I plan to come back here tomorrow morning and take pictures by the lake. After all, I'm here to catch the *essence* of Latvala, lakes and landscape included." If it took her all night to find her way back to the castle, then it was well worth the satisfaction she felt at not allowing him to order her around. Turning away, she brushed at her clothing and approached the buckskin mare.

"You're going to get yourself hurt, that's what. Do you even know your way home, little lady?" He strode up to his steed and swung up into the saddle with effortless ease.

"If I don't know the way home, surely the mare does." Chey, sore from the tumble, refused to acknowledge it. Setting her foot in the stirrup, she mounted up and settled into the saddle. One look around confirmed her worst fear; she had no idea which way to go. Everything looked the same with the tall trees blocking sight of the castle and the darkness obliterating any trail she might have left in her headlong rush to evade him.

"I won't have more serious injuries on my conscious because you're too stubborn to ask for help. Follow me back to the main trail." He reined his horse around and let it pick its way through the underbrush.

"And why should I ask *anything* from a man who sees fit to tackle innocent women to the ground?" Reluctantly, Chey gave her mare lead to follow.

"If you don't, you'll get lost out here. There are worse creatures to run across out here than myself," he said with a laugh.

"Ugh."

"What was that?"

"I had a bug in my throat."

"Of course you did."

"What was your name again?" she asked, feeling truculent and impatient to be away from his presence.

"Sander. That's S a n d--"

"I think I know how to spell it."

"Sander Fisk, in case you need my last name when you turn me in to the proper authorities."

Chey was grateful for the shadows that hid the stain on her cheeks. That had been precisely why she'd wanted to know his name. "That's funny. I thought *you* were the proper authorities."

"I'm the head of security. That doesn't mean I'm exempt from reprimand. Watch the low branch." He ducked under a heavy bough.

Chey did the same. "And how long have you worked for the Royal family?"

"All my life. I was raised here. My mother was a chef up until her death a few years back."

No wonder he didn't seem worried over his job. Even if she mentioned his actions to Allar or Urmas, it was unlikely Sander would get so much as a dressing down. It was his job to protect the Royal family no matter what. She'd been a trespasser for all he knew.

Still. The entire ordeal irritated her.

"So quiet all of a sudden," he said.

"I'm thinking."

"It takes that much effort?" His voice was rife with laughter.

Chey glared at the back of his head. Or what she could see of it in the gloom. He was impossible. Refusing to be baited, she said nothing as they re-entered the main trail and turned toward the castle. She presumed, anyway. It was hidden behind the forest they rode through. Picking pieces of leaves and twigs from her clothing, she flicked them onto the ground. Then she gave the hem of the sweater a neat tug.

At the head of the path, where the meadow broke open away from the trees, Sander brought his horse to a halt. Chey drew alongside, breathing a sigh of relief to see the enormous castle in the near distance. Lights illuminated the surrounding wall and spilled out windows from many rooms and towers. It was beautiful even at night.

"I'm sure you can find your way from here," he said, apparently not going any further.

"Of course I can. The stables are just over there." She kneed her mare into a walk, anxious to put distance between them.

"You're welcome," he said to her departing back, for gratitude she hadn't given him in leading her back to open ground. "Maybe next time you'll actually remember to bring your camera."

Chapter Three

"Infuriating bastard." Chey stared at the ceiling of her bedroom, unable to sleep despite the jet lag dragging at her bones. The unexpected meeting in the woods was still on her mind. She'd made her way back to the stables, and then the castle, with little trouble. After finding the kitchen and a late dinner, she'd retreated to her room to begin sorting through the photos she'd taken on her first day in Latvala.

Now the hour was somewhere beyond midnight and the encounter kept flashing behind her eyelids, replete with soundbites from their conversation. It even eclipsed her meeting with Mattias.

Sitting up, she pushed the covers back and swung her legs to the ground. For bed, she'd worn a velveteen track suit the color of butter. It was soft against her skin and modest should she decide to wander the halls when everyone was was asleep.

Which was what she wanted to do.

Grabbing her camera off the desk, she checked the batteries and, still barefoot, exited her bedroom. The castle at night proved to be just as intimidating as it was during the day. There was something ancient and mysterious about the feel in the air, as if the castle had absorbed all the joys and horrors of its occupants over the centuries.

She wished she could capture that on film. Somehow portray the structure's longevity and the sensation of secrecy.

Drawn toward the stained glass window at the end of the hall, she found several interesting angles to capture the spill of colored light by. From there she headed downstairs, snapping a pale marble bust of who might have been an ancestor. Milky eyes stared sightlessly into the hall, the lush mouth and hard jaw even more defined in half shadow. A big library drew her next, the shelves illuminated from moonbeams falling in through the panes of a tall window. Books with leather spines crammed every shelf, perfect for shots from the side. Because she couldn't help herself, she straightened one or two books from their crooked lean.

She became aware that she wasn't alone when the faint tink of ice in a glass hit her ears. Glancing toward one of the high-backed chairs facing the fireplace, Chey groaned. Someone was sitting there. All she could see was an arm, a hand, and a tumbler.

"Can't sleep?" Mattias asked.

"I'm sorry, I didn't know anyone was in here. Excuse--"

"You needn't rush off. Come, sit." He used his glass to gesture at the opposite, empty chair.

It was the last thing Chey wanted to do. While he intrigued her, she also knew he was involved, and she didn't want anyone else walking in and getting the wrong idea. On the other hand, she might not get this kind of opportunity again. It wasn't every day that she got to sit and chat with Royalty.

Chey crossed the room and eased down into the chair, sitting on the edge rather than making herself comfortable in the plush confines.

Mattias, bare chested and bare foot, wore only a sleek pair of black lounge pants that sat low on his hips. A swirl of dark hair started on his chest, made a line down his stomach, and disappeared beneath the band at his waist. He was in excellent physical condition. Muscular, honed.

She took all that in with a quick glance, heat rising in her cheeks. "Do you always sit and contemplate cold fireplaces?"

Mattias regarded her in that way he had, as if he was trying to figure out all her most personal thoughts and feelings. "Sometimes. Especially when I have much on my mind. I didn't expect to see you taking pictures this late."

His tone said, *I didn't expect to see you at all this late.*

"As you guessed, I couldn't sleep. It's difficult to when you're staying in a castle for the first time. I'm restless or something." The urge to explore distracted her as much as her unique circumstances did.

"I imagine so. Tell me what you think of our home, then." He invited her to elaborate as if they'd known each other a lot longer than one day.

Chey exhaled and glanced around the extensive library. The mantle over the fireplace held what looked to be priceless statuettes and brass candlesticks.

"It's hard to put into words this soon," she admitted. "Of course I think it's lovely. But there is something else, too. Almost as if the castle is brooding."

She glanced back to Mattias in time to see his brow arch.

"That is an interesting way of putting it," he said.

"That's how it appears to me. And secretive. If these walls could talk, I can only imagine what they would say."

"Don't you think most ancestral homes are like that?" He swirled the remains of his drink around his glass and lifted it for a sip. Watching her over the rim.

Chey shifted on the seat. "I don't know. I've never been to other ancestral homes. This is just how yours strikes me."

"Like most castles, this one has roots in dark parts of history. Men—and women—have been killed here. One of my ancestors, Prince Gustav, was hanged in what is now the East garden. This castle has been laid siege to, has seen Royalty born within its walls, and has weathered its share of scandal." Mattias finished his drink and set the glass aside on a small table.

Fascinated, Chey studied his eyes. "Is that the garden that is off limits to me?"

"Yes. It is one my mother and sister favor and they do not like to be disturbed. Would you like to see it?" His mouth curved into a somewhat devilish smile.

"Are you certain I won't get in trouble?" Chey wanted to see the garden more than ever now, but Allar's strict warnings echoed through her mind. Under no circumstances was she to enter the garden.

Mattias pushed up from the chair with leonine ease. "When a Prince invites you *anywhere* here, take that as a golden access pass. If anyone troubles you over it, send them to me."

Chey was tempted to tell him about the incident with Sander earlier in the woods, even if it wasn't related, and promptly dismissed it. She wasn't prone to 'tattling' and in reality, no harm had really been done. It didn't mean she wasn't still irked at Sander Fisk, but she wasn't going to out him.

"I'll remember you said that." Chey stood when Mattias did, hyper-aware of his naked chest, the lean angles of his hips. Any woman would be, she told herself, and tried to put it from her mind.

"If you don't take any pictures, no one will ever know you were there but me anyway, and

I promise not to tell." He winked over his shoulder.

"You know, you almost seem normal." Chey blurted the thought before it had time to run through the filter between her brain and her mouth. Cringing, she braced herself for his anger.

Instead, Mattias laughed. Leading her out of the library, he padded along the floor with a languid, unhurried stride. "We're people, above all things, with feelings and emotions and whatever else. I might be Royalty, but I'm not untouchable."

"You all seem that way. Or you did when I was taking the photos. I guess it's just status. You have loads, I have none." Chey paced at his flank, eyes ahead on the hallway and not aside on his back. Safer that way.

"We're born what we are. Some of us have no choice but to follow the course expected of us."

"Well. I mean, you *could* decide you didn't want to be a Royal and go live elsewhere. Right? That's still your choice." Chey rounded the corner when Mattias did, heading down a restricted hallway. Already her skin started to prickle with nerves.

"That's where duty and honor step in. I *could,* but where does that leave my family? Where does that leave the people of this fine country who believe in us? Our ancestors lived and died to make this a country we could be proud of—and I am *very* proud of our country

—and I would not consider abandoning the duty of carrying on." He glanced aside, a brow arched.

Chey chewed in the inside of her lip. She realized just how outclassed she was, how small in comparison to his position. It was quite a shocking revelation to comprehend the gap of separation. At the same time, standing next to him in his half clothed state—he seemed like any other man.

Meeting his gaze, Chey tilted her head in a way that said she understood. Mostly. "I get it. About honor and duty. At least as much as I'm able to coming from the background I have. Family is important, but we only answer to ourselves and those we come in contact with. It's not like we have an entire country to think about as well."

"Some think it a burden, and it can be. At times, I wish nothing more than to sink into the ranks of the unknown, so that I may move about the world without a camera always in my face. Yet there is no other position I would like to hold than to be second in line to the throne." Mattias guided her through another turn, and another, entering a short hallway with double french doors at the end.

"I don't think the first in line was at the photo shoot today," she said, fishing for a little more information. "In fact, two of your brothers were absent, yes?"

"Mm, yes. Dare, who will be crowned King when father passes, has been...set up to meet a woman mother dearly wishes he would consider taking to wife. They were in Italy last I heard. Gunnar, the youngest brother, returns tomorrow from vacation with his wife, Krislin. Otherwise, you've met Paavo and me as well as our sister, Natalia."

"I'm never going to keep all this straight," Chey muttered.

Mattias chuckled and opened one of the french doors, allowing her to enter first. "Dare, Mattias, Paavo, Gunnar and Natalia. Easy."

Chey repeated the names under her breath as she stepped from the castle into the secretive, walled garden.

. . .

She understood immediately why the garden was the queen's favorite, and why it was off limits to everyone else. Stepping into the walled space was like stepping into Eden. Chey guessed it was a half an acre, impressive considering it was attached to the castle itself, with cobbled walkways, extensive foliage and stone fountains in the shape of cherubs. Water burbled from each one, and from a meandering creek that fed into a small pond. Tiny white lights decorated trees, adding a whimsical flare.

Right away, Chey brought the camera up to snap a few shots. If Mattias brought her here to begin with, she doubted he would say anything about the photos. He didn't. He paced alongside, hands behind his back, watching both her and the surroundings.

Chey could see his attention swing out and then back every few steps.

"It's really beautiful. I can see why they love it so." She stepped over a small bridge that straddled the creek to get a shot of a gazebo smothered in vines and tiny pink flowers.

"I suppose. Personally, I prefer more rugged pursuits." Mattias sounded unimpressed with the garden.

"Such as?" Chey swung the camera around and snapped off a shot of Mattias framed by the castle, just about to cross the bridge.

His gaze met the camera, enigmatic and as secretive as the garden they stood in.

Chey lowered the camera and smiled. "I figure Viia will enjoy that as much as you will enjoy the ones I take of her."

His lips ticked into a somewhat wry smile. "Perhaps she will."

"Stop there on the bridge and I'll take another. That's a great shot." Chey pointed with a finger right where she wanted him. To her surprise, Mattias complied. He leaned a sleek hip against the arching rail, slid his hands into the pockets of the lounge pants and crossed one bare foot over the other.

He was the picture of a rake, dark hair sweeping his brow. Even in repose, Mattias commanded the same sense of animal magnetism and regal bearing as he had earlier, dressed in his fine suit.

Chey tried to capture that aspect of him, though really, she thought to herself, it wasn't hard when Mattias exuded it with such ease.

"What the *hell* do you think you're doing?" a feminine voice snapped from the shadows.

Startled, Chey lowered the camera. Natalia stood on the footpath, tumbler in her fingers, glaring straight at Chey. She wore a diaphanous gown of white that lapped at her ankles and scooped low on her chest.

It didn't take Chey but a second to realize Natalia was six sheets to the wind. Not drunk enough to stagger or slur, but drunk nevertheless.

"I'm--" Chey, about to explain, got cut off by Mattias.

"She's with me. Stay your tongue, sister," Mattias said, warning clear in his tone.

Natalia never looked away from Chey. She pointed a finger around the glass. "She is *not* supposed to be here. What will mother say?"

"She will marvel over the pictures of her favorite private place." Mattias stepped away from the rail, sliding his hands out of his pockets. When he glanced at Chey, there was a message easily read in his dark eyes: *Do not ever speak of what you see here.*

Chey nodded and crossed the bridge back to the other side.

"*Our* private place! She's violated it and now we can never come here without wondering if she's skulking in the shadows, taking pictures of us!" Natalia screeched in fury, her beautiful face torqued into a mask of disdain. Cocking her arm back, she hurled the glass at Chey's head.

Mattias shot a hand out, but wasn't quick enough to block the hurtling tumbler.

Lucky for Chey, she'd been watching the altercation like a hawk, and ducked her head away from the projectile. Glass shattered against the edge of a fountain. Shards rained over the cobbled walk like bits of diamond. Shocked at the woman's anger, Chey made eye contact once more with Mattias, who had been scowling at his sister. He inclined his head toward the double doors, indicating it was high time to leave.

"Don't you *ever* come here again!" Natalia shouted.

Chey departed the garden with quick strides, concerned that Natalia's bellow would bring the guards. Breaking into a trot, she found her way along the private corridor, sure that someone was going to catch her here by herself and raise the alarm. The hallways, so far, were empty.

Chey made it back to the main hall, which was common ground for her, and breathed a sigh of relief. Taking the stairs at a jog, she headed for her bedroom, wondering if Natalia's drinking was routine. Mattias hadn't seemed surprised to find her inebriated. In fact, his whole demeanor had become one of spare tolerance, as if he had to deal with it more often than he preferred.

In the safety of her bedroom, Chey closed the door and leaned against it, out of breath from the stairs. What a way to end her first full day in the Royal castle.

Hopefully, it wouldn't be her last.

Chapter Four

The little hidden lake at sunrise was spectacular. Chey stood behind the tripod, lining up a stunning shot lengthwise across the water. She'd risen at dawn and hit the stables right after, intending on capturing the photos she wanted despite the previous day, and the previous evening's events.

Tugging habitually on the hem of the pale blue sweater she wore over jeans, Chey straightened out a wrinkle in the material before turning the tripod a click to the left. It gave her a whole other vantage with a different section of the lake to focus on.

Behind her, tied to a tree stump, the buckskin mare nibbled grass, tail swishing flies away from her flanks.

All in all it was a peaceful morning. A good way to start the day. Later, after lunch, Chey had another photo shoot with the family. This, however, was her time, and she put it to good use.

Worried over the garden escapade, she refused to dwell on it. She knew Mattias would keep their confidence.

The question was—would Natalia? She would have to admit being drunk and unruly, though perhaps that wasn't unusual and no one would care.

"You're up early," a masculine voice said behind her.

Chey yelped and nearly knocked her camera over. She caught the tripod as it started to tilt and fall. A hand shot past her to catch it, too, leaving her entire right side pressed up against Sander's.

"...don't sneak up on people like that! I almost ruined a very expensive camera." Annoyed, she got the tripod upright—with his help—and stepped far enough away that she could swing around and glare at him without their bodies touching.

He had his hair pulled back into a low tail this morning, the ends brushing the collar of a palomino suede coat. He wore layers beneath: steel gray flannel and a white tee shirt. He'd left the zipper and buttons undone so that the white showed all the way to the waist of his jeans. Boots that matched the suede, engraved with a brogue design on the the arch and the toe, completed his attire.

Chey took all that in with a quick sweep of his person.

"I wouldn't have let it fall. Didn't you hear me coming? You should pay more attention to your surroundings," he countered in a blasé tone.

"I'm sorry. I'm busy with *work*. You know, that thing you should be doing? I have no doubt you've gotten all the information on me, so you know I'm allowed to be here." Chey huffed and stepped back behind the camera.

Now she was distracted.

Fantastic.

"Are you always this bitchy?" he asked, crossing his arms over his chest.

Chey straightened again, set a hand on her hip, and gave him a withering look. "I'm not bitchy. You're simply impossible to deal with."

"Most women think I'm charming."

"Well, I'm not most women."

"Really." It wasn't a question.

"What is it you want, exactly, Mister Fisk?" Chey hoped she put enough irritation in her voice to make him hurry along. The way he looked her over just then was one hundred percent male. Annoyed that it made her skin prickle and hear heart pick up speed, she narrowed her eyes and glared.

"To let you know where you may and may not go. To the lake, the creek dividing the property on *this* side, but no further into the forest. And not at all on the east side." He pronged his fingers and held his arm out in the direction she was not allowed to wander. His eyes never left hers.

"But I'm supposed to capture the countryside--"

"*Not* beyond the lake or the creek, and not at all to the east," he repeated with an edge to his voice. "Capture as much of the countryside over here as you like."

"Why?" Chey wanted answers.

"Because I said so, and since I'm head of

security, you'll do as I say." He crossed his arms over his chest once more, staring at her like he dared her to defy him.

Chey flashed her palms at him in the traditional sign of surrender. If he was going to be *that* adamant, she wouldn't push it. "All right, all right. I won't wander beyond those--"

A gunshot ripped through the early morning mist.

Close enough to be easily heard, yet far enough not to be directly in their vicinity.

Before the echo died, Chey found herself on her back, flattened by Sander. She gasped, the wind knocked from her lungs, staring up at him with his suddenly sharp eyes, thin mouth and predatory air. He snapped looks across the lake, in every direction, even behind them.

"Was that a--"

"Yes," he hissed, then brought a finger to rest against her lips. In effect silencing her. When he glanced down, he conveyed his wish for her to be quiet. Danger, he told her without speaking a word, lurked in the forest with them.

Chey shuddered beneath him. Every breath she took was laced with the scent of him; sandalwood, musk and spice, a subtle note of amber and leather oil. She felt every contour of his muscular body, from his toned chest to the cut of his abdomen and the thick pressure of his thighs.

There was no way she could get up, even if she wanted to.

66

Reaching back, he dug out his phone. After another sweep of the area, he glanced down at the face while he thumbed over the surface.

Chey couldn't see what he typed. It was brief, that was all she knew, because he used one finger and only for a few moments. Code, perhaps, sent to other cell phones to put people on alert.

He ducked when another shot rang through the day. Breath hot on her throat, he spoke there near her ear.

"We're going to leave here. Stay low, follow me and follow my lead. Do *not* stand up, and do not speak."

Chey nodded her understanding rather than agree vocally. He wanted her silent, she would be silent. Fear licked along her spine and spread out through her limbs. Someone was shooting—but at who? Them? The thought made her blood run cold. Surely it was just a mistake, someone out shooting at birds or engaged in target practice.

But then why was Sander on alert like this? He wouldn't be, she argued with herself, unless he knew the shooting was unscheduled or out of the ordinary.

He stared down at her face while he slid the phone back into his pocket. His eyes glittered, mouth pinched into a thin line. Then he was moving. Sliding off her with too much ease, staying low to the ground as he belly crawled toward the nearest trunk of a tree.

Chey, lamenting leaving her camera out in

the open, rolled onto her stomach and did exactly as he did. Any second she expected to hear another shot or feel the whiz of a bullet pass her head.

When Sander reached the tree, he used it for cover, rising to a crouch. He gestured for her to come up to her feet at the tree next to his and made a point of indicating she should face the same direction, blocking sight of them from the east.

Chey reached her tree and climbed to her feet, positioning herself as he wished. This skulking about was not her forte; she left the decisions to someone who obviously knew better.

He inclined his head, holding her gaze. Telling her she'd done well. After another few moments, he crept from his tree to her own, using a hand on her hip to guide her to another tree, and another, then behind a cluster of boulders that gave them broader coverage.

Leaving the horses tethered, they exited the area near the lake in the most clandestine manner they possibly could, with pauses every so often so Sander could listen. No other shots had been fired since the last.

Using foliage for cover, he grasped her hand and led her into a light jog, moving quicker through the forest. Chey felt safer the further they got from the initial starting point, but not safe enough to run fully upright or to speak.

It seemed to her they jogged for several miles, enough to begin to put a stitch in her side. She wasn't a runner by nature. Chey preferred fast walks with little hand weights on flat ground. Hardly in a position to complain, she sucked it up and kept going, one hand cinching the spot near her ribs that ached.

A clearing broke open ahead, giving Chey a glimpse of a cabin nestled on a few acres surrounded by trees. One story, it had a large wrap around porch, a peaked roof and several rocking chairs adjacent to the front door.

Sander paused at the last tree before the clearing and pulled his phone from his pocket. Chey watched him scan through a few menus and draw up what looked to be a blueprint.

He pulled her by the hand into the clearing itself after that, traversing the distance between the forest and the cabin at a quick jog. Chey felt strangely exposed even for that short time.

Loping up the front steps, he released her and opened a screen door, then the regular wooden door, holding it for her to pass through first. Chey ducked under his arm and stepped across the threshold. The inside matched the outside for quaintness. Pine walls made the atmosphere cozy, along with plush leather furniture in shades of brown and sage green. A rock fireplace took up an entire corner, with a mantle stretching across the front. To the left sat a dining area leading into a well equipped kitchen. The open floor plan made it seem like there was more square footage than there actually was, though the cabin was not small by a long shot. A hallway divided the cabin down the middle with a handful of doors leading left or right.

Sander closed both doors and engaged two dead bolts on the latter.

"We're going to stay holed up here while the military sweeps the grounds, all right? This is bullet proof, the whole thing, even the windows, so you don't need to worry about anyone taking pot shots at us from the trees." He thumbed in another message on the screen of his phone before sliding it away into his pocket.

"What's going on? Why would someone be shooting?" Chey stood near the back of one of the sofas, tearing her eyes off the warm décor to glance at Sander. He seemed to fill the cabin with his presence.

"Don't know yet, sweetheart." Sander passed her for a closet in the hall where he took out a handgun and a fresh magazine. After sliding the clip into place, he checked the safety, closed the closet door, and tucked the weapon into the back of his pants.

Chey watched him retrieve the gun and wondered why he hadn't had one on him already. Distracted by the circumstances, she asked, "Were they shooting at the castle, trying to pick off one of the Royals?"

"The castle would be an almost impossible

target to hit from where we were. Too many trees. None of the Royal family are out on the property, so it's unlikely any of them were the target." He stepped past her into the kitchen, pulling two bottles of water from the fridge. Sander offered one out when he returned.

"Thanks. But I don't understand," she said, taking the bottle and cracking the lid. She hadn't realized how thirsty she was until she saw the bottle.

"It could be any number of things. A new maintenance member foregoing the rules about guns and shooting game in the woods. Someone who entered the property overland, from the back, making a statement." He drank from his bottle, gaze cutting to the windows every so often, on guard despite the military sweep or the bullet proof cabin.

"But don't they have the whole perimeter monitored? How could someone just walk onto the property?" Chey couldn't get comfortable. She paced a few feet one way and then another. Already a quarter of her water was gone. An askew coaster sitting on a side table was re-centered as she passed by. Somehow, she resisted the urge to fluff and straighten the pillows on the sofas.

Sander chuckled. A deep, resonant sound that shook his chest. "Chey, the family seat sits on more than two thousand acres of land. Do you realize how many miles of terrain that is to monitor? Not to mention it backs up to a preserve that is totally rugged, almost impassable unless you're a climber or a hiking enthusiast. We save the strict monitoring for the immediate acreage surrounding the castle. It's easier to catch someone coming in for a direct strike that way than to waste manpower prowling every inch of the property markers. Don't get me wrong—we have measures in place in the woods, but nothing like what we have closer to the castle itself."

"I guess that makes sense." She had another swallow of water, then glanced at his eyes to find him following her progress with his own. "So you don't think we were the target, do you?"

"'We'? No. *We* weren't. *You* might have been, but not we," he said.

Shocked, Chey stopped pacing. "What? Why would anyone want to shoot at me? I just arrived yesterday. I don't even know anyone that well yet for crying out loud."

"Simple deduction, sweetheart. No one knew I was going to check the lake today to see if you were going to come back like you said you were, so they couldn't have known I'd be there. Not to mention that whoever it was, if they *were* shooting at you, had to have followed you into the woods from the castle. It was a preplanned event, and I am not a part of that equation." He sounded matter of fact.

Chey frowned. What he said made perfect sense. All except the *why* of it. Could Natalia have been so angry over Chey seeing her drunk that she hired someone on the property to get rid of her?

Surely not. Such an extreme measure wasn't necessary, not when the Princess could have stomped her foot and barked orders for Chey to simply be fired. There were less hectic ways to get her off the property than murder.

"It wasn't me, then. Couldn't have been. I'm thinking it was something other, like you mentioned. Someone shooting when they shouldn't have been. An accident, or just an oversight." That suited her mind much better than the alternative.

"Mm." The sound Sander made was nothing more than a low murmur of either agreement or consideration.

"How long will I have to stay here? I'm supposed to have a photo shoot with the family this afternoon." Chey finished her water and walked the bottle to the trash. It was full, almost needing to be emptied. If this was a vacant cabin, why was there so much trash?

"Until they sound the all clear."

"Does someone live here?" she asked, changing the subject. On her way past the counter, she straightened a fishing magazine that had been sitting cockeyed. Old habits died hard.

"I do. The King had this place built fifteen years ago, then lost his taste for 'adventuring' on his own property not long after, and it sat empty for almost a decade. Since I'm here so much, they had no problem with me moving in."

"I see." That seemed reasonable. He'd been raised on the property, and probably lived in quarters up near the castle previously. Having his 'own' private space was probably preferable to a standard room. "Until they sound the all clear? When might that be?"

Sander finished off his water and pushed off his lean from the sofa. "When they're done with the sweep, they'll call."

"I'm just looking for a time frame, here. Two hours, four? More?" Chey paced through the living room, pausing here or there to straighten a thing, even if it didn't technically need it.

"Chey. They'll be done when they're done."

She glanced up and caught his gaze over the back of a couch. He didn't sound angry, only decisive. His tone said that she might as well make herself comfortable for the duration. She wasn't going anywhere for a while.

. . .

"*Flore* is not a word." Chey stared at the game of Scrabble, at the word Sander had spelled out, with a wary eye.

"Yes it is." He sat across from her, coat stripped from his shoulders, the gray flannel shed in its wake. It left him in an unassuming white tee shirt that fit his muscular torso well.

Chey hated that it was such a distraction. "What does it mean then?"

"It's what you do when you're not exactly engaging in foreplay, but sort of. *Flor-ay.* The in between. That stage when you think you like someone enough to flirt, and they're flirting back, but it's still first-base with a bunch of crap batters up next who might or might not advance you to the next level." His expression was utterly deadpan.

Chey laughed outright. "You're so full of it. I call *crap* on your word. You get no points."

"See? The next batter just struck out, leaving Joe on first base." He lamented the faux first-baser's loss with a melodramatic sigh.

Their game had been ongoing for more than a half hour. Much to Chey's surprise, Sander proved to be more than willing to pass the time badgering her about her knowledge of English, and attempting to use non-words to gain an advantage. He was comical when he wasn't being an ass, and shockingly good natured overall. Every few minutes he glanced at the windows or his phone, still on high alert despite his banter.

"That's all right. Joe needs to learn *strategy.* Which happens to be my next word, meaning I just won the game." Chey snapped down her final tile with a pleased grin.

Sander frowned and bumped the board with his thigh when he stood up out of his chair. The tiles scattered across the table, and his, *"Oops"* was so contrived that Chey gasped, pointing a finger at his subterfuge.

"You did that on purpose. Cheater."

He smiled a wolfish smile, tipping the board up so the rest of the tiles would fall to the table top. He closed the board after that and set it back inside the box.

"So what if I did? What're you going to do about it? Take my picture?"

"Cheaters and losers are required to make the winner lunch," she retorted. His smart comments amused her now, rather than annoyed her. A welcome change from their abrasive first meeting.

"You're on. You get to clean up the rest of this, then, while I get started." He waved dismissively at the remains of their Scrabble game.

Chey muttered loud enough for him to hear. She was positive that he wouldn't know the first thing about cooking. He'd probably filched meals from the castle as a child like everyone else, leaving him short on culinary knowledge. Scooping the tiles into her palm, she dumped them into a baggie, then situated everything in the Scrabble box just so before sliding on the lid.

"You want something more potent to drink? Wine, a mixed cocktail?" he asked from the kitchen.

"Isn't it a little early to hit the alcohol?" Chey wondered if he was a drinker. He seemed familiar with booze. She set the Scrabble box exactly against the edge of the table, perfectly aligned and straight.

76

"It's supposed to be my day off, and I'm pretty sure it's noon somewhere, to use a familiar phrase." He took down two highball glasses from a cupboard, then opened the refrigerator door.

"Supposed to be? Oh. Me. I almost forgot that this is *work* for you." She approached the bar at the edge of the kitchen and plopped down onto a barstool. From her vantage, she could see everything Sander was doing. As well as the gun still poking up from the back of his jeans.

He cut another wolfish grin over his shoulder. "I'm not officially on the clock, so I'm allowed a drink. What's your favorite?"

"Lately it's been watermelon vodka over Sprite. It changes monthly."

"Mm. I know I don't have watermelon vodka, but I have the makings for a Tequila Sunrise."

"That actually sounds pretty good. It was my drink about two years ago." Chey watched him fish out the tequila, a top shelf brand, orange juice from the fridge and grenadine last.

"So, what, you cycle through drinks as soon as you're sick of them?" he asked, deftly pouring the ingredients into one of the highball glasses.

"Pretty much. Doesn't everyone?" She murmured her thanks when he delivered the glass to the counter top.

"I don't know. I think people usually find

something they like and mostly stick to that. Not that you can't order whatever else, but I tend to see people picking favorites." He returned to the alcohol and poured himself wine instead of a mixed drink. Then he started taking out packages and things from the fridge.

There were worse places she could be, Chey decided, than sitting in a fine cabin in the middle of the woods watching a man with a physique like *that* make lunch. Even if the lunch would probably taste like shredded cardboard. If only there hadn't been a shooter in the woods earlier, this would have turned out to be a rather pleasant day. A shocking revelation considering the first meeting she'd had with Sander.

"You sound like you know from experience." Chey sipped at the Sunrise, finding it perfectly mixed.

He took a frying pan out from under a cupboard and arched a brow over his shoulder at her. "I *do* get out once in a while, you know. It's not all work, all the time."

"Yes? And what do you do for fun? Besides provoke innocent women." Chey buried a grin into her drink when he snorted.

"I provoke *non*-innocent women." He leveled a specific look at her, laughter in his eyes, and turned back to the stove. Shortly, the distinct scent of cooking steak filled the kitchen.

"Are you saying I'm one of the non-innocent? Sander Fisk, how dare you." Playfully petulant, she leaned an arm on the counter, glass curled in her fingers.

"I know, right? I'm playing with fire." He worked while he talked, more efficient in the kitchen than Chey would have given him credit for.

"What else?" she asked.

"It might be more appropriate to ask what I *don't* do. I enjoy hiking, fishing, rock climbing, canoeing, skiing—pretty much all outdoor sports. You?" He shredded lettuce and cheese and brought out a bevy of peppers, tomatoes, cilantro and other hot sauce ingredients.

Chey arched a brow. He was going to make hot sauce from scratch? "I like taking pictures of all those things. Before my mother passed, we used to go horseback riding and spend time at the beach."

"Not bad pursuits. You should try canoeing before the weather turns. Latvala has some fantastic rivers." He paused, then added, "I'm sorry to hear about your mother. That must be difficult."

"It was. *Is.* It's only been just under nine months since the accident that took her and my father." Chey had a longer drink, turning her mind from the painful recent past to thoughts of the future. It was better that way. The topic of her parents was still fresh and hurtful. "Maybe I will try the canoeing, then. You should suggest the best place to go."

"I'll do you one better," he said, stirring the

meat. "I'll take you myself."

Chey twitched in surprise. It wasn't an unpleasant prospect when she thought about it. He knew Latvala much better than she did.

He glanced over his shoulder, both brows arched.

Realizing she hadn't answered, and that he probably thought she didn't want to go, she nodded. "Yes. Sorry. I was imagining what it would be like and whether I should bring a camera or not."

"I won't let us tip over. Bring the camera," he said, turning back to the food. He dumped the hot sauce ingredients into a food processor and turned it to grind. In short order, the meal finished cooking. He carried plates of hot steak strips to the counter along with the shredded lettuce and cheese. Sliced tomatoes, avocado dip and chips accompanied the flour tortillas he heated over the stove.

"I can't believe you made all this," Chey said. She set her glass down and accepted a plate from Sander before beginning to fill a tortilla with fajita fixings.

He set the hot sauce, now in a small bowl, beside everything else. Using the toe of his boot, he pulled a stool around to his side and straddled it so they were facing each other across the counter.

"I *did* mention that my mother was a chef, right?"

"I know, but I didn't think you actually learned anything from her." Chey smiled, sheepish at the confession.

He laughed. "Why wouldn't I? It wasn't like she shooed me out of the kitchens at every turn. She was the type, anyway, that demanded I learn how to take care of myself."

"It seems like it worked out pretty well for you," she said, leaning over her plate to take a first bite.

"I suppose it has." Sander filled three fajitas for himself, dolloped guacamole on his plate and added a few chips. After a quick scan of the windows and a check of his phone, he dug in.

"Anything?" Chey asked when he glanced at the phone.

"You'll have to put up with me for another two or three hours, then you can head back to the castle." Sander eyed her while he ate. He took large bites, holding the fajita in two hands.

"Did they say whether the photo session is still on?" Chey watched his mouth instead of his eyes for a long minute, then dropped her gaze to her plate.

"Mm. Yeah. They're pushing the time back a little. You'll get details when you return. Something about the big garden, I guess." Sounding unimpressed and disinterested in the Royal pictures, he took another bite of his food. "They have your camera, too, and the mare."

"Oh good." Chey, relieved to know her camera hadn't been left to the elements, dipped a chip into the guacamole and ate it. The guacamole was as good as everything else. "Thanks. For all this. Keeping me entertained while we have to wait, making lunch. I have to admit—it's really good."

"Don't worry about it. I don't get company out here all that often. It's nice for a change." He chuckled and finished off fajita number two. "Thanks," he said after he chewed and swallowed.

Chey wondered if Sander was involved with anyone, a thought that struck her out of the blue. There were no signs a woman lived here with him, which meant little to nothing. He could be dating someone outside the compound, preferring to meet up with her on his off time away from the castle. A quick check of his left hand turned up no ring on his finger. It wasn't concrete proof that he was single, but it indicated he wasn't married, at least. Feeling the weight of his stare, she glanced up from her plate to find him watching her.

Holding his eyes, she let the chemistry between them build until the air all but sizzled. Unable to deny the attraction, she finally concentrated on finishing her lunch. What were the odds that she would run into two attractive men on this trip? Mattias had the intrigue of Royalty going for him and Sander...was just Sander. Blunt, abrupt, cocky, self assured. Although they had a rocky start, she found herself enjoying his company more and more.

Sliding off the seat, Chey ferried her plate and glass to the sink. Rinsing it along with her glass, she set each in the dishwasher, helping herself to his facilities. He'd made it, the least she could do was clean up.

Stepping up behind her, right at her back, he leaned over to set his plate and glass in the sink. The dishwasher still open at her side, Chey froze when he leaned so close. She could feel the heat bleeding off his body, the warmth of his breath graze her throat. It was dizzying.

"Did they give you a phone?" he asked, bracing a hand against the counter. He didn't move otherwise, crowding her space by the sink.

Chey stayed facing forward, looking out the little window with a view of the trees. "Yes, they did."

"Here. Let me give you my number and I'll take yours. That way, I can contact you directly and we can plan the canoeing trip."

She glanced aside and up. Sander studied her eyes, a back and forth tick before dipping to her mouth. Chey would have bet half her paycheck that Sander was about to kiss her. Did she want him to? The man who had tackled her off the horse, the man she'd just slapped only yesterday?

Or was she reading too much into it?

"All right. I just need to grab—oh. It's with my camera equipment. In one of the bags." It took all Chey's willpower to keep her gaze on his and not glance at his mouth.

"Not to worry. I'll write mine down. Shoot me a text later and then I'll save yours to my phone." He grinned, all teeth and sudden charm. Turning away, he opened a smaller drawer in the kitchen and took out a notepad along with a pen. With slanting, sharp script, he wrote down his number, tore the paper off, and handed it to her.

Chey watched Sander the whole time. How his muscles played under the shirt, the ease with which he moved. He was entirely too distracting. Accepting the paper, she glanced down at it, before folding it twice and sliding it into the front pocket of her jeans. "Thanks."

He put the pad and pen back and closed the drawer. "Thank me when we're on the river." Winking, he started clearing the remains of their meal off the counter.

"Here, I'll help--" Interrupted by a series of hard knocks—two short, followed by three more—Chey glanced at the door.

Sander set down the plates in his hands and drew his gun before the second knock rang through the cabin. His demeanor changed, becoming predatory and alert. There must have been a signal in the pattern of the knocks because he lowered his weapon and held it down against his thigh.

"They're here early. C'mon. Don't worry about this. I'll get it," he said, indicating the left over dishes.

"I thought I had another couple hours?"

Chey discovered she was disappointed to be leaving earlier than planned.

"You sound disappointed you won't be staying," he pointed out with a devilish grin.

Chey scoffed and followed him toward the door. "I wanted to hear more about the trip and what things I might be photographing."

"Mhm." He didn't sound convinced. At the door, he issued brisk words in his mother tongue. A sharp answer came from the other side. Swinging the door open, he traded another few terse sentences with a man dressed in a dark business suit. After a moment, Sander nodded once, a curt gesture, then glanced at Chey. "He'll drive you back to the castle."

The suited man glanced from Sander to Chey, then stepped aside to indicate he wanted her to go first. Parked not far from the cabin, a rugged Jeep sat with the engine idling. Chey hadn't heard it pull up.

"All right. Thanks again for...everything." Chey glanced once more at Sander, who cut her a brief smile, and stepped out to the porch.

From there, the suited man escorted her to the Jeep, head on a swivel to study his surroundings, and opened the door to the passenger side. Chey climbed in with a murmur of gratitude for his help. He closed the door with a quiet thump, rounded the nose of the Jeep, and got in. Chey watched Sander, who stood in the open doorway, until the Jeep swerved around and headed away down a narrow path in the opposite direction.

Questions about the intentions of the shooter lurked in the back of her mind all the way back to the castle.

Chapter Five

Chey stood in the big garden, or the *King's Garden,* as dusk fell across the landscape. She studied the angle she'd set the camera up to capture, a picturesque view of a square arch overflowing with small, climbing roses. Greenery surrounded it and not far beyond, a fountain of cherubs burbled merrily. It would make a great backdrop for a family photo.

Since her return to the castle, security had been tightened even more than usual. Men and military stood guard in the halls, at the doors, and around the courtyards and perimeter of the grounds. Allar had no new information to give her. He reassured her everything was being done to track down the perpetrator and left it at that.

Not that Chey expected regular updates. She was sure she probably wouldn't ever hear what became of the incident in the woods. The security didn't owe her any explanations.

She had her equipment back in one piece and for that she was grateful. While she waited for the family, she found her phone among the bags and entered Sander's number into the short contact list. She sent a text as promised.

Back safe and sound. Look forward to

canoeing. C.

Putting the phone away just as she heard a mild commotion at the doors to the garden, Chey smoothed her palm over the new suit she'd changed into. Dove gray with a pink shirt beneath, it made her feel businesslike and professional. For this assignment, she knew she needed to dress appropriately and had brought every suit she owned.

Into the King's Garden swept Viia, heels cracking over the stone walkway. She looked smart and sharp in a black skirt suit with white accents. Pulled back into a sleek chignon, the severe style of her blonde hair accentuated the high perfection of her cheekbones and the lush shape of her red painted mouth. She glanced briefly at Chey on the way by, dismissing her just as fast.

Remembering Mattias' request, Chey stepped behind the camera and snapped a few shots without the flash. She caught Viia looking somewhat perturbed—which was, as far as Chey could tell, a normal expression for her—and impatient.

It wasn't her fault the woman was constantly in a sour mood.

Aurora entered the garden next, subdued in a fragile peach dress that swished around her calves.

"It would have made for a better portrait, Aurora, if you'd worn something less...frilly," Viia said with a skeptical look at Aurora's dress.

"Paavo wanted me to wear this one. He's in his gray suit." Aurora didn't glance at Chey as she approached Viia and the rose covered arch. "Besides. You're not *quite* of the family yet. If and when you are, then you'll be wearing more appropriate clothing."

The stinging words caught Chey by surprise. She straightened behind the camera just as Viia leveled a scathing look on Aurora.

"Need I remind you, Aurora, that *should* I become his wife, you'll be ranked lower than me?" Viia said. "And then *I'll* be setting the standard for what's proper and what's not."

The complications of being involved in a Royal setting became clear to Chey in less than two days on the property. A fight for power and position reigned, with the lower ranking women squabbling over who would set trends and standards. The hierarchy was tedious, tenuous. She wondered how many more secrets the family harbored besides a possibly alcoholic Princess.

"Frankly, Viia, if you haven't secured a ring and a proposal by now, I'd wonder over his intentions. Are you sure he's not using you to keep his mother from setting up another situation, like what she's done with Dare? Trying to force him into marriage?" Aurora faced Viia down, flicking the floating hem of her peach dress around her calves.

Any other time, Chey would have loved to capture some of the looks these women were trading on camera. It added a whole new sphere to understanding the intricacies of the Royals. Things not seen by the general public.

She didn't dare, however. If either woman caught her at it they would throw fits, she was sure of it. As it was, she pretended like she wasn't paying any attention to the tension, fiddling with the camera instead.

"Did you catch any of that?" a masculine voice said near her ear.

Chey twitched in surprise and straightened. Mattias stood at her side, so close she could smell his masculine cologne. She hadn't heard him enter the garden, too caught up in the melodrama with the girls.

"I...no. I didn't think it wise." Chey whispered, as if that might help keep her and Mattias's conversation under the radar. It did not. A hush fell over the garden, broken only by the trickle of water from the fountains and the chirp of birds. In periphery, she saw Viia and Aurora both staring their way. The guards at the doors stared, too. Fidgeting, Chey glanced from Mattias's chin to his eyes. He looked both devious and mischievous, like he knew very well the scene he was creating. Chey widened her own eyes a little, as if to say, *What the hell are you doing?*

He touched her shoulder with his palm. "You're doing a fantastic job. Keep up the good work."

"Thank you, your Highness." Chey matched the slight raise in volume to allow everyone else to hear what they were saying.

Mattias winked and stepped away, strolling with familiar leonine grace toward the formerly arguing women. "Ladies."

Chey caught an absolutely feral look from Viia. Refusing to show any kind of emotion or response, she went back to adjusting her gear, preparing for the session.

A round of greetings ensued with the group, in their own tongue, and shortly after, Paavo joined them. He passed a cordial, distracted smile to Chey and gathered Aurora into the circle of his arm.

Mattias's voice sharpened enough to draw Chey's attention back to the quartet in time to see Viia's expression falter. Whatever he said must have been withering for her to lose her austere poise.

"It will just be us this afternoon, Miss Sinclair. Commence when ready," Mattias said after turning away from Viia.

And so the session began. Chey knew ahead of time what the Royals wanted in general terms for photos. The women alone, with their man, the brothers both together and separate. She had been informed that the King and Queen would not be attending as originally planned, probably due to the shooting though no one confirmed it. Allar and Urmas hovered in periphery, ready to go between should it be necessary.

Once, when Chey made eye contact with Viia, she recognized a clear warning in the other woman's gaze. What did Viia think she was going to do...make a try for Mattias? The thought was laughable. Mattias flirted with Chey because he had an agenda. He wanted private pictures of Viia, that was all. Maybe it was in his nature to be a rogue as well as a Royal.

At least he didn't have a stick lodged up his backside, like some of the women.

Finishing the session just before dark, Chey began breaking down her equipment. As the Royals filed out of the King's garden, Chey caught Mattias's gaze.

He smiled with his eyes instead of his mouth before escorting a haughty, openly irritated Viia into the castle proper. Bemused, Chey carried the camera and the tripod back toward her room. An aid assigned to help Chey with her equipment followed in her wake with the rest.

Arriving at her bedroom, Chey discovered the door open and a cart sitting outside in the hallway. Ingel, the head of the household staff, was inside with another, younger woman with fresh towels folded in her arms.

"Miss Sinclair, we will be out of your way shortly," Ingel said with a friendly smile. She wore her silver streaked brown hair secured into a tight knot at the back of her head, one hand smoothing the strands near her nape.

"No rush, Ingel. Take your time." Chey, who had several interactions with Ingel already, returned her smile with a sincere one of her own. The woman, who exuded professionalism from top to bottom, also had a motherly air Chey found appealing. Ingel's eyes warmed with affection often and the faint wrinkles around the sides of her mouth only made her look sweeter, instead of older.

The younger woman, black haired and brown eyed, bobbed a nod before taking the new towels into the expansive bathroom to replace the old ones that had been already removed.

Chey set down her camera and the tripod, mouthing a *hello* to the young woman, and gestured for the aid to leave the rest of the equipment by the door.

"Thanks, I'll get it from here," Chey said.

He gave Chey a curt nod and departed.

"You have finished another session?" Ingel inquired, straightening the corner of the coverlet on the bed.

"Yes. My second full shoot since I've been here." Chey moved the equipment closer to the wall out of their way. The young woman swept past on her way to the cart, bringing in a few little bottles of body oil and lotion, among other things. It was almost, Chey thought, like being in an upscale hotel.

"Very good," Ingel said, walking over to pick up a duster off the dresser. "If you need anything else, please ring down."

"I will. I'll see you tomorrow."

"Good night, darling." Ingel shooed the younger woman out ahead of her and closed the door in her wake.

Left alone with her thoughts, Chey exhaled. What a long, complicated day. The staff and the Royals functioned as if there hadn't been an unknown shooter in the woods—maybe the perpetrator had been caught, or someone came forth to admit they'd been shooting when they weren't supposed to be. It drove Chey a little crazy to be just enough out of the loop that she wouldn't be told that kind of information. And why should she? She was a stranger here, brought in to work, not get embroiled into Royal affairs.

And yet that's exactly where she found herself after the confrontation with Natalia in the Queen's garden.

Catching sight of her equipment by the door, Chey remembered the text she'd sent to Sander earlier. Walking over, she crouched down and fished her phone from one of the bags. Set to vibrate so it wouldn't disturb her session, she turned it on and checked her messages.

There, as promised, was a text from Sander: *Day after tomorrow. Meet me at the lake. 6 a.m. sharp.*

Chey didn't have a session that day at all, as far as she knew. Getting her fingers on the screen, she typed in a reply: *Perfect. See you then. C.*

Ready to call it a day, suffering another bout of jet lag, Chey slipped the phone away and got ready for bed.

Tomorrow was a private photo shoot with

the King and Queen. She wanted to be well rested and prepared for anything.

. . .

The only warning Chey had for the impending attack was a prickle at the back of her mind. That faint inner alert that kicked in as if the subconscious knew that danger was imminent. Caught in a dream, it took her too long to rise out of the haze and respond to the threat.

Two things happened simultaneously; a knee jammed itself into her diaphragm and a strong pair of hands pinned her head to the pillow with a blindfold stretched between them. The pressure of the knee made it difficult to breathe, much less scream.

"Listen," a voice whispered near Chey's cheek. It was rough, like the person spoke through a mask or some other muffling device.

Chey grabbed the intruder's gloved wrists and yanked to no avail. The attacker had the advantage of leverage, which they used with merciless precision.

"Stop moving and listen or you won't like what happens next."

Unable to make out whether the voice was male or female, Chey ceased struggling. Breath short in her throat, she could do nothing but what the attacker wanted. The knee in her stomach made every respiration burn.

"There will be no more midnight forays through the castle taking pictures. No more clandestine visits to the garden. That is not a part of your job."

Chey wanted to argue that it *was* her job to wander· the castle at any hour, the walled garden excluded, to take as many pictures as she deemed fit.

"*Do* you understand?" the voice hissed, applying more pressure with their knee.

Chey wheezed, squirming uncomfortably on the mattress. "Yes, yes."

"And there will be no more dallying with the Royal heir, Mattias, when you think no one else is watching. Someone here is *always* watching."

"All right, all right." Was this Natalia? Viia? Chey couldn't see the latter woman going to this extreme to press a point home. Then again, desperate people did desperate things and if she thought her position was threatened by a mere photographer, then there was no guarantee she wouldn't stoop to this.

"It would be most unfortunate for Allar or Urmas or someone else to find a precious artifact belonging to the Royals tucked away in your room."

"I would never steal--"

"And if that is not enough incentive, then you should realize how easy it is to fall from the top of the stairs or a balcony to your death. It's happened before in this house." The intruder grated out their threats with eerie confidence.

Had it really come to this in a matter of three days? Was her presence so threatening, so unwanted? She believed every word the attacker said. This was no random show of petulance or irritation. They would follow through if she did not do as they asked.

"I understand." Chey, forced to shape the words more than speak them, groaned at the pain in her stomach. It was approaching intolerable.

"That is not good enough." The attacker added more pressure with their knee.

"I said okay!" Little stars winked in and out at the edge of Chey's vision. She felt dizzy, nauseated.

The hands pinning the blindfold drew away with abrupt swiftness. Before Chey could sit up, take a swing or call out, the attacker struck with the back of their hand. A violent blow with enough force to knock her into the pillows. Stunned, temple throbbing, she saw the attacker's retreat as a flicker of shadow through a haze like dream. The snick of the closing door was the only sound the person made upon their exit.

It took Chey a full sixty seconds to blink away the fuzz and the nausea. Staggering out of bed, she propped herself up against the nightstand and concentrated on getting her breath back. Furious that someone had the audacity to attack her in her own bedroom, she shuffled to the door and threw it open. She wouldn't let them get away with this. Sticking her head out, she looked left and right along the broad, long hallway.

Nothing.

No shadow moving away.

It took Chey a second to realize why it was so hard to see; someone had doused all the lights along the walls. The only available illumination was what fell in the tall window panes at the far end of the hallway, which didn't reach all the way to her bedroom. Easing back, Chey closed her door. Leaning against it, she fought off another wave of dizziness and engaged the locks. That was something she hadn't done in her time here yet, but she would do so from now on.

Leaving the door, she made her way to the bathroom and flipped on the light. The long, gilt framed mirror above the clamshell sink reflected newly pale skin, a blush of color on her temple and eyes that looked haunted, even to Chey. Touching fingertips to what would become a bruise by morning, she winced and picked up the washcloth she'd used earlier to scrub her face. Rinsing it under the water, she dabbed it over the abrasion and braced the other hand against the edge of the counter.

She wasn't sure whether to get on her phone and call Allar or Urmas right now, or wait until morning. This couldn't go unreported. She wouldn't allow the intruder to threaten her, keep her from doing what she wanted to do in the off hours. If she wanted to walk the halls at night, taking pictures, or speak to Mattias, then she would.

For all her belligerence and rebellion, however, a little voice niggled in the back of her head. *What if they follow through and plant false evidence in your room? The Royals will kick you out, possibly even have you arrested. At the very least, they'll ship you home and demand their money back. Money you've already spent.* Some of it, anyway. Several thousand dollars that she couldn't replace.

And in no way shape or form did she want to end up in a foreign jail.

She also didn't want to end up dead.

Somehow, some way, her presence here was a threat to someone else. It threw new light on the shooting incident and for the first time, Chey felt certain it had been aimed toward her. A warning, perhaps, to go with the one she'd received tonight. It would explain the absence of anyone being apprehended for the shooting after a thorough search. Anyone in the castle from the guards to the staff to the drivers to the military to security could have shot that gun and not been caught. All they had to do was sink back into their position and go unnoticed as the search began.

Viia and Natalia both, the people with the most motive in Chey's mind, had the power and money to make it happen. They could have hired anyone and paid handsomely for the shooter to keep their mouth shut. Setting the washcloth down, Chey turned out the light and made her way back to bed. Unsettled, she crawled between the sheets and pulled the covers to her chin.

Any thoughts of sleep had been vanquished with the attack. All she could do now was wait until morning.

Chapter Six

All the make up in the world couldn't cover the ugly bruise spreading from her hairline toward the corner of her eye. Chey did the best she could, dabbing foundation and concealer over the area to little avail. Fresh from a hot shower, standing in her robe in the bathroom, she grunted in disgust and tossed the little make-up sponge down. What was she going to tell people when she had to show up for the photo shoot with the King and Queen?

I fell down the stairs just wouldn't cut it.

She'd decided against telling Allar or Urmas what happened. Now she needed a plausible excuse. Maybe she could say she'd bumped her head on an open cabinet drawer in here. One glance at the extensive sink area and the linen closet with its six doors assured her it *could* have happened. Whether anyone would believe it was another story.

A timid knock at her door drew Chey out of the bathroom. Opening it, she found Ingel and Elise, the younger, dark haired woman there with trays for breakfast in their hands. One had the makings for hot tea, the other toast and fruit.

Ingel gasped when she saw the markings on Chey's temple. "Darling, what happened?"

Elise peered around Ingel's head, frowning.

"I left the door to the linen closet open and cracked myself a good one last night," Chey said, hating to lie. She stepped aside to let the women in. Their arrival at exactly eight every morning had already become routine.

Ingel made a *tsk* sound and swept inside. "Do you need anything for it? I can bring you cotton and antiseptic, or ointment--"

"No, no, thanks. It's just a bruise. It'll take a couple days to go away." Chey left the door open and followed the women to the small table they took her breakfast to.

She watched as Ingel expertly prepared her a cup of tea. Steam roiled out of the expensive china. Setting the teapot down, Ingel faced Chey and got a closer look at the injury. Her eyes were filled with kind concern.

"You need anything, you call me, yes?" Ingel said.

"I will. Thanks for breakfast." Chey still felt strange having anyone wait hand and foot on her.

Ingel smiled a motherly smile for the gratitude. "It is nothing. Good luck with your photos today. Come, Elise."

Elise bid Chey good morning and followed Ingel to the door.

Once the women were gone, Chey sank down into a chair and nibbled on the toast. Her mind busy with the events of last evening, she sipped at the tea and ate several slices of fruit.

What a predicament to be in.

More than anything else, Chey wondered who had something to hide. Only a desperate person would sneak into someone's room and threaten them with blackmail—or worse. Desperate for what, or over what, however, Chey could not fathom. Her acquaintance with Mattias was a clear problem, one she would have to tread lightly around. Now that he had secured her agreement to photograph Viia, perhaps his attention would wane.

Wouldn't that be an ironic and tragic coincidence, she thought, if Viia had paid someone to threaten her while her own boyfriend had been the one to seek Chey out in the first place.

Chey, cynical straight from the womb, didn't believe in coincidences like that. If it *had* been Viia, there was something else driving her. Something more secretive than a matter of conversation between herself and Mattias and a few harmless pictures.

Finishing breakfast, Chey returned to the bathroom and dressed for the day. For the private shoot with the King and Queen, she broke out the best suit she owned. Dark navy, with a modest hem on the skirt, the outfit sported white piping on the lapels, cuffs and hem of the shortcoat. Sliding her feet into a pair of three inch, sensible heels, she gathered her camera and deposited the rest of the equipment outside in the hall to be brought down by the aid.

Today, for the first time, she locked her bedroom door when she left.

Urmas waited at the head of the stairs leading to the third floor. The one that was off limits to Chey unless she had a direct escort. He watched her come up and checked the time on his watch.

Chey knew she was ten minutes early. She liked being punctual and was relieved that Urmas shared her tendency.

"Oh, Miss Sinclair, I--" Urmas paused after glancing up from his watch. He frowned. "What happened?"

Chey breezed to the top of the landing, desperately curious about this floor of the castle, yet unwilling to stare and gawk in the presence of Urmas.

"Misjudged an open cabinet door," she said. The lie didn't come any easier the second time around.

Urmas looked dubious. He lifted his chin and studied the mark with frank curiosity. "Did you have Ingel bring you something for it?"

"No. It's just a bruise." Chey decided it was a good thing she'd gone into photography instead of stage make-up, where she would have obviously failed spectacularly.

"Hm." Urmas hummed, then pivoted and guided her toward a tall arch at the beginning of a broad hallway.

Chey forced herself not to squirm under his scrutiny, and breathed a sigh of relief when he led her on. Adjusting the camera case strap on her shoulder, she finally absorbed the detail of the off limits third floor.

And what detail it was. White walls accented by gold trim provided a pristine backdrop for paintings taller than she was. Opulent chandeliers hung from the hallway they turned into, the ceiling inset with crown molding and hand paintings reminiscent of Michaelangelo. The atmosphere was somewhere between a museum and a cathedral, with archways leading into private parlors, a huge library and other formal sitting areas. Smaller hallways branched off left and right, with gilt doors leading into what Chey assumed were the private suites of the Royals.

Shocked all over again that people actually lived like this, Chey tried to fathom the money, the responsibility, the centuries it must have taken to ascend to this seat of power. Every so often she was struck with a sense of the surreal, like she might wake up from a vivid dream in her tiny apartment back in Seattle.

"Remember, no pictures of anything up here besides the formal sitting room we'll be using," Urmas reminded her. He turned into an archway between two marble statuettes of draped cherubs wearing solemn expressions.

Following, Chey entered the sitting room of the King and Queen. One wall was nothing but windows, the panes alternating between clear and stained glass arches. All the furniture matched the white-on-gold theme of the walls. Modern looking divans with gold scroll sat next to sleek sofas with gold tasseled pillows and ottomans with burnished gold buttons. Two high backed chairs situated near an enormous fireplace was the spot Urmas led her to.

"This is where you'll set up. Decide how you want the furniture and a few staff members will be in shortly to move it for you," Urmas said with a gesture.

"All right. Thank you." Chey set down her camera case. Urmas stepped away, cell phone already in hand.

Chey got down to work, more than glad to put her troubles from her mind.

. . .

The session with the King and Queen went exactly as Chey expected. Urmas, the go between, transferred new sitting positions after Chey snapped the angles she wanted. Aksel and Helina made little fuss, moving and posing as directed. Helina looked about as bored as she might have watching grass grow for an extended period of time. Chey struggled to snap shots that didn't convey her boredom to the public. Or her indifference. Aksel was a little more animated with the few people he deigned to speak to during the ordeal, once even laughing over this comment or that.

After, when the Royal pair had left the

room and Chey was breaking down her equipment, Allar surprised her with a question.

"A cabinet door, hm?"

Straightening, Chey turned to meet his inquisitive gaze. "I see good news travels fast in these halls. Yes, an unfortunate accident."

He quirked his lips and studied the injury with as much doubt as Urmas. "You should be more careful, Miss Sinclair," he said in a quiet voice. "Next thing we know, you'll be falling down the stairs."

Chey sucked in a breath. For a moment, she wondered if Allar had been behind the event. What were the chances he would suggest exactly the same circumstance the attacker had?

He arched his brows and cocked his chin like he was waiting for her to say something.

"...yes. Of course. I'll be more careful. Excuse me." Chey stepped around him, snagged the camera case strap and exited the sitting room. Urmas stood in the hall, ready to escort her back to the lower level. Back to the territory she was allowed to roam.

Along the way, Chey ran through the reasons Allar might do such a thing. Unfortunately, they weren't many. In fact, she couldn't come up with a single explanation that would motivate him to threaten her.

Unless—unless she'd unknowingly snapped a compromising picture. But of what? She'd only gone out on her own twice, once inside, and once out. Oh, and the walled garden, which turned out to be a failure on all fronts.

"You're starting to make suspects of everyone," she muttered under her breath.

"Pardon, Miss Sinclair?" Urmas paused on the stairs to glance back.

Chey met his eyes. Realizing he'd heard, she said, "Oh, nothing. Just talking to myself. I do that sometimes."

No she didn't. She needed a cover for her muttering, however, and the excuse was a handy one.

He held her gaze before continuing. At the juncture of the hallway to her bedroom, Chey paused when Urmas detailed her schedule.

"You'll have the next three days to shoot the castle and the grounds. Then we have a session scheduled for an outdoor event with the young Royals. When you're out and about, see what setting looks good to you. Find a few choice locations that capture the fall foliage and some of the landscape. Let me know if you'd like an escort to drive you deeper into the property." Urmas glanced up from his phone.

Chey inclined her head. "I'll let you know. Thank you, Mister Urmas."

"I'll be by to collect the photos you took today in the morning, as usual. Enjoy your day." He departed, walking with a brisk stride back toward the stairs leading to the third floor.

"Good day." Chey watched him only for a

moment. Then she headed down the hall to her room, ready to change and get some fresh air.

Donning a pair of kelly green khakis and a thin ribbed sweater in peach to combat any chill in the air, Chey scooped her dark hair back and secured it into a messy knot atop her head. A few stray wisps tickled her jaw and throat. When she stepped in front of the bathroom mirror to make sure it didn't look *too* messy, she gasped to see how dark the bruise had become at her temple and the corner of her eye. Blue and purple now, the mark definitely looked like more of a backhand than any encounter with a cabinet door.

There was nothing she could do about the lie now.

Collecting a smaller, more portable camera, she laid the strap around her neck and went to the door, swinging it wide. There stood Mattias with his hand raised like he was just about to knock.

"Miss Sinclair, I--" He paused when he got a look at her temple. His dark eyes darkened further. "What happened?" he demanded.

Surprised to see him, she blustered over an answer. "I...well it was silly, really. I misjudged one of the cabinet doors. In the bathroom."

Mattias, wearing black slacks and a crisp white button down with tiny black pinstripes, frowned. "You did that on a cabinet door?"

Why didn't anyone believe her? *Because it's*

a piss poor lie. "Yes. Urmas has already urged me to be more careful."

Mattias took a step forward. Using just his fingertips, he whispered a touch across the edge of the bruise. Then he met her eyes. "You would tell me if a guard got out of line or something like that, wouldn't you?"

Chey stared up at Mattias, close enough now to catch a scent of his masculine cologne. "Of course. Are you here to inquire about Viia's pictures? I haven't finished editing them yet."

A subject change was in order. Chey hurried to distract him. She pinned her gaze on his throat and left it there for the time being, diffusing the heat and friction they were starting to generate between them. It bothered her for more than the threat she received about spending time in Mattias's company. After Scrabble with Sander, and their upcoming canoe trip, Chey wanted to squelch any attraction she had to Mattias. Not that she'd egged it on by any means. What woman wouldn't be affected by his easy charisma and charm? Only daft, blind, really old women on their deathbed, she assured herself.

Mattias eased his touch away from her temple. "No, actually. I am not here about Viia's photos."

"You're not?" Chey risked a glance at his eyes.

"I thought to take you into the city. Shopping, lunch, sight seeing. It will be a

110

prime opportunity for you to take aerial pictures as well as those of the city. Are you interested?" he asked.

Was he kidding? Chey would have chopped off her little toe for the opportunity to shop, sight see and take photos in such an exotic location. She wasn't sure any city trips were on her agenda—though she could be mistaken. Urmas didn't tell her anything that far in advance.

Then she remembered the threat. Her expression waned from a gleam of excitement to one...less excited. She felt the shift and could do nothing to correct it in time.

"I'm...actually, I'd love to go, Mister Ahtissari, except I have an assignment I'm supposed to be getting ready for. I need to scour the property for a place to set up our next photo shoot." How she hated to miss out on such a golden opportunity. There was no help for it, though.

Mattias's brows arched high. "Well, *Miss* Sinclair, I have a helicopter waiting, so you'll forgive me if I would like to upset your schedule for a handful of hours. I promise to have you back early enough that you may wander the property at your leisure."

Damn the man. A helicopter? How was she supposed to say no to that? Chey glanced past Mattias to the hallway. As if she thought a dark shadow would be lurking in the nearest crevice to glean all her secrets.

Mattias glanced behind him, too. Then he

twisted back, a clear question on his features.

If she wasn't careful, she was going to tip her hand that something else was wrong. For a moment, Chey hovered on the verge of confession. She wanted to tell him everything. Would he believe her? Chey couldn't be sure. Never mind that one of her prime suspects was his own girlfriend. And speaking of his girlfriend, what would Viia think of this little foray into town? Already the woman had been shooting her warning glances, and perhaps had sent someone into her room to warn her away from the Prince.

"You know, if I was a less observant man, I might think you were just shy or intimidated by the offer to accompany me into town. But I'm not, and I don't believe for a second that you're shy, which leaves me thinking that there is something you're not telling me," Mattias said.

He *was* observant, disturbingly so, and she didn't know how to talk her way out of this without lying her backside off. The longer she stood there debating, the more suspicious he was going to become.

"Chey?" he prompted.

She glanced down at her hands. "I can't go with you."

"Why not?"

"I'd rather choose my next photo shoot location. I'm sorry."

"There is definitely something you're not telling me," he said matter-of-factly.

Chey understood then that Mattias—probably all of the Royals—were used to getting their way. He might push and push until it became even more clear than it was now that she was avoiding him for reasons other than choosing a picturesque location.

Caught between a rock and a hard place, Chey fidgeted. When she glanced at his eyes, she found him staring at her with puzzled curiosity. Perhaps a sliver of concern. Since *he* was inviting *her,* wouldn't that take the pressure off spending time with him according to her attacker? It wasn't like Chey could easily turn down a request from a member of the Royal family.

Right?

She considered it.

Maybe, just maybe, Mattias's invitation would spare her any blame.

Lifting her chin with a renewed sense of belligerence, Chey decided the hell with it.

"All right, Mis—*Mattias.* I would love to go with you to the city. Should I change into something more businesslike?"

Mattias didn't immediately relent from the incisive look he was giving her. But when he smiled, he *really* smiled. It changed his whole face, making him even more handsome than usual.

"No. Go just as you are, if you're comfortable in that. You'll prefer it over suits and heels, trust me. Meet Allar at the back entrance and he will escort you to the helicopter, where I'll be waiting. Ten minutes," he said, and left.

Chapter Seven

The flight from the family seat to the main city of Kalev was short but packed with breathtaking scenery. Chey was able to snap aerial shots of the castle from several angles, thanks to Mattias ordering the pilot to circle the property. The landscape along the way varied between open meadows, farmland, forest and wild coastline. Once or twice, a smaller town tucked itself into the terrain, but by and large, it was acres of green and trees.

Kalev, their oldest and largest city, was a mix of old architecture and modern construction. They flew over the parts of the town preserved through the centuries by former Kings, the buildings colored like sandstone weathering the pass of time rather well. She got a few pictures from her unique vantage, and more when they approached a helipad located atop a newer highrise overlooking the ocean.

Mattias pointed it all out himself, gesturing to this or that out the windows. Dressed in the same clothes as he had been in at the castle, he looked every inch a Prince.

Landing and disembarking, Chey followed the entourage through a door on the roof and into an elevator. It skimmed down the shaft with enough speed to make Chey's stomach lurch. Done in royal blue and silver, it reminded her of the ruling family. Expensive, classy, ornate.

She understood why when the elevator opened into a private lobby, and from there to a hallway that seemed as if they'd stepped straight from the castle into the hotel. Rich furnishings, gilt mirrors and top notch design suggested the hotel paid homage to its King.

A small furor erupted as the security, followed by Mattias and Chey, entered an elaborate foyer that housed the information and registration desk. Employees greeted the men and waved, some gushing, others pointing. Several tourists paused to watch the entourage walk by.

Mattias, who carried himself regally, exuded the same magnetism that had very first drawn Chey's eye. She imagined there wasn't anything he couldn't do or achieve. This was a man used to the limelight, who *owned* the limelight, and passed among his people with confidence and the assurance they respected and loved him.

He inclined his head to several staff and a tourist or two, enduring a flurry of photographs with a smile. Exiting onto the sidewalk in front of the hotel, Mattias glanced back, catching her eye, and led her to a waiting limousine at the curb.

Chey, overwhelmed with the entire ordeal, gave Mattias an uncertain smile.

Flashes went off from nearby cameras as the paparazzi arrived. Restrained by the security team, the photographers called Mattias's name and shouted all manner of enticements to look their way.

Expecting Mattias to disappear into the limousine ahead of her, she found him gesturing for her to go first instead. Chey ducked into the lavish vehicle and got comfortable on the seat. She wasn't surprised to find a blue and silver theme inside the limo. A small bar took up a little space to the right and another seat curved opposite the one she sat on with the Prince.

Mattias waved to the throng and slid inside.

"How do you deal with that all the time?" Chey blurted.

Mattias laughed and glanced sidelong. "We grew up this way, remember? It's nothing when you've done it all your life."

"I wouldn't call it 'nothing'," she countered with a faint snort.

"What would you call it?" He sat with his knees slightly parted, the expensive material of his pants rustling quietly every time he moved or shifted.

"I really don't know. The right words elude me. But I don't think just anyone can pull that off." She found it easy to be candid with the Prince despite feeling somewhat out of her element.

"Perhaps not. It's easier for me than it is for

you because it's what I know. You know photography, so you're comfortable with a camera. You handle it rather than let it handle you. Me? I wouldn't know the first thing about it. The last time I held a camera of any worth, I bumbled it and nearly dropped it on the ground. It's about comfort zones and practice. With time, you get better."

"I don't know that I would ever get better in front of all those people," she confessed.

"All what people? That was just a handful. For the festivals, births, deaths and all that, there are thousands."

"You like to contradict me, don't you?" she said, glancing aside.

He laughed, a dimple creasing his cheek. "You make it a delight to do so."

"I'm going to start returning the favor."

"You already do."

"I don't contradict you!" Chey gaped.

He just arched his brows.

"This isn't contradicting, it's debating."

"It's contrary," he argued.

"Which is hardly the same as contradicting."

Mattias cut a sharp grin her way. "You're missing Kalev."

"What?" Chey snapped a look out the windows. He was right; the city rolled by as the limousine cruised the streets, decadent and rich with history. There was an ancient feel to the air, even where the more modern buildings encroached on the old, as if all one had to do was close their eyes to be transported back in time.

Mattias began filling her in about the city. Who settled it, the violent past, when it came under siege by an enemy. He pointed out specific spots dedicated to the remembrance of warriors who had won their country back, and bade the driver stop numerous times so she could get out and take pictures.

He was an excellent tour guide, Chey discovered, eager to introduce her to Latvala's history. Charmed by the striking architecture and the quaint feel of the shops sitting right at the edge of the street, Chey indulged every whim to take photos.

When the limousine came to a stop outside a two story, older structure, Chey immediately reached for the door handle. Mattias rested a hand on her wrist to stay her.

"Leave the camera this time, hm?" he asked.

"What for? That's a beautiful building--"

"You'll see. Trust me." He smiled with just his eyes.

Chey set the camera on the seat between them. "All right."

"Excellent." After the driver opened the door, Mattias exited the limousine and extended a hand down.

Chey took it, charmed all over by his chivalry. Of course, she wondered if it was all for show. For the cameras, even if there weren't any on the sidewalk right at that moment.

"Thanks." Once she was out, she released him.

The security team flanked the front doors to the building on all sides, leaving a swath of sidewalk for Mattias and Chey to navigate. One of the employees, a manager perhaps, opened the door with a broad smile, cheeks flushed, head bowed.

"Welcome to Kesska's, your Highness," the man said, gesturing grandly.

Mattias inclined his head and gestured for Chey to precede him.

Stepping inside, she understood why Mattias asked her to leave the camera behind. This wasn't a historical landmark but a retail store. A store for the affluent, judging by the quiet violin music spilling over from a small stage in the corner, the remarkable displays, and the ultra-sleek layout.

Chey fretted over the prices even before she saw a price tag. Although she'd been paid well for this trip, she didn't want to spend seven or eight grand on an outfit. Too embarrassed to admit this shop was out of her price range, Chey looked for the rounders that she thought would have the least priced articles rather than the ones on more prominent display.

"Get whatever you like. This trip is on me. Oh, and pick something on the formal side," Mattias said near her ear. He split off from her, wandering along the walkway between sections of clothing toward a table set up with the fixings for coffee.

"But...I--" Too late. He was already gone.

All Chey could think was that if her attacker heard Mattias fronted the shopping trip, they might make another visit to her room just to hack and slash the clothes while they planted torrid evidence that would land her in jail.

She groaned. Maybe no one would find out.

After a half an hour, she warmed to her task. She found much of the designs to her liking and tried on a handful of different outfits. Unsure why she needed something 'on the formal side', she chose a demure suit of the palest gray with stunning embroidery on the collar, cuffs and hemline of the jacket. It all but screamed elegance.

Several times she caught Mattias's gaze on her, watching while he sipped coffee and lounged in a chair situated close to the coffee bar. The employees didn't bother him, nor did his security.

Just when she thought she had what she wanted, Mattias was there at her ear, having crossed the store unseen.

"The gray is nice," he said. "But think state dinner or formal ball for the dress, hm?"

"Formal ball?" Chey glanced over her shoulder and up at his eyes. "Who's having a formal ball?"

"You ask many questions. Choose something longer." He winked and stepped away.

And so the shopping began again. What she settled on, finally, was a snug fitting mermaid dress in palest blue that accentuated her curves and left her shoulders completely bare. The color highlighted her eyes and offset her dark hair. She added nude heels that spiked her height up a modest three inches.

Mattias, in conversation with the manager, apparently paid for it all with a gesture and a smile. Chey never saw a credit card change hands. The entire Royal family probably had carte blanche at any of the shops in town, with the bills sent to their accountants. It was all overwhelming and enlightening and Chey tried not to fret about the thousands of dollars she'd just inadvertently spent.

The retinue swept out like a tide, surrounding the limousine while she and Mattias embarked.

"That was excessive," Chey said as the doors closed.

"Not unusual," Mattias replied. "One would think you don't enjoy shopping. Perhaps the only female on the entire planet."

Chey laughed and glanced aside as the limousine pulled away from the curb. "It's not that I didn't *enjoy* myself, it's just..." She flailed a hand, at a loss for words. Or, more appropriately, hesitant to explain the guilt at spending that kind of money.

"Expensive?"

"How did you know?" Chey flushed and looked out the window.

"It's not difficult to guess. It's the least I can do for--"

"For me taking pictures of Viia." This time, Chey interrupted him.

The silence in the limousine prompted Chey to glance across the seat. Mattias watched her with a pensive expression. He made an almost flippant gesture in the air with his hand.

"Sure, yes. For taking pictures of Viia." His tone indicated he was less than pleased with that answer.

Chey wanted to ask him what he expected of her. What he wanted, if it wasn't her talent with photography. He had to know that she was unsure why a member of the Royal household had shown her this much attention.

He couldn't be interested in her other than for work purposes. She was unconnected politically, lacking an inheritance, a foreigner and of the working class, to boot. His mother, at least, seemed to think all those things mattered more than whether love was involved or not.

A light bulb went off over Chey's head when the real reason presented itself for his interest. It had been staring her in the face this whole time.

Mattias wanted to make her his temporary mistress.

The sparks between them hadn't been a fabrication or her imagination, and he probably saw a perfect opportunity to take advantage of the situation. Now he'd spent money on her, too, and that she'd allowed it was likely some secret code between almost-lovers that she would come willingly to his bed.

Mattias pressed a button on the car door and spoke quickly in his own tongue. Maybe he'd changed his mind about their day and had ordered the driver to return them to the helicopter.

"Why the silence?" Mattias asked, proving he was not immune to her mood shift.

She ground her molars together and stared out the window.

"I have a sudden headache. Probably from the...from hitting my head." She flickered her fingers up near her temple.

"My apologies. You should have said something sooner. Would you like to cut the day short and go home instead?"

Why did he have to sound so courteous? Now she was going to miss out on taking more pictures of the city, and who knew when she would get the opportunity to come here again.

Just because she thought he wanted to make her his mistress didn't require her to become that.

"No, I'll be fine. What else is on the agenda?" Chey glanced over.

He was still regarding her in his serious, sober way. "Lunch, first, and then a stop at the Royal park. Are you hungry?"

Chey discovered that she was. Looking out the window instead of at Mattias, she absorbed the details of the city. "Yes, actually."

"Excellent. You will enjoy this restaurant, I believe."

The restaurant turned out to be an old mission right on the shoreline. Much of the structure remained as it had been, preserved well enough to function as a skeleton for the upscale dining experience it offered. Inside, the owners had added paintings of the mission in its heyday, a few potted plants and plush chairs fitting a spartan, mission style theme.

On the third floor, a waiter led them to a private balcony overlooking the water. Hydrangea and bougainvillea clustered at each end, filling pots and trailing up wrought iron scroll work attached to the outside walls.

"This is stunning," Chey said, setting her camera down in an empty chair. The owner had, of course, been gracious about her taking as many pictures as she wanted. Nothing would be denied a guest of the Prince.

Mattias settled into a chair and waved security back through the balcony doors, leaving them with a modicum of privacy. "And the food is as good as it seems it should be. Would you like wine?"

Getting comfortable in her chair, inhaling the scent of salt on the air, she glanced across at Mattias. He watched her rather than the scenery.

"Please. I'm going to request you order for me, too. You know the cuisine better than I do."

"Oh, getting brave, I see. Very well." Mattias didn't need to look at a menu. He gestured and a waiter appeared as if by magic. Rattling off an order in his native tongue, he dismissed the waiter and reclined in his seat.

"As long as you didn't just order snails or goat's feet, I should be all right." She quirked a smile. He looked entirely regal and masculine, and, on impulse, Chey snatched up her camera.

He didn't pose or posture; Mattias smiled indulgently when she lined him up in her sights. Slightly slouched in his chair, he gave off an air of capable command and alluring negligence.

When she lowered the camera, Mattias held out his hand.

Chey stared at it, confused at first over what he wanted her to do. Did he want to hold hands?

Laughing, as if he guessed her thoughts, he reached across and gently eased the camera from her fingers.

"I thought you said you were terrible with cameras?" she said, releasing the camera to his care.

"I am. Let's hope I don't drop it."

"You're not very reassuring."

Grinning, he lifted the camera and sighted her in. Chey always felt weirdly conspicuous when someone else took her picture. She noted that Mattias held the equipment with poise and confidence, not like someone who was uncomfortable with it.

"You're a fibber," she accused.

He snapped off three photos, then peered at her over the top of the camera. "A what? I am not."

"Yes. You've used one of those before. Extensively, if I had to guess."

"Nonsense." He lifted it and leaned to get a different angle of her face. "Smile."

She quirked her mouth and laughed when he caught a picture of it. "Stop that. Give me my camera back."

"I rather think I like this picture taking thing. One more."

Chey flashed her teeth, because she knew that's what he was waiting for.

"Good, perfect." He depressed the shutter and finally set her camera down on the chair next to him. "That wasn't hard, was it?"

"Yes. I'm not very photogenic."

"What you are," he said, cocking his chin. "Is modest. I bet all of those photos will flatter you."

The waiter returned with their wine, pausing to pour each a glass before retreating.

"Shall we bet on it? I say I blinked in at least three, and have a funny expression in the rest." She picked up her glass, brows lifted in challenge.

Mattias lifted his glass to scent the wine

and give it a slow swirl. "You're on. What are we betting?"

"You tell me what the formal dress is for if I look dorky in the majority of the photos. If I don't, then you tell me what the formal dress is for anyway."

"So this is something like...what's yours is mine, and what's mine is mine, yes?" He swirled the wine once more, dark eyes glinting with amusement.

Chey laughed. "That's right. I can't lose."

"Hardly a fair proposition. If you look decent in the photos, you agree to a horseback ride tomorrow afternoon." This time it was Mattias who arched his brows in challenge.

Tomorrow she was supposed to go on the canoe trip with Sander. She really wanted to go, and didn't know how to get out of the suggestion of horse back riding.

"Can't do it. Something else."

"Have a hot date?" he asked with an incisive look.

Chey felt her cheeks grow hot. "What? No. I've made plans though that involve work."

"Horseback riding. Tomorrow afternoon." Mattias didn't back down and didn't change his request.

Chey saw an opportunity and took it. "Are you sure that's wise? I mean, after the shooting?"

"The threat has been eliminated. We will be perfectly safe. Agreed?"

She couldn't go horseback riding tomorrow

with Mattias. The canoe trip wasn't something she was willing to give up. All she could hope was that she looked as awkward in the photos as she usually did.

In the meantime, she wondered exactly what 'eliminated' meant.

"Agreed." She lifted her glass to toast him and seal the deal.

He tapped the rim of his gently against her own, eyes holding hers. "To a long ride."

Was that a euphemism for something else? Maybe he was really asking to meet her for a tryst. Panic settled in her chest.

"To...knowing what the formal gown is for." She almost forgot what she'd bargained him with. Tapping glasses, she took a sip of the wine, finding it sweet and pleasant on the tongue.

Setting the wine glass down, she held her hand out for the camera. Time to find out who was right.

He picked it up and held it out.

Chey flipped the viewfinder around and scanned through the pictures, praying silently for the bet to swing in her favor.

"Ha! What did I tell you? Look there, blinking in two photos, a half blink in another two." Triumphant, Chey leaned over to show him the viewfinder.

Mattias leaned as well, putting them almost shoulder to shoulder. Chey hated how potent he was this close. She could smell his cologne again, feel the heat of his skin. Hadn't she just been annoyed with him, deciding he was trying to seduce her and make her his mistress?

Mattias made a considering noise in the back of his throat and settled once more in his chair. He studied her contemplatively while he sipped his wine.

"I told you. I'm a terrible model." Turning the camera off, she set it aside.

"Even you have to admit that the last one, with you smiling, is exemplary however."

Chey couldn't deny it. He'd snapped a one in a million shot. "I'll give you that one. But it's not the majority, so I win."

He smiled and set down his glass, fingers toying with the stem. "The dress is for tomorrow evening. We're hosting several important dignitaries. You'll accompany me as my date."

. . .

She bobbled the wine glass while lifting it to her mouth. Saving herself the embarrassment of a spill, she gawked at Mattias. "*What?*"

He repeated himself. Slowly. "The dress is for tomorrow--"

"I heard you. Mattias, are you sure about that?" Chey set her glass down without remembering to take a drink.

"Why wouldn't I be?" He watched her like he didn't understand her shock.

Of course not. He was a Prince. Most women would jump at the chance just to have this lunch with him, much less be his date to anything.

Forced to pause when the waiter brought their lunch—sauteed scallions over filet minion, grilled zucchini and caesar salad—Chey considered what to say. Her usual way was to be blunt and honest, especially when she felt out of her depth. Like now.

She sliced off a delectable bite of the filet, then toyed with it on the end of her fork. Finally, she met his eyes. "What are you doing?"

"I'm about to eat. And I'm waiting to hear why you shouldn't accompany me tomorrow evening." He lifted a brow and picked up his utensils.

Chey set down her fork and leaned a few inches forward. She took the proverbial bull by the horns. "What is Viia going to say?"

"Make no mistake, Miss Sinclair. *I* choose who I am escorting to what event, not Viia. She is not my wife, nor my keeper," he informed her with a matter-of-fact, no nonsense tone.

Chey took several small bites of the food. It was as good as he'd promised it would be. Brow furrowed, she thought over what to say next. He'd effectively put her in her place about his position of power—Mattias could do any damn thing he wanted—and at the same time, indicated Viia's standing was not as solid as Viia would have everyone believe.

The threats from her attacker rolled through her mind. She was doing exactly what that person told her not to. What she *should* do, is confess about her head. She should explain the attack, lay out the details of the threats.

Yet what came out of her mouth wasn't what she expected to say.

"What are your intentions with me, Mattias?"

"To finish lunch, take you to the Royal Park after, and tomorrow night, attend the event with you." He didn't hesitate to answer and watched her across the table the whole time.

"I think you know what I mean."

He forked up a bite of salad, dabbed at the corner of his mouth with his napkin, then tossed it down before leaning back in his chair. Washing down the food with a swallow of wine, Mattias took his time answering her question.

"Are you asking whether I'm thinking of having an affair with you on the side? Because you're living in the castle, an easy 'target'?"

Unprepared for him to hit so close to the truth on the first try, Chey looked down at her plate.

"No. I'm not. It's not my style to seduce women in a clandestine way. If I'm going to seduce you, I'll just come out and do it," he said.

"Good. I feel better knowing what's on your

mind." Even if he'd flustered her with his candor, Chey didn't regret her forward question. At least now she knew.

"I can understand why you'd think so. There's no denying the spark, hm? And your position puts you within easy reach."

"Then why? This can't all be because of my job. I won't even be bringing the camera tomorrow night." Chey knew instinctively that it would be taboo to snap shots at a formal function unless invited to do so.

"Because you're different than the women I'm usually subjected to. You speak your mind, you're candid, and you don't look at me like I'm a title instead of a person. Isn't that enough? I may be a Prince, Chey, but I'm also human and like to be treated as such." He paused to take a drink. "Besides. I enjoy the way your eyes light up at all the new and different things. The jaded women I officially court lost that quality a long time ago. If they ever had it to begin with."

"You almost make it sound like courting Viia is an act of tolerance." Holding his eyes, she had another sip of wine. Mattias was nothing if not honest. At least about this.

"Choosing a woman who will bear the title of Princess is a tedious process. There is a lot more to it than meets the eye. I admit that I am not enamored with any of it." He smiled, a wry twist of his lips, and finished off his zucchini.

"Like your older brother, the one your

mother tried to set up with someone else?" Chey recalled the mention of Dare and the mystery woman.

"Yes, except Dare has it ten times worse than I do," Mattias said with a wry laugh. "He is considered one of the top ten bachelors in the world."

"What a hardship." Chey muttered the quip without thinking.

He laughed. "It can be. Imagine that everyone you meet wants you only for the title you'll provide them. Rarely is love, real love, involved in all this. We know it, our parents knew it, and our ancestors before that. Viia has an esteemed background, comes from a notable family, is well educated and because of her extensive family tree, is a good bet to bear several heirs. She is one of five children, and her aunts and uncles all have three to five children each. That's what they look for. It's not always a guarantee that offspring will be as fertile, but it's a better bet than choosing someone whose family has histories of miscarriages or trouble conceiving."

Fascinated, Chey sliced off a few more bites of meat and scallions while she listened. "If I didn't know better, I'd say you were describing a brood mare."

"Yes, it does sound like that, doesn't it?" His tone implied that it was exactly what Viia was being judged for.

"How do you live in a loveless marriage? And don't give me *I do it for my country,* bunk, either. There has to be more to it." She watched him while she chewed. Mattias, Chey discovered, hid most of his reactions behind a casual veneer that was difficult to penetrate. Except when he laughed.

"Not just for my country, but for my lineage, my family. It's my duty to marry well." Finishing his lunch, Mattias lounged in his seat with the last of his wine.

"I could never do it," she confessed, picking at a last bite of salad. "I'm poor company when I'm miserable, and that sounds like a miserable life."

"It's only as miserable as you make it."

"Or as miserable as the other person makes you," she countered.

"Does Viia seem that hateful, then?"

"Not hateful, exactly." Chey didn't know the woman very well and had only seen a few interactions with her and everyone else. Then again, she could be biased thinking Viia might be the culprit of her attack.

"Then what?"

"I'm not really sure I'm in a position to say. I don't know her well." Chey pushed her plate away and picked up her wine.

"You're thinking of that little dust up with Viia and Aurora."

"Yes."

"Would you be surprised to know that it's typical in these circles? Most women want to be the one setting trends, to be looked up to and admired."

"Probably not surprised, I guess. Actually—I really don't know how any of this works. This is my first time anywhere near Royalty." Chey laughed, a quiet sound that didn't travel farther than their table. She finished her wine and set the glass down.

"You'll be more experienced than most at the end of your term with us," Mattias said. He too finished his wine. "Would you like more wine? Dessert?"

"I suspect I will. Especially if I keep having lunch with Princes." She smiled for her tease, then shook her head. "No, but thank you. This was excellent and I'm full."

Mattias's eyes gleamed a moment. Then he pushed his chair back to stand and held her chair for her to do the same.

"On to the Royal Park. There are several things there I think you'll find interesting."

Chapter Eight

As Mattias guessed, there were quite a few things Chey found interesting, not the least of which were the bronze statues of his ancestors. They stood in a segregated part of the park overlooking the ocean, carved in exquisite detail. Life sized, Chey got a good idea of what each man was like.

She took hundreds of photos consisting of the Queen's Pagoda, the playground, and rows of hedges that spelled out *Latvala.* Mattias drew a small crowd, and he paused several times to greet the citizens, hold a child, or shake hands.

The people seemed to genuinely love him. There was a reverence in the way they interacted that struck Chey as sincere and respectful. These were the emotions she tried to capture with her camera. Never mind that Mattias handled it all with easy aplomb, causing women both young and old to flutter their lashes and laugh behind their hands. Now and then he met her gaze and held it, before moving on.

Whatever else Chey had thought, she found Mattias charming and affable. It offset the magnetism that drew people like flies, or perhaps it enhanced it.

Either way, Chey reminded herself who he was, and of his status.

On the flight back to the castle, she was again tempted to confide in Mattias about the attack. The words hovered on the end of her tongue, ready to spill forth at a moment's notice.

By the time they landed at the private strip, the words remained unsaid. She couldn't decide why she found it so difficult to tell him the truth. Maybe she thought he would find something at fault with her, as if she'd drawn the unwanted attack upon herself. And maybe, too, she didn't want to tell him that the brood mare he was courting might be behind it.

That was a shock the Royal family wouldn't take well.

Or would they? Was this how the upper echelon of society worked? Thrived? Was subterfuge, threats, attacks and machinations merely another facet of their lives, like breathing?

Forced to at least consider it, Chey stared out the window of the limousine as it ferried them back to the castle. Mattias was companionably silent the entire ride. Now and then, Chey felt his gaze boring into the side of her head.

The gate rolled up to admit them. Cruising along the drive, the limousine came to a halt in front of the broad steps. Chey got out when the driver came around to open her door, and paused when she saw who stood on the top step to receive them.

Viia, with an expression straight from a striking viper, stared down from her lofty height. Attired in an immaculate skirt suit of dark gray and cream, her gaze landed on Chey and locked there.

Chey, caught in the snare of Viia's obvious displeasure, looked away when Mattias collected her elbow and guided her nonchalantly up the stairs. It was like being led right into the lion's den.

"Viia," Mattias said, as calm and controlled as you please.

"Mattias." Viia greeted him but never looked away from Chey.

"Miss Sinclair, thank you for your company. I look forward to seeing the photos you took today." Mattias released Chey's elbow and smiled a rogue's smile.

Chey might have laughed at his blatant show of indifference to Viia's silent fury if it hadn't been for the attack the night before.

"And thank *you* for the invitation. I'm positive I couldn't have had a better escort. If you'll excuse me?" Chey, anxious to point out that it had been Mattias's idea to take her to town, as it were, dismissed herself from their company.

Viia did not deign to offer a parting goodbye.

With a guard holding the door, she disappeared inside. There were enough hours left in the day to grab a bite of dinner and go scouting the landscape for a place to have the next photo shoot. Later, when evening fell, would be time enough to edit the pictures she'd taken and turn them in to Urmas come morning.

If she planned to blockade her bedroom door while she worked, no one would be the wiser.

. . .

Chey escaped the castle at the crack of dawn the next morning. On horseback, she fled through the mist, dew flying off the hooves of her mare. After an evening locked and barricaded in her room, she was ready to spend time outdoors.

No matter how much make up she'd used, or how much ice she'd applied, the bruising was worse today than yesterday. A blight on her otherwise golden skin, it covered the entire side of her temple, the corner of her eye, and part of her cheek. There was no help for it.

Attired in jeans and a hunter green sweater with sleeves to her wrist, she was comfortable and warm enough with the slight chill pervading the air. A pair of hiking boots with a thick tread was her choice of footwear. Angled over her head and across her body, the strap of the camera case fit snug and secure. It was all she'd brought.

Slowing the mare to an easy canter once they entered the woods, Chey let the horse clop along with the reins loose between her fingers. She trusted the mare to find the best footing.

A good thing, too, because she was distracted with thoughts of Mattias and Viia. Of the attack. Of who might be watching even as she rode out this early in the morning. She was under no illusions that her comings and goings were being observed.

With any luck, whoever might be watching would lose her now that she was obscured by the trees.

Coming upon the lake, she ducked a low branch and straightened. A heavier veil of mist hung just above the water, floating like old ghosts. Surreal and slightly eerie, Chey panned a look left and right for Sander.

"You're late," he said somewhere behind her.

Startled, Chey twisted in the seat. Sander leaned against the trunk of a large tree, arms crossed over his chest. The camouflage pants he wore fit his hips well, as did the snug, long sleeved shirt of indiscriminate green. A pair of sturdy boots, laced up the front, had a thicker tread than her own. He blended in with the forest, as she knew he'd meant to.

"I'm right on time. Should I have--"

"...what the hell happened?" Sander's amiable tone fled. In its place, something cold and unforgiving.

Chey turned the mare toward him so she wouldn't have to keep craning her neck around. He pushed off the tree, giving her a first glimpse of the shoulder holster he wore. It was the same color as his shirt and she hadn't noticed it upon first glance. His eyes were pinned on her face.

On the bruise.

"I accidentally bumped into the cabinet door. In the bathroom."

"And does the cabinet door have knuckles?"

Chey arched a brow. How had he discerned that? "What?"

"You heard me. Who hit you?" He strode up and rested a hand on the mare's bridle. His eyes were sharp on the wound.

Chey shifted on the saddle. It creaked under her meager weight. What was she supposed to say to his adamant declaration? He'd caught her off guard with his forward assessment. And the longer she took to answer, the more guilty she probably looked.

Licking her lips, she toyed with the dark withers of the horse's mane.

"Chey..." There was a warning in his tone.

"Look, Sander. Can we just have our day? I've been looking forward to the canoe trip. I promise I'll explain everything afterward." She met his eyes. His were sharp, taking in every detail.

"The river isn't going anywhere," he pointed out. "It wasn't Mattias, was it?"

She shouldn't have been surprised Sander knew about her trip to the city yesterday. The entire castle and all the staff probably knew. It *did* surprise her he thought Mattias capable of such an act.

"Of course not. He's always a gentleman."

"Always? That makes it sound like you've had several interactions with him."

"Well, I *do* live at the castle," she countered.

"And how many interactions have you had with Paavo?"

"...point taken. Paavo doesn't seek out my company."

"And Mattias does?" Sander looked away from her bruise to her eyes. He didn't sound or look accusing, only curious. As if he was narrowing down suspects in his mind about who might have hit her.

"Once or twice. Don't say anything, but he wants me to capture some private, personal pictures of Viia. You know, candid, soft shots when she's not aware I'm taking them." Chey stressed the business aspect of their impromptu meetings, and at the same time, asserted that she knew he was involved.

"I see. Who else seeks your company out?"

"You?" She couldn't help but add a liberal dose of sass to her reply.

Finally, he smiled. It wasn't the easy going smile she'd seen in the cabin, but it was a smile nevertheless. "Yes, but we both know *I* didn't strike you."

"I don't picture you as the type to hit women. Just the type to tackle them off their horses." A smile trembled at the corners of her mouth.

He eyed her, then laughed. A raspy, quiet sound that echoed over the water. "Half of that statement is true. You know which half."

"I do. Now then. Can we go? I'll tell you what you want to know later."

He stroked his hand down the nose of the mare, like he was considering it.

"Come on, Sander. What's done is done. Why waste a perfectly good canoe trip?" Chey couldn't believe she was cajoling him like this. The longer she sat there, however, the more time she wanted to spend in his company.

"I want every detail," he said, turning away to issue a quiet whistle into the woods.

His horse threaded through the trees and went right to him.

"I don't make promises lightly. I'll tell you everything." Chey wondered what he would do about it. As head of security, it was his job, probably, to interrogate people if there had been an attack. It made her nervous and she was thankful to put the confession off until later.

"You bet your ass you will." He swung up into the saddle with little effort.

Chey laughed. "Did you ever think that maybe I just don't want to talk about it?"

He reined his steed around. "That goes without saying. If you'd wanted to talk about

144

it, the entire castle would already know the details. You've tried to brush this under the rug for reasons I can only guess at."

"Stop being so astute." Chey chose to combat her nerves with light humor. Once she confessed, there was no going back. She didn't know exactly what Sander might do, but she suspected he was the type of man who wouldn't rest on his laurels. He was a man of action and conviction. Sander would, eventually, get to the bottom of it.

Maybe that was a good thing.

The mare picked her way along the trail behind his horse, shaking her head and mane out.

"It's my job."

"So? You could pretend indifference."

"What kind of a man would that make me?" he asked, ducking a branch.

Chey ducked it, too. "An indulgent one."

"But that's not what you really want."

"How do you know what I really want?" Chey stared at the back of his head. He'd pulled the top half of his hair into a small ponytail again. The rest hung loose around his neck.

"If you didn't want someone to know the truth, you wouldn't have shown your face in public. You would have claimed the flu and stayed in your room to heal as much as possible."

"I can't do that. I have to work."

"Mm, not a good enough excuse. Everyone

gets sick. You could have made a plausible argument until the bruise faded. Instead, you lied."

"Everyone else bought it but you," she pointed out.

He twisted his shoulders to glance back. A brief moment of eye contact before facing front. "Really."

She wasn't sure she liked the implication. "You don't sound like you believe that."

"Because I don't. Even Ingel wouldn't buy that load of crap."

Chey scoffed. "She didn't say otherwise."

"She's head of the house staff. What do you think she's going to say?"

"Mattias didn't say anything, either." Which wasn't exactly true. He'd seemed suspicious of her 'cabinet' story.

"He knows better. Trust me. A five year old child would know better."

In the face of Sander's conviction that someone had hit her, Chey decided maybe she shouldn't have fabricated a tale about the bruise after all. Now they were all going to think she lied on a regular basis.

"If it makes any difference, I respect that you're attempting to either protect who did it, or spare someone the humiliation of discovery. It's just not the right choice if whoever it is needs reprimanding."

She couldn't decide if it was the words or his tone that prompted the sudden confession.

"They showed up in the night. While I was

146

sleeping. Pinned my head down with a blindfold and stuck a knee in my chest. Made it hard to breathe." At some point, she became aware that the mare stopped walking and that his steed had, too. He turned in his seat, staring back at her.

"I tried to fight back, but each time they applied more pressure with their knee. He, or she—I'm not sure which—told me that I had to stop taking late walks through the castle. That I shouldn't spend any more time with Mattias. They said there are eyes everywhere, and if I didn't do as they said, that they would plant false evidence in my room. Some Ahtissari artifact and blame the theft on me. Or," she paused to swallow and meet his eyes. "That a long fall down the stairs was a common occurrence in the castle."

Sander turned his steed around. Approached slowly, until he was side by side facing the opposite direction so he could look directly into her eyes.

"Then they took the blindfold away but before I could see who it was, they backhanded me. *That's* how I got the bruise, Sander."

He didn't say anything for a full minute. Chey started to wonder at his silence. Finally, he spoke.

"Do you have any ideas who it might be? Has anything else happened to spark suspicion in your mind?"

"Yes." She saw no reason to lie. Not now.

"Mattias showed me the Queen's garden--"

"Even though you both knew it was off limits?"

"Yes."

"All right. Go on."

"I took a few pictures. We had only just arrived, more or less, when Natalia found us there. She...she was..." Chey hesitated to out the girl for her drinking.

"Drunk," Sander guessed.

"That's right." Maybe it wasn't the secret Chey thought it was. "And very angry I was there. She threw her glass at me."

Sander arched a brow. He ran his hand under his horse's mane and gave the strong neck a pat. "Did it strike you?"

"No. She missed. All the same, she was unhappy I was there. So I suppose she had some motive. The other is...Viia. Due to the nature of the threats regarding Mattias and myself, and the venomous stares she's been giving me, she's the other that came to mind. Beyond that, I don't know." Chey watched Sander's expressions. He looked thoughtful, considering. And not judgmental.

"Tell me your impressions of your attacker. Off the cuff, first things that come to mind. Don't think too hard about it," he said.

Chey shifted in the saddle. "I couldn't tell if it was a man or a woman. But they were strong enough to pin my head down, at least. I didn't get the impression of...size. What am I trying to say..." She trailed, struggling to

148

define what she meant.

"It wasn't the same as if I was leaning over you," he guessed.

Chey realized he was right. "Yes, exactly. I didn't have the impression of bulk, of someone obliterating the rest of the room."

"Good. What else? Just say whatever strikes you. Often your subconscious picks up more than you realize."

"They were angry. Frustrated."

"How so?"

"It was the terse way they whispered. You know how when someone is irate and speaking in clipped syllables? Even with the accent, I noticed it." She hadn't pinpointed that until Sander goaded her into speaking freely of the attack.

"What about smell? Did you catch a scent of anything?" Sander slowly circled his horse around her own.

Chey followed the animal as far as she could see to one side, then picked up on the other. Watching with her eyes. She frowned, thinking about his question. "I don't recall smelling anything."

"Think hard. Something sweet, something masculine? A certain soap, sweat?" He didn't take his eyes off her as his horse clopped front to back and around again.

The methodical motion lulled Chey a little. "Nothing. I don't remember any scent associated with the event," she finally said.

"All right. And you're certain you don't lean

one way or another as far as a female or male voice?"

"No. It wasn't just whispering, but...I want to say they were speaking through something that changed their voice. Maybe. Or they did it on purpose to throw me off. It was so middle of the road that I couldn't tell if it was a man or woman at all." That part frustrated Chey more than she wanted to admit. It would have been an easy clue to home in on.

"On a scale of one to ten, how hard did they strike you?"

Chey met his eyes and cocked her chin in consideration. "Seven? I've been clocked before. This person has some strength to them. It could have been stronger though. So I say about a seven."

"Did the fist feel bigger or smaller?"

"I'm not sure. It didn't feel like a sledgehammer, but it also wasn't a feminine slap. They got their knuckles into it. My head snapped to the side with the force, so whoever it was has some decently honed muscles."

"Very good. Just one moment." Sander reined his steed out of the circles he'd been making and angled away while he took out his phone. He spent three minutes, no more, giving orders in his mother tongue.

Chey wished she knew what he was saying. Or who he was talking to. Would this change everything? Would the family send her home, thinking she was too much trouble to bother with? God, she hoped not. She hadn't worked long enough to pay back what money she'd already spent.

Sander tucked his phone away and guided the horse back her direction.

"What will happen now?" she asked.

"The appropriate people know. What I want you to do is pretend like everything is going as it would if you hadn't told me. Do the same things, take the same precautions. Don't let on that you've confessed, all right?" He brought his horse to a halt facing the opposite way again.

It gave her an excellent view of his face. His sharp eyes. "I can do that. The Royals won't send me home, will they?"

"No. We're going to take care of it. However, I can't have someone shadow you all the time or they'll know what's going on. So you're going to have to watch your own back in the castle. Try not to make it easy for someone to hurt you."

"Well that makes me feel all fuzzy inside." Unease brought out her natural sarcasm.

He smiled, but didn't laugh. "Yeah, it's not the best circumstances. Hopefully, they'll tip their hand sooner than later, and you won't have to worry about it anymore."

"What about them planting a relic in my room and framing me for theft? I really don't want to go to jail."

"We're aware. The security in the castle know what's going on. Two of them be going through your room while you're out here with me to make sure no one has pre-planted anything in your absence. Sorry for the intrusive nature of their search, but it's for your benefit." He swung the horse around and started off again through the forest at a brisk walk.

Chey noted that he wasn't heading back toward the castle. She kneed the mare into a walk. "Sander, wait. Where are we going?"

He glanced back. "Canoeing?"

"...after what I just told you?"

"There's nothing we can do but wait, Chey. Wait and check your belongings and work the investigation until a solid lead presents itself. And it will. One way or another, we'll find out who did this." He sounded sure.

"I guess you're right." Frowning, she let the mare pick her path behind Sander's horse. She watched how relaxed and at ease he was in the saddle, moving with the gait as if he'd been born with one foot in the stirrup. She supposed he probably had, with easy access to the stables his whole life.

"Right now, you're safer out here with me than anywhere else."

"Unless the person starts taking pot shots at us again."

"We'd know. There are extra security measures in place after the last incident. No one will be taking any unexpected shots at anyone today."

"What you really mean to say is that other people know where we're going, and have cleared the way." It made the most sense in Chey's mind, rather than spread the military out over thousands of acres of land.

He twisted his shoulders to look back, grinning. "Excellent deduction. Actually, they've cleared the way up to a certain point. No one but you and I know where we're going. If anyone was to try and follow, the guards would see."

Chey smiled, a wry curve of her lips that lingered even after he turned to face front. "You think of everything."

"I try. Come on. The fog is starting to burn away. I want to be on the water before it's all gone." He dug his heels into his mount's sides, encouraging the horse into a canter once he hit a small trail.

Chey's mare automatically matched the pace. For now, Chey set aside worries and questions and concentrated on the trip ahead.

Chapter Nine

Chey understood exactly why Sander wanted to hit the water before the mist lifted completely. With the sun on the rise, it created a surreal veil over the river and through the trees that was stunning and beautiful. Balanced on a seat in the rather crude canoe, Chey snapped picture after picture.

After they'd arrived at the cabana at the edge of the river, Sander had tied the horses to posts near a water trough and pushed one of three canoes halfway into the water. He'd pre-loaded it at some point with food, water and a few other necessities. After she'd boarded, he pushed off and hopped in.

Now the river snaked ahead through terrain she could only describe as rugged. A high cliff flanked the left side after the forest broke away to rock. The right was a mix of shore, boulders and trees. Twice, with caution, she turned on the seat to take several pictures of Sander. He smirked instead of smiled.

"Oh, come on. It won't hurt you to smile just once."

He flashed a devastating smile while her camera was hanging around her neck instead of up at her eye.

"That's not fair! Do it again." She raised the camera.

"You're supposed to be taking pictures of the landscape, not me."

Chey wanted to say that he made the landscape much more interesting but didn't dare. "One more smile."

Sander angled the oar across his lap, the paddle hanging over the water. Beads of gold dripped from the blade into the river. He looked as rugged as the terrain drenched in colors of the sunrise, and Chey didn't waste the opportunity to get a few more pictures.

He indulged her and smiled, all teeth and charismatic charm.

"Thank you. Was that so hard?" She teased him while she turned to face straight, one hand shooting out to the bench she sat on when the canoe rocked side to side.

"Yes," he retorted with a dry tone. "You didn't rock the boat that much, don't worry. This baby can take a lot more than a gentle sway before it tips over."

"It does feel pretty balanced," she admitted. Chey was a novice to canoeing. Any kind of tilt prompted her to hold on whether she needed to or not. "Do you do this often?"

"When work permits. I do get days off like other normal people." The slice of the paddle through the water was quiet yet effective.

"And you control all of the security for the Royals?"

"Yes. I have managers that oversee the castle itself, the front gates, and the back property here. A whole different crew represents the guards who protect the family on a more personal basis."

"Do you ever protect the Royal family on a more personal basis?" She glanced over her shoulder. He snorted.

"I prefer to worry about security as a whole."

"That was a diplomatic answer if I've ever heard one."

"I can be diplomatic when the situation calls for it."

She laughed. "Like when you tackled me off the horse?"

"You should learn to mind. Then I wouldn't have had to tackle you at all."

"I only mind when the situation calls for it." Chey should have checked her sass at the door, but couldn't care enough to do so.

He barked a short laugh. The sound carried across the water. "*Really* now. Isn't that interesting. I wonder what situation that could possibly be," he said in a way that suggested he knew exactly which situation it was.

"Quit wallowing in the gutter. I can all but hear your dastardly thoughts from here." It amused her that he thought it had something to do with bed or sex. Most men would though. They were hardwired that way.

"What I'm wondering, is if you're ever going to pick up the oar and row."

"You're doing a splendid job."

"You can't fully experience canoeing unless you actually do some of the work. Come on."

Laying the camera against her chest, checking the strap around her neck twice to make sure it was secure, she grabbed hold of the oar tucked inside the canoe and got a good grip on it. Then she glanced back once to time her stroke to his. The pull on the oar was stronger than she thought it might be.

"Don't dig it all the way in to the grip you have on the handle. Let the paddle do more of the work."

In her attempt to fix her stroke, she accidentally sliced the paddle into the water too soon, creating a splash that washed over the front of the canoe.

"That's why I sat in the back." He sounded amused.

Feeling mischievous, Chey reversed the slap of the paddle, sending an arc behind her.

He grunted, then spewed a few sentences in his mother tongue.

Laughing, she dipped the oar again, this time without any splash. "That's what you get for being smug."

"Do it again, and I'll show you what you get for being petulant." A playful growl laced his threat.

"I wasn't being petulant."

"Yes you were. Semantics, though. Just understand that my paybacks are serious business."

"You wouldn't dump me into the water."
She glanced behind her, a brow arched.

He arched one back. Wouldn't he? That's
what his expression said.

"My camera!"

"Can be replaced. Though the pictures
you've taken cannot. Pity."

He won that round. With a silent laugh,
Chey faced forward and got down to the
business of rowing.

. . .

The breadth of the river narrowed and
widened, pinching between cliffs and then
shallowing out as the craggy rock fell away to
forest or the flat of the river's edge. Sander
knew his way well, Chey discovered, steering
them through the deeper part of the shallows,
through swifter currents and around boulders
thrusting up from the depths that might have
otherwise caused problems. He guided her in
rowing and in the sights at the same time,
explaining how untouched some of the terrain
in these distant acres really was. Few hikers
or Royals ever ventured this far back in the
property attached to the castle, leaving it
pristine and wild.

Chey got several amazing photos of birds,
fish that swam close to the canoe near the
surface of the shallows, and gnarled trees with
branches twisting toward a blue sky.

Finally, Sander steered the canoe toward a

flat part of the shore just in front of a sloping rise of rock. She could see it climbed into another craggy cliff overlooking the river.

Encouraging her to disembark, Sander pulled the canoe up onto the sandy loam and used a tether to secure it to a fallen tree. He tugged out a small cooler and a backpack from between the bench seats, then led her up a rather steep incline made of boulders in various sizes and shape. Sure footed as a mountain goat, he didn't need to hold onto the rock like she did. Up to the challenge, Chey ascended until they crested the top of the cliff —and what a sight greeted her from that lofty height.

Spread out before them was a panoramic vista of forest and wildlands that stretched as far as the eye could see. The river cut across the landscape like a glistening snake, sidewinding its way through foliage and rock on its way inland toward another lake. In the far distance, she saw the low outline of what looked like mountains.

"This is breathtaking. Some of these pictures will be perfect, I think, to give a clearer picture of what Latvala is really like. The untamed parts, anyway." She lowered her camera and glanced at Sander.

He stared out at the landscape with a look of pride and serenity. "Exactly. Our homeland is more than the shopping district or the busy ports in the city. That has its charm—but I think this is a necessary and overlooked part of the country."

"How far does the Royal land extend from here?" Chey knew there had to be smaller cities between the castle and those distant mountains.

"Quite a ways. There is actually another, smaller castle that sits right on the big lake. You can't see it from here." He pointed in an easterly direction, beyond a thick forest that obliterated most everything for a half mile or more. "Twenty miles past that castle is a small city called Herfshire, and then another three or four towns leading up to the mountains. The Royals only allowed so many cities to crop up within a certain area near the castles. Most other cities, with more citizens, sit further up the coast and inland to the east of the mountains there. People of Latvala like to spread out, rather than cluster together."

"Who lives in that smaller castle? And just how small is small?" Chey couldn't imagine a 'small' castle.

Sander hooked his thumbs into the pockets of his jeans and stared out at the impressive landscape. "No one lives in it now. It was built before the other one—in fact there are a few castles in Latvala that predate the current family seat—to house the King and Queen during their reign at that time. It was in the thirteen hundreds, so although the structure has withstood the test of time fairly well, it's pretty much unlivable in its current state. The Royal family has kept it preserved and will

160

continue to do so."

"Is it open to the public? Like for tours and everything?" Chey lowered her camera after snapping another few shots. She glanced at Sander, studying the handsome shape of his profile.

"No, no. None of the Royal family ever opened it up and even if they did, the locals wouldn't go. Only tourists who don't know the old stories."

"What old stories? Why wouldn't the locals go?"

"Because there are those who say it's haunted." He met her gaze.

Chey scoffed. "Ghosts aren't real."

"Aren't they? How do you know?"

"Well how do you know they *are?*" she countered.

"I've spent a night up in the south tower, that's why." He cut a sharp, knowing grin.

Chey waved a hand dismissively in the air. "Please. You can't seriously think I'll believe you had some paranormal experience."

"Are you calling me a liar?"

"I'm saying that you probably thought you saw or heard something. People's minds go into overdrive in those situations." Chey absolutely did not believe in ghosts. She couldn't decide if that look in Sander's eyes was a spark of mischief or challenge.

"I think that even if a ghost walked up and smiled right in your face, you would deny that you'd seen it," he said, bending down to the cooler he'd set on the ground. Opening the lid, he took out two bottles of cold water and handed one to her.

She accepted it with a disbelieving snort. "That's not true. But it won't happen because they don't exist, like I said."

He twisted the lid off the bottle and tipped it back, draining it to half. "All right. How about we put the theory to the test?"

"What do you mean?" She sipped from her own bottle.

"You, alone, in the abandoned castle. I'll wait outside nearby so when you start screaming, it won't take me long to get there." He looked as smug as he sounded.

Chey's eyes widened. Recapping the water, she glanced out at the vista of woods and rocky terrain. She couldn't see the castle from there, more was the pity. Catching a quick denial on her tongue, Chey rethought her initial reaction. Why say no? She was almost sure the old castle wasn't on her list of places to visit while she was here, which meant an extra photo opportunity.

Not only that, but how many people would love to wander an ancient ruin steeped in so much history?

"Tell me first why you think it's haunted." She wanted all the details.

Sander set down his water on a nearby rock and started unpacking their lunch. He'd gone to some trouble to bring everything they needed, right down to napkins and toothpicks.

162

He unloaded deli style sandwiches, pickle spears and small baggies of berries and almonds. While he passed hers over, he answered her question at length.

"The King and Queen had nine children. Six boys, and three girls. The youngest girl was known as a handful, very willful and hard headed. She taunted her older brothers, the house staff, even her parents. As she grew older, none of the most prominent, well suited men wanted anything to do with her. They'd heard the stories of her devilry and coupled with the fact that she was so difficult to please, they steered clear. There were plenty of other, less tiresome women to choose from, even though they weren't as titled. Anyway, she became unbearable to live with, blaming everyone else for her lack of a beau or husband. She threw tantrums daily and made life hell for everyone in the castle. One day, when she was twenty-three, the staff realized no one had heard or seen Andra since the evening before. Two maids went up to her room—in the south tower—and found her hanging from a high beam. Dead." By the time he'd reached that point in the story, Sander was sitting atop a low, flat boulder, sandwich in hand.

Chey sat on the other end, caught up in the tale of Andra. The position brushed her side against Sanders now and again. "So she killed herself out of sheer misery?"

"Mm, no. No, she was murdered." He took a

bite of his sandwich.

"Sounds like suicide to me."

"It does, until you know that she was hanging from the middle of the room—and there wasn't anything close by for her to stand on. The only chair was sitting against a wall near a chest of drawers and the bed wasn't either high enough nor close enough to provide a launching off point. It was just Andra, hanging from a rope in the middle of the south tower. She couldn't have thrown the rope over the beam and hauled herself up, couldn't have jumped up and touched the beam itself for that matter because of how high the ceiling is." He glanced at her eyes and took a bite of his sandwich.

Chey used a napkin to dab at the corner of her mouth. Every time the breeze gusted by, she could smell the scent of his cologne. Masculine, appealing, sensual. It was distracting.

"But who would have murdered her—well that's a silly question. Everyone in the castle probably wanted her dead." Chey frowned and took a drink of water.

"Exactly."

"Did they ever find out who did it?"

"No. It's remained a mystery all this time. Everyone was appropriately distraught and upset, so no one could even point fingers and blame. Two generations later, it happened again. In the same tower, from the same beam. Murder for sure, because all the furniture had been taken out after Andra's death and the tower was bare."

"...what? Another murder? Who died this time?" Chey couldn't fathom living in those circumstances.

"The youngest daughter of the reigning King and Queen. This girl, though, according to legend, had been the exact opposite of Andra. Sweet, kind, compassionate. Everyone loved her. No one ever confessed and no one ever figured out who did it." He finished off the sandwich and popped a few almonds in his mouth.

"I'm wondering about the why of it, myself. What could she have done to deserve it?" Chey, slower to finish her sandwich, watched Sander sidelong.

"Who knows. The perpetrator wasn't going to admit doing it, much less why. It was an obvious reference to Andra though, so there was a lot of speculation about reincarnation and all that."

Chey scoffed. "That's a likely excuse. Why not the more reasonable explanation, which would be something along the lines of a jealous companion who took their rival out in a most dramatic way."

"Which is probably exactly what happened." He looked like he was trying not to grin.

"Wait—is all this even true? Or are you just making it all up to give me the heebie jeebies when I visit the castle?" She narrowed her eyes.

Sander laughed. "No, I swear it's all true. You can read about it. There are books in the castle library somewhere that outline the history of the Royal family. It's all there."

"So you don't really believe in reincarnation too, then. That was just what the superstitious people came up with." Finishing her sandwich, finally, she stuffed the baggie away into the backpack and fished out a handful of raspberries.

"No, I don't believe in reincarnation."

"But you believe in ghosts."

"You'll see tomorrow evening."

"You didn't answer my question," she retorted.

"Yes, I did." He winked and got up off the rock. "You ready to get back on the river?"

"Definitely. This was fantastic though. A view and ghost stories. You know how to entertain a girl." Teasing him, she finished her berries and packed everything away.

"You haven't seen anything yet, sweetheart." He swung the backpack strap over a shoulder and picked the cooler up. Sander led her back down the boulder trail to the shore. After stowing the cooler and the backpack, and making sure she was settled on her bench, he shoved the canoe off to start the next leg of their trip.

. . .

Liberated by her truths, Chey enjoyed herself more than she thought she would. Sander, fast with quips and wit, entertained her with his dry sarcasm as the miles fell away under their oars.

She knew something had changed with the river when the formerly smooth ride started to get bumpy and rough. A large boulder made an appearance in the middle of the water that they steered around. The landscape on either side of the bank had flattened out, stretching away into woods instead of high cliffs.

"All right. This is where you're going to need to pay closer attention. I can't see ahead as well with you in the front, so you're going to have to tell me when those big rocks stick up out of the water. I know where most of the large ones are. It's the smaller ones we have to watch," Sander said.

"Are we heading into rapids?" she asked, using her oar to point out a rock coming up on their right.

"Yes. It's nothing major, though we do have to be vigilant when we're passing through. The easiest way to see the submerged ones are to watch the water. When it splits and passes around something you can't see, tell me. We'll go to the left or right, following the current. Can you do that?"

"I think so, yes. It doesn't look too bad from here." Looking ahead, Chey only saw a few places where the calm surface rippled into white rapids.

"Like I said, this patch isn't bad. Just steer us around the boulders."

"Are there places along the river where it's worse?" Chey guided them around another, smaller rock that just broke the surface.

"Yes. Several rapids along the river are serious business. No one but an experienced rafter or kayaker would undertake it."

"You sound like you know firsthand." She glanced over her shoulder. Sander looked away from the water to her eyes and smiled in a way that said she was right.

"Of course I do. I have mentioned, have I not, that I spend a lot of time outdoors?"

"Yes. But there has to be a cut off point, right? Where it's too dangerous or risky?" She looked forward when he gestured. The canoe followed a swift current that made Chey's stomach flip-flop. The sensation of speed tapered off almost as quick as it began.

"What's life without a little risk?" he countered.

"You know what I mean." The current smoothed out, though the canoe traveled just as fast along the surface, speeding through a wide gap between boulders.

"And my answer remains the same. You can't hold back just because you think the risk is too high. Don't get me wrong—I won't jump off a cliff with no bungee attached or toss myself out of a plane with no parachute, but I've done both those things with the proper protection and have no regrets."

"There is no way I would jump out of a plane. For any reason." She shuddered at the thought. That risk, in her mind, was just too high.

"You don't know what you're missing. Or are you the type that thinks 'risk' is battling twenty other women at the sales rack at the local store? Bit of hair pulling, tug-of-war over a bra--"

Chey guffawed and slapped her paddle backwards in the water. Rewarded with his grunt of surprise, she concentrated on the river lest she miss a change in current and land them on the rocks.

In her distraction, she didn't think about the attack, or the threats, or what might happen from here. Chey enjoyed the moment, yelping in shock when the canoe dipped down and splashed back up, spraying her with water. She checked her camera, grateful to see only a faint sheen on the outside.

The rapids dwindled to a calm flow once more, leaving Chey with a racing heart and a grin on her mouth. Although tame by Sander's standards, it had been wild enough to be exciting for her.

From there, Sander guided them through another gorge and eventually onto a bank when the rock sloped down to flat shoreline once more. He climbed out and tugged the canoe further up onto the sand and offered her a hand to disembark. Accepting it, she grabbed the strap of the duffel and stepped down onto the ground. Sander plucked the cooler out after that, and hitched the canoe all the way up a rail where he secured the vessel by rope. The area showed signs of being used as a common 'input' for river travelers. A few benches sat near the long rail to tether canoes or rafts or other water equipment to and a small building sat further in. Restrooms, noted by the distinctive graphics on the doors.

"Are we hiking all the way back?" she asked, slinging the duffel strap over her shoulder.

"No. We're better than twelve miles from our starting point." He picked up the cooler and gestured the other direction.

Chey spotted a medium sized parking lot with a shiny, new white truck waiting in a slot. "You've thought of everything, haven't you?"

He led her toward the truck. "It pays to think ahead. We wouldn't make it back to my cabin before dark, and out here, you don't want to wander around with the creatures of the night."

At the truck, he lifted the cooler into the back with little effort. Taking the bag from her once she reached him, he set that in the back and unlocked the doors with a number code instead of keys.

"I've heard wolves before. Is that what you mean?" She climbed into the passenger seat and closed her door.

"Yes. Normally they won't attack humans,

but why take the chance." He started the engine and backed out of the space. "There are bears this deep in the woods, too. And you definitely don't want to run across a mother with her cub."

Chey fastened her belt and watched Sander rather than the appealing terrain they drove through. He handled the truck with confidence and familiar ease. There were damp spots on his shirt and pants from her flap with the paddle, bringing a grin to her lips.

He glanced over just in time to see it. "What?"

"Nothing."

"You're staring."

"And you're not watching the road."

He swerved back onto the dirt lane when the tire rumbled over a rough patch of small rocks to the side.

"Then quit distracting me."

She laughed. "I didn't do anything!"

"You're staring." He glared playfully sideways, then put his attention forward.

Chey wanted to tell him that he couldn't find it a surprise. Surely many women stared when they were in his presence. He was so casual, so self-contained. And he had chest and shoulders to die for. No, Chey was certain Sander Fisk was not immune to extra attention from women.

"Is that uncommon?" Chey could be counted upon to speak her mind, at least.

"No," he retorted with wolfish charm.

"Then why are you surprised?"

"Because it's you. You don't seem like the staring type."

"What type do you think I am?"

"The type to come over here and do something about it." A rasp laced itself through his words, as appealing as the seductive glance he leveled across the cab at her.

Oh, he was a brazen bastard.

And he was absolutely right. She *was* the type to take action when the desire arose. Under the right circumstances, Chey could be forward and blunt.

Her belt came loose with a quiet click.

He cut his eyes to their corners, a quick check, before finding the road.

Scooting across the bench seat, she cupped her hand on the other side of his whiskered jaw and set her teeth to the nearest, scraping her way to a kiss. His stubble tickled her skin, not an unpleasant sensation.

"Can you kiss and drive at the same time?" she asked before slanting her mouth over his. Chey caved to the attraction between them and slipped her tongue past his lips. She had nothing to lose and everything to gain. He wanted it, or he wouldn't have goaded her into action.

He applied the brakes steadily and wrapped one hand in her hair, switching from passive participant to sudden aggressor. Sliding his

172

tongue over hers, he kissed her thoroughly, dipping into the hollows behind her teeth and along the roof of her mouth. He kissed her like a man skilled in the art of passion, who knew exactly what he wanted and meant to take it.

Chey would have sworn the temperature in the truck rose a hundred degrees in seconds. Breathless, she nipped his lip and eased back enough to see his eyes. He searched hers with a predatory gleam, fingers giving her hair a testing tug. Automatically, she moved her head to counter, just to see what he would do. He increased the grip and brought her mouth to his, changing the angle, his other hand gliding down her ribs to her hip.

Lost in the heat and friction, Chey didn't so much as twitch when he slid his hand under the hem of her shirt and found skin. Sander made it easy to want him, to throw caution to the wind and give in. He was all male, solid and strong, with a subtle scent of masculine cologne tickling her senses. The river left its mark on his clothes, as well as the trees and sand, adding something untamed and wild to his skin. When he groaned, she swallowed it and returned a more feminine version of her own.

Breaking the kiss, he teethed her lip and pressed a whisper there. "My cabin?"

"Yes."

. . .

Carrying her with one arm around her hips, like she weighed nothing, Sander toted her from the truck to the front door of the cabin. Chey, arms wrapped around his neck, barely registered that the horses were tethered to the post alongside the structure as he unlocked the front door. Feet dangling a half foot off the ground, she tongued his jaw, his ear, his throat. Each glide earned her a groan or a growl, encouraging her to do it all over again. Under her palms, his muscles flexed and shifted, causing her to knead circles across his back and shoulder.

Nudging the door closed with the heel of his boot, he tossed his keys negligently aside and skimmed her shirt up her body. The peeling of layers came as he drove her backward: shoes and socks, shirts and pants, bra and boxers. He was as glorious naked as she imagined he would be, all sinew and hard strength. Clasping an arm around her waist, he carried her like that into what must have once been the King's old bedroom. Periphery picked out all the details because she didn't want to stop kissing him long enough to take a good look.

A high ceiling wrought with heavy beams arched over a large room with several windows in two walls. The massive bed sat to the left with other sturdy furniture flanking a stone fireplace that ran floor to ceiling.

Laying her down on the mattress, he covered her with kisses from her navel to her throat, and slid between her thighs with an

174

experienced slice of his pelvis. He gave no quarter, the way he loved her, consuming all of her with his demanding mouth, strong hands and stronger hips. Pounding her into submission, he swallowed her lusty cries and fed her a snarl of his own at the end. She thought it sounded suspiciously like her name.

Sweat covered and boneless, Chey recovered from the bliss wrapped in his arms, legs tangled endlessly. Every now and then, a stray spasm shook her. He squeezed her tighter against him, kissed her temple, then turned just his shoulders flush with the bed. Raking a hand through his damp hair, he stared at the peaked ceiling.

"Penny for your thoughts," she ventured, kissing his chest. He looked like a fallen God, honed and golden skinned.

"I'm wondering how much of a ripple it would cause in the castle if you spent the night here."

"Well, they said I could come and go as I please when I'm not photographing the Royals--" It dawned on Chey then that she had plans for the evening. Sitting straight up, she glanced at the windows to gauge the time. From the sharp slant of the sun, she guessed it was late afternoon. Four, maybe five o'clock. Oh *crap.* She was supposed to be getting ready for the dinner this evening with Mattias. Did she even want to go? It didn't matter. She couldn't just stand Mattias up, not after the shopping trip. Never mind she'd agreed to go.

"What's wrong?" he asked, voice alluringly raspy.

"Actually, as much as I'd like to stay, I can't. I just remembered I have something to do this evening." Chey gave him an apologetic glance and leaned over to kiss him. He grunted but returned it.

"Plans?"

"Sort of. I promised someone I'd be there at the castle this evening. Or trust me, I'd stay." She smiled down into his face.

He cocked a brow, obviously curious at what she wasn't saying. "All right."

"We're still on for tomorrow, right? Where am I supposed to meet you again? I can come here if you want. I know my way well enough now." She kissed him once more before sliding out of bed. With every inch she put between them, Chey regretted having to leave more and more. Things felt good between her and Sander. She wanted to explore him, spend time getting to know his habits.

Aware his gaze followed her every movement, she picked her clothes up off the floor and started pulling them on.

Sander, as lazy as a lion basking in the sun, arched a hand behind his head and set the other on his stomach. The sheets barely covered his hips.

"Sure, meet me here. Remember that you need to act like everything is normal at the castle, hm? Don't give the game away. And don't be surprised if you notice someone tailing you at a distance when you come and go. I've got a few men discreetly following you, just in case. The mare's outside, but you can take the truck to the castle if you need to get there faster."

His willingness to work with her, and not antagonize her for leaving so abruptly, endeared Sander to her. Once she had her clothes and shoes on, she set a knee to the mattress and leaned over to brush another kiss across his mouth.

"Thank you. I'll take the truck. Can I just drive it back tomorrow? I love riding the mare, but I think I feel safer with the vehicle."

He kissed her, a lingering press of lips. "Of course. Don't worry about the horse. I'll see to it she gets back to the stables tonight."

"Excellent. I'll see you tomorrow evening, then."

He caught her around the nape and hauled her down for a more thorough kiss. Then he released her. "Go on, get out of here before I forget all my good intentions and drag you back into bed."

Laughing, Chey pinched his stomach hard enough to make him grunt and swat at her hand. "*Maybe* I'd let you."

"Maybe?" He arched a brow like she'd just issued a challenge.

Chey eased off the bed before he followed through and snagged her. "Okay, probably. I'd probably let you," she teased. "I'll see you tomorrow."

He said nothing in the way of goodbye, but the hot look he leveled on her gave Chey goosebumps. Raiding his pants for keys, she left him there with a last glance back. Then she hurried out the door to the truck, aware time was ticking off the clock.

She had a Royal party to attend.

Chapter Ten

At precisely seven o'clock, Chey answered a subtle knock at her door. Expecting to see Mattias on the other side, she swung it wide, a smile in place. Elise stood there in her typical uniform, a box in her hands. The maid looked surprised to see Chey dressed in such elaborate finery.

"Oh, Miss, did I disturb you? I have a delivery," Elise said with another glance at Chey's gown.

"No, I thought you were someone else. What's this and who is it from?" she asked, taking the box from Elise's fingers. It was blue, almost exactly the same color as her dress. A sheer white bow sat on top.

"I do not know, Miss. Mister Urmas sent me to deliver it and to tell you that you are to meet him at the end of the hallway in five minutes."

Chey smiled at Elise. "Perfect, thank you."

Elise returned the smile and added a conspiratorial whisper. "You look very beautiful. Good evening."

"Thank you. Good evening, Elise." Chey waited until the maid was gone before opening the lid to the box. Nestled inside on a bed of pale blue velvet was a diamond solitaire on a delicate silver chain. The princess cut diamond, three or four carats at least, sparkled and shined. Chey gasped. Had Mattias loaned her this so she would blend in with the company better?

Hurrying to the vanity, she set the box down and fastened the necklace around her throat. The clasp was easy to latch and felt secure once she was done. An exquisite addition to the outfit, she admired its beauty for several minutes, stunned that Mattias would entrust her with such a thing. It offset the corset style bodice of the gown perfectly, adding just enough elegance without being gaudy.

Smoothing her palms over the snug fit of the gown, she assessed herself in the mirror one last time. Her make up, applied with a bit heavier hand to help cover the bruise, accentuated her eyes with dusky shadow and smudges of kohl. On her cheeks, a tint of rose rouge which matched a subtle stroke of matte color on her lips. The dress fit like a dream, nipping in at her narrow waist and hugging her curves toward her feet, where the hem flared just so over her shoes. Dark and curled into soft waves, the front of her hair had been affixed atop her head with a clip, the rest left to cascade down her back.

For a moment, Chey lamented that Sander couldn't see her like this. She was always in jeans and sweaters, clothing fitting to keep the chill of late fall at bay.

She didn't think she'd ever dressed so fine for any occasion.

Aware of the time, she left her room, locking the door behind her, and joined Urmas at the end of the hallway. He did a classic double take when he saw her.

Did the man even know she was attending the soiree? Or had Mattias kept it a secret from even the liaison, bent on making a surprise of her presence?

"...Miss Sinclair, I do say, you look stunning. Is there something I should know?" Urmas sounded complimentary and also wary. Dressed in a typical, subtle suit, he offered his elbow as he'd been born and bred to do.

"I don't know. Is there?" She smiled up into his face and slid her hand through the crook of his arm. Instead of asking him where he was escorting her, she acted like she already knew. She suspected Urmas was to escort her to some parlor or another, where Mattias would be waiting.

Urmas narrowed his eyes and grunted. He led her along the hall and as she'd guessed, guided her toward one of the formal sitting rooms available to guests staying on this floor of the castle. When they arrived at the doors, which were both open, Chey saw Mattias standing near the roaring fireplace with a glass of wine in hand. She wouldn't be human, or female, not to notice how fine he filled out his clothes. Looking straight off the cover of GQ, dark hair combed carefully back from his face, he was freshly shaven and sported an expensive looking set of cuff links, a silver tie and a silver watch that screamed money and power.

Mattias spoke without looking over at the doorway. "Thank you, Urmas. You may go."

Urmas opened his mouth, then closed it again. This time when he glanced at Chey, there was clear suspicion in his eyes. Chey gave nothing away. She murmured her thanks and stepped into the sitting room. Urmas turned on a heel and marched away.

Chey waited a few feet from the entrance. Waited for Mattias to address her. He took his time about it, finally slanting a look across the room. His eyes swept her head to toe, lingering on her waist and the sparkle at her throat. Once again, he exuded a sense of animal magnetism so strong it was almost impossible to ignore.

Fresh from her romp with Sander, Chey could look at Mattias now and not be moved as she once might have been. Oh, he was handsome. And a Prince. In line to the throne. Any woman in her right mind would fight for a shot at his affection. How ironic, she thought, that she preferred the rough-and-tumble head of security to the pristine elegance of a Prince. Not that Mattias had romantic designs on her. He'd made that clear at lunch the day before.

"You'll be the most exquisite woman in the room," Mattias predicted. He toasted her with his wine glass and had a long drink.

Chey lifted her chin and smiled, performing a small curtsy that was less clumsy than the ones before it. She'd watched and learned from other staff members.

"Thank you, Mister Ahtissari. The gift you loaned me is extraordinarily beautiful and I'm proud to wear it tonight." Her fingers lifted to brush gently across the diamond at her throat.

He set his glass on a table and strolled over. Without pause, he circled her, looking at every inch of the dress. Of her flesh. "It is not a loan, Chey. It's a gift. *Your* gift. I'm pleased you like it."

She gasped. "What? Mattias, I can't--"

"Can you not?" he asked, arriving before her. He reached out to touch a carefully arranged curl.

"No. It's far too fine. I'm happy to wear it tonight, however." She stuck to her guns, denying the gift out of hand. He was spending too much money on her. Money she hadn't earned or deserved.

He leaned his head toward her. The subtle scent of his cologne was alluring and seductive. "It's a gift. Has no one ever told you it's rude to deny one given in gratitude?"

Chey swallowed and held his eyes. "Gratitude for what?"

"For being my companion this evening, of course." He leaned out of her personal space and offered his elbow in a fashion much more regal than Urmas had.

183

"It's an awfully expensive gift to attend a one night function," she said. Slipping her fingers under the bend of his elbow, she followed when he led her from the room and into the hallway.

"I think you should worry less about how much things cost and more about the thought behind it." His expression waned contemplative.

"I have. It's still extravagant." Chey walked with him to the end of the hall, where a guard opened a door not easily seen unless you were standing right in front of it.

Mattias led her through the arch and down a flight of broad, red velvet covered stairs. Low lights in sconces on the walls cast off an ambient glow. "It doesn't come with any strings attached, if that's what you're worried about."

Maybe part of that had been the reason for her hesitance. Like with the dress. "I suspected not. I guess I'm unused to gifts of this nature, that's all."

"Then get used to it." He cut her a half smile and led her through another arch to a door that opened on cue by another guard.

From there, another, longer hall with windows along one wall stretched away deeper into the castle. Mattias escorted her toward the front instead of the back, where faint strains of music could be heard coming from one of the great ballrooms.

The double doors he aimed for were not the

184

main entrance to the room. Chey knew because she'd seen the expansive archways leading into both ballrooms and this wasn't it. A private entrance, then, probably only used by the Royals. Bracing herself, she fortified her resolve and stepped into the ballroom on Mattias's arm.

Transformed into a gilded paradise, it took Chey's breath away. Gold lamae draped the walls, accented by red and gold shields keeping the material shaped like a swag. Red linen covered tables lining the edge of the room, the tall chairs carved in a baroque style reminiscent of early French designers. Candelabra stood at certain points along the walls, the flame flickering shadows across the tables and guests. Two enormous crystal chandeliers hung from the high ceiling, casting light down over the center dance floor where a few dancers gathered to waltz.

Already, a collection of guests mingled over extensive food tables and a wine fountain, with Latvala Royals liberally interspersed. The King and Queen were already in attendance, flanked by diplomats in fine suits and cordial smiles. Natalia, with her petulant face and haughty demeanor, stood amongst a throng of what Chey presumed were admirers, drawing laughs from the men along with appreciative glances over her body. She didn't appear drunk—so far. Paavo and Aurora, engaged with an elderly, affluent looking couple, both had wine in their hands and pleasant expressions on their faces.

Chey wondered at Mattias entering *after* the King and Queen. Shouldn't he have arrived before? Clueless over Royal events and staging, Chey waited for Mattias to lead her forward. In the few seconds since they'd entered the room, no one had, so far, glanced their way.

"His Royal Highness, Mattias Ahtissari," a voice said over well hidden speakers.

And then just like that, Mattias and Chey were in the proverbial spotlight. She wasn't sure whether she wanted to sink through the floor or faint. Many pairs of eyes swung their way. Struggling to act like she belonged on Mattias's arm, she pasted what she hoped was a natural looking smile on her mouth. Why on earth had she agreed to this?

Mattias, smooth and cultured, finally advanced her deeper into the room.

Chey caught flickers of shock on the King and Queen's faces. On Paavo and Aurora's. Afraid to glance at Natalia, Chey studiously avoided eye contact with her. If the others were all but gaping, Chey figured Natalia would be outright scowling. The guests greeted Mattias with warm enthusiasm, apparently unaware of the sudden tension his arrival had created within the Royal family. He shook hands with important looking men and kissed the knuckles of their wives. Several times he introduced her as 'Miss Sinclair', and Chey extended her courtesies with every bit of

186

grace she owned. The titles Mattias delivered—Ambassador, Liaison, Prince—all went right over Chey's head. She would never remember them all. That other Royalty was present in the room shouldn't have shocked her, yet it did.

Approaching the King and Queen, Mattias presented her with casual elegance.

"Father, Mother, I'm sure you remember Miss Sinclair," he said with a glance aside to Chey.

Flustered, made more so by the way Aksel and Helina pinned her with sharp looks, Chey curtsied carefully and straightened. "Your Highnesses."

What was she supposed to say after that? How the hell are ya? What about them Seahawks? Unnerved, Chey left her greeting simple.

"Miss Sinclair." Aksel, though polite, nevertheless projected an air of displeasure. It was the slow way he enunciated each syllable of her name and the hint of warning that matched the stare he leveled on Mattias.

Helina, nostrils flaring, did not deign to acknowledge her.

"If you'll excuse us," Mattias said with a slight bow of his head. He did not seem the least bit perturbed at the chilly exchange from his parents. Moving away from the Royal pair, Mattias paused when a server with a tray of wine glasses offered them drinks. He picked one up and handed it to Chey.

She accepted it and resisted the urge to gulp the entire thing down at once. After Mattias had his and the server retreated, Chey whispered, "I should kick you right in the shin."

The resonance of his baritone laugh drew several glances their way. "I dare you," he whispered back.

Chey gasped. Were they really having this conversation? Right here, right now?

"You should know that I rarely ever turn down a dare. If we weren't where we are, I would absolutely do it." She sipped her wine. Just then, she caught Natalia's glance by accident. The woman wore a murderous expression. Her companions all stared Chey and Mattias's way, as if trying to figure out what got the Princesses ire up. Feeling puckish and truculent, Chey toasted Natalia with her glass.

In for a penny, in for a pound. If Natalia was behind the attack, then at least Chey could give the girl a real reason to shove her down the stairs.

"You're doing very well," Mattias said with a subtle switch of subject. "But then, I knew you would."

"It's not that hard to be cordial, you know. We heathen Americans *do* possess some diplomatic skill." She countered his praise with a healthy dose of dry sarcasm.

His shoulders shook with silent laughter. Mattias sipped his wine. "And you possess--"

"Mattias Ahtissari! It's been too long. How are you?" A gentleman with ink black hair and equally dark eyes intruded on their conversation, smiling broadly with one hand extended to Mattias.

"Prince Severian, I think you're getting fat." Mattias shook the man's hand, grinning like the devil himself. "I'm well. This is Miss Sinclair. Miss Sinclair, Prince Severian of Weithan Isle."

Prince Severian laughed and clapped Mattias on the shoulder. "Always the charmer. Miss Sinclair, my pleasure." He turned to Chey and extended his hand in the way that men do when they kiss the back instead of shake.

Chey let him have her fingers. "The pleasure is mine, Prince Severian."

He lifted her knuckles to his lips for a brief brush, and released her. "Now then, not to be rude, but may I steal your date for a moment or two?"

Mattias arched a brow at Severian.

Chey couldn't decide if Mattias was surprised by the request or surprised that the Prince was asking *her* permission. "Of course. Prince Ahtissari, you know where to find me."

She stepped away to let the men discuss what they would. The affairs of the state or other political intrigue. Not three steps from them, she heard Severian lower his voice and address Mattias. His voice carried despite his best attempt to be discreet.

"I won't keep you, Matt. But what's the rumor I hear that there's been assassination chatter intercepted by your security?"

Damn. Chey wanted to linger and hear Mattias's answer. Assassination chatter for who? The King? The Queen? By the time she heard the low rumble of Mattias's voice, she was too far away to make out specific words. Threading her way to the edge of the crowd, she positioned herself near a vacant table and sipped at her wine. She wasn't daunted by standing alone in a crowd of dignitaries. It gave her an opportunity to see how this level of society worked, how the women congregated in groups and how the men branched off, puffing on cigars or tossing back brandy. She wondered at the number of Royalty present that didn't belong to the Ahtissari name and what their visit was about. Surely, some sort of deal making was happening, or being introduced for the rest to consider. Trade, import and export, military might, positions on war. It could be a number of things.

"Left to your own devices already. I'm not surprised. Why don't you make a quiet exit while no one's watching," Natalia hissed at her side.

Distracted by Mattias and Severian, Chey didn't see Natalia's approach.

"Or what? You'll pitch another tantrum and throw your glass at me?" Chey, shocked at her own audacity, couldn't quell her sudden fit of impatient annoyance. She didn't owe Natalia anything, hadn't *done* anything wrong, and she was growing tired of the woman's vitriol every time she turned around.

Natalia narrowed her eyes and leaned closer, until her mouth was right at Chey's ear. "I'll have you and your precious camera thrown out on your ass. Watch and see if I don't. Speak to me like that one more time, and you'll find yourself on a fast track back to whatever hovel you crawled out of."

If there was anywhere Natalia could strike a winning blow, it was with the threat of being forced to leave the castle. She hadn't yet worked off the money she'd put in the bank, and the damage to her reputation might never recover if word got out that she'd been fired for lack of professionalism at her job. She was sure Natalia would do as much damage on the international front as she could, wrecking Chey's chance to work with other members of high society.

Still. It galled her to swallow her pride and feign regret. "My apologies, Princess Natalia."

"You don't sound very convincing."

Chey wanted to ask Natalia if she didn't have better things to do than stand here and heckle the hired help. Curbing her wayward tongue, she lifted her glass and sipped the wine instead. It kept her mouth busy until she reined in her temper. Across the room, she saw Mattias glance her way. His eyes narrowed when he spied Natalia standing in such close proximity. Chey knew she needn't convey the tension between herself and Natalia. A moment later, he disengaged from Severian and headed her way.

Rather than repeat an apology she didn't feel or mean, Chey took another drink. Natalia chose that moment to 'accidentally' bump her shoulder in the guise of reaching for a napkin on the table behind them. A small bit of wine spilled down the front of Chey's dress, splashing droplets onto the skin of her chest.

Gasping in outrage, Chey had half a mind to throw the remains of her drink right in Natalia's face. Of course she couldn't. That would land her in very hot water.

"*Natalia,*" Mattias snarled, arriving in time to see the blatant collision.

"I'm so sorry, Miss Sinclair. You'll have to forgive me." Natalia simpered, offering Chey the napkin with a smirk in her eyes but not on her mouth.

Mattias, in a low voice, ripped a stinging reprimand in their mother tongue and snatched the napkin from her hand.

Chey, unable to understand the language, nevertheless had no trouble discerning his anger at Natalia. Rather than blot the napkin on her chest and the front of her dress, he set his wine down and cupped Chey's elbow to escort her to the private exit. The guard opened the door and they stepped through into the hall. Now she felt like she needed to apologize to Mattias for cutting his evening short.

"I'm sorry--"

"Don't apologize for her, Chey." He spoke in a quiet, no-nonsense voice.

Chey picked up her pace to match his long strides. A quick glance aside showed her his profile and the compressed line of his mouth. Mattias was *not* happy.

"I'm not apologizing for her, I'm apologizing because your evening was cut short. You don't have to walk me all the way back to my room. I can find my way from the stairs." She brushed ineffectually at the stain on the dress. What a waste. Thousands of dollars down the drain.

"I'm not leaving you to walk alone back to your room. That was the preliminary greeting round—the more serious talks begin tomorrow morning. I won't be missed." He guided her up the private staircase and out the door leading to the hallway on her floor.

"I overheard Severian," she confessed. Her curiosity was killing her. "At least the part about the assassination."

Mattias snapped a sharp look at her. "It's best to forget it."

"Someone in this house, yes? The King or Queen?"

"There are often rumors. More than you might think. Separating the real from the fake threats can be trying and tiresome."

"You didn't answer the question."

"Yes, someone in the Royal family."

"You're not going to tell me who, are you?"

"Trust me. The less you know, the better off you are. It's not safe to have knowledge of too many insider secrets." He winked, but his expression remained hard.

Chey considered his words and found wisdom there. The more she knew, the more danger she probably put herself in.

At her door, Mattias released her elbow and faced her. "Thank you for accompanying me. Your presence was notable and noted."

"Oh, I have no doubt," she said with a wry smile.

For the first time since leaving the event, he smiled too. "It's good to do the unexpected once in a while. Keeps them on their toes."

"So that's what my function was. The 'Surprise Factor'." Chey wasn't all that shocked to hear it.

He reached up to run his fingers along the delicate angle of her jaw. "No, your function was to entertain me and provide me an escort worthy of such esteemed company."

"Viia isn't a worthy escort?" Chey arched a brow in disbelief.

"I think we have discussed what Viia's more prominent qualities are. It would not be seemly for me to discuss what I perceive her failings to be." His fingers slid off the end of her chin.

"Right. Broodmare status. Mattias—it's disappointing to hear that. I've heard your reasons and I understand your position. Still. You seem like a strong enough man to make up your own mind and do what you want to." Chey realized that she spoke from an inexperienced viewpoint, that she had no idea what life for a Royal must be like. All she knew was that she wouldn't be able to live that way, under such strict control and expectation. She'd been spoiled by the ability to make her own decisions and decide her own fate.

He regarded her with serious, dark eyes. Then, he whispered, "And *this* is why I am second in line to the throne, and someone like you is not."

Any other time, Chey might have taken serious offense to what sounded like an insult. Except he spoke the truth, and Chey acknowledged it with a tip of her head. "Yes. No matter what else, thank you for inviting me. I would have never had the privilege of experiencing anything like it otherwise."

"You're welcome. I'm sorry we were not able to squeeze in a dance. Maybe next time. If you leave the dress outside your door, I can have someone attempt to fix it."

"Maybe next time," she agreed, all while thinking of a dance with Sander instead. In the living room of the cabin, perhaps, or under the stars and moonlight. She glanced down at the front of the pretty gown. "There's an old saying: if it's red, you're dead. I don't think it will come out, but I'll leave it out here anyway when I change."

"Very well. Good night, Chey." Mattias

bowed his head and pivoted to head down the hallway.

Fishing the key out of her bodice, because there wasn't a spare inch anywhere else on the snug dress, she unlocked her door and let herself inside.

Time to change and reflect on a very unusual day—and night.

. . .

In the spill of light falling in her window, Chey removed the stunning pendant and laid it on the dresser. The diamond shined despite the otherwise dim state of the bedroom. Struggling to get out of the dress, she kicked off her shoes and wiggled the zipper down her spine. What a pity Sander hadn't seen her in it before the advent of the bright red stain. She wondered what he would have thought, and whether he would have liked it.

Preoccupied with pulling a track suit out of her drawers, she made the change and walked the dress to the door. Folding it carefully, she left it just outside. Re-engaging the locks, she padded to the dresser and picked up the necklace. It went back into the original box Elise delivered it in and into her sock drawer. She felt conspicuous leaving it out where anyone might stumble across it. The only people who came and went in her room were the maids, however, and they never touched her personal things. Only the bedding, towels and general cleaning duties.

Stopping by the window, she stared in the direction of the woods. Sander was out there somewhere, doing who knew what at this late hour. Shuffling paperwork, taking care of security business, making plans for their outing tomorrow to the haunted castle. Despite her shower, she could still feel the imprint of his hands on her hips, the texture of his mouth on hers. It would be far too easy to allow that man to really get under her skin in the short time she had to spend here.

And yet, she couldn't imagine *not* taking advantage of every hour she could. Once she left Latvala, she would probably never see him again. Wasn't that a sobering thought.

Turning toward her bed, she reached down to snag the comforter and tug it back, when something on the surface caught her attention. She hadn't noticed it before, from a distance, because the squares were flat and flush with the material. Letting go of the cover before she could draw it down, she picked up one of the squares. That was when she realized they were paper cutouts, thin and crinkly in her fingers.

Snapping on the bedside table lamp, Chey got her first real look at the nightmare before her. A handful of photos from some local newspaper—or a rag, as Mattias called it—had been arranged haphazardly on the bed. All of them were shots of she and Mattias during their trip to Kalev. Taken with a high powered telephoto lens, it captured their jaunt into the exclusive store, their lunch on the balcony of the restaurant, and the stop at the park.

The message could not be more clear. *Someone* knew they were going, and had been watching the whole time.

A chill raced down Chey's spine. One of the papers had cutout letters taped to the bottom: *You have been warned.*

Dropping the papers, Chey straightened and glanced around the room. She hadn't checked the bathroom or the deep, walk in closet since she'd arrived. What if the person was there, waiting to hurt her?

Shuffling to the end of the bed, she jammed her feet into her tennis shoes, foregoing socks in her panic, and backtracked for the cutouts. Gathering them as quietly as she could, she tip-toed to the desk, the hair standing up on the back of her neck, and fished the keys to the truck out of the top drawer.

Any second she expected a shadow to part from the wall, or a corner, and stalk her.

Hurrying to the door, she exited her bedroom and broke into a run down the hall. At the top of the stairs, she cautioned herself to make sure no one was there. After a quick look around, seeing no one close by, she went down as quick as she dared to the main floor. From there she doubled back toward the kitchens and a rear exit, bypassing all the other security at the front of the castle due to the guests. There was security here, too, though none stopped her headlong rush through the bailey toward the back gate.

If they thought her eccentric, so be it. All Chey cared about was reaching the truck. At the stables, she found the vehicle sitting right where she'd left it. Once inside, she fired up the engine and spun the tires, tearing off into the night for the safety of Sander's cabin.

Chapter Eleven

The bright shaft of headlights speared the gloom as she sped into the clearing. Applying the brakes a little too hard, the truck skid the last five feet to a halt. Cutting the engine, Chey scrambled from the vehicle and jogged to the door of the cabin.

"Sander? It's Chey. Hello?" She rapped her knuckles against the wood, impatient. He was head of security overall, he was the one who should see the pictures first. When he didn't answer, she knocked again.

Nothing.

Stepping down the porch, she cupped her hand near her eyes and peered in the front window. She could see a small light had been left on in the kitchen and another in the living room, but that was all. There was no movement inside to indicate Sander was home. Damn. That wasn't a possibility she had considered during her flight from the castle. She just expected, at this time of night, that he would be home.

Now what? Should she wait? Go back to the castle? Sit in the truck? Was she safe out here without Sander close by? Questions crowded her mind. If she went back to the castle, to her bedroom, and someone was in there waiting, they might get to her before *she* could get to a phone or scream for help. Maybe she should find Urmas, or Allar. One or both men would be prowling the front half of the castle with the gathering of dignitaries.

Before she could make up her mind, the distant sound of an approaching engine echoed through the woods. That must be Sander. Had to be Sander.

What if it's the attacker, following you from the castle? What if they know Sander is busy elsewhere? The thought galvanized her into action. Jumping off the porch, she darted into the stand of trees adjacent to the cabin. Hiding behind a thick trunked tree, she waited to see who emerged from the darkness.

Headlights cut through the gloom, announcing the vehicle's approach. A rugged Jeep emerged from the same trail she'd driven down, and halted next to the truck. There was something unhurried about its progress that alarmed her.

She couldn't pinpoint why.

Your imagination is running away with itself. Stop it, she chided herself. Adding more fear onto the already tense situation would do her no good. A fighter by nature, Chey nevertheless knew when to be cautious. She was out of her element here, dealing with the unknown.

The door to the Jeep opened and a figure got out. Tall, muscular. *Sander.* Chey left the cover of the trees.

"Sander!"

He looked away from the truck, which he'd been approaching, and faced her when he saw her running from the forest. "Chey, what the hell are you doing hiding in the trees?"

In the few seconds it took to reach him, she glimpsed his attire: green and black camouflage khakis, sage green shirt with sleeves pushed to his elbows, and lace up boots of black. Nothing unusual where Sander was concerned. He must have been out patrolling the grounds.

"Something happened. I found these when I got back to my room tonight." Chey came to a stop right in front of him and held out the squares of paper she'd found on her bed. They crinkled in her shaking fingers.

"Got back from where—I can't see these in the dark. Are you all right?" Sander took the papers from her and guided her with his other hand to the cabin door.

"I'm all right. I just didn't know what else to do. I didn't think to check my room when I got back, and after I saw this lying on my bed, I just grabbed them and ran." She stepped inside after he unlocked the door.

Sander entered on her heels and threw both bolts. Taking the papers to the kitchen table, he snapped on an overhead light and spread them out across the surface. "Tell me what happened. Everything."

"Mattias invited me to an event, some gathering of dignitaries and other important people. We didn't stay too long because Natalia grew angry again and spilled wine on my dress. I got back to my room and found these in there." Chey crossed her arms over her chest and watched him position each piece just so.

"She was angry because you were there with Mattias?" he asked, glancing over to meet her eyes.

Chey nodded. "She doesn't want me interacting on that personal of a level with him. With any of the Royals, I think."

"Did she threaten you?"

"Not physically. She said she would have me thrown out if I spoke to her that way again. I got a little...testy...when she ordered me to leave."

Sander looked back at the pictures, then pushed away from the table. Out of a deep pocket on the thigh of his pants, he fished out his phone. Moments later he was speaking quietly in his mother tongue, stalking through the living room.

Chey waited, watched. She wished, not for the first time, that she understood his language. And although the situation was serious, Chey couldn't help but admire the breadth of his shoulders under the shirt or the way his hips filled the pants out. He resembled a prowling lion pacing its cage.

Finally, after fifteen long minutes, he hung up. "My men put cameras in your room, so we might catch whoever keeps visiting. But they didn't get them activated before being called away for the event, so there's no evidence to look at, unfortunately. And because they were pulled off duty, no one was there watching your room in person. I gave them orders not to balk or argue, because right now, I'm not trying to alert too many people that I'm having you watched and followed."

"I see. Just missed an opportunity, then. Could there be fingerprints on the papers, maybe some on my door? Would that even help?"

"There could be. I'll keep those with your permission and have them checked. My men are doing another search of your room right now to make sure no one stayed behind or planted anything, like they said they would." He pushed the phone into his pocket and closed the distance.

"No, keep them. I don't mind. Do what you need to. I just hate that whoever this is, is not backing down." Chey reached out to tentatively touch his arm.

He turned his hand over, skimmed it down her forearm, and caught her fingers in his. Bending his head, he brushed a quick but warm kiss on her lips.

"Don't worry. We're closing the net, little by little. They'll slip up, make a mistake, and we'll have them. It doesn't please me to know it could be Natalia or Viia, though. The person acting on their behalf probably thinks they'll be immune to prosecution if they just say it was one of the girls who hired them," he said.

Chey breathed him in when he kissed her. The scent, his scent, was familiar and soothing. Already she attributed safety and security with Sander. He was well suited to his job.

"I know you are. I have every confidence you'll figure this out sooner than later. Tell me, though. What happens to Viia or Natalia if it turns out that they're behind this?" Taking initiative, Chey slid her arms around Sander's middle. She had to tilt her chin up to see his eyes due to height differences.

"Natalia will get reprimanded, of course. In private. The Royals will attempt to hide her involvement, especially considering she's been into trouble for her drinking. As far as Viia?" Sander arched a brow. "She's not a member of the family yet. Last I knew, Mattias hadn't proposed, which means she's not afforded the same protections as the others. I imagine Mattias will break it off with her, despite the Queen's inevitable protests."

"Why would the Queen protest?"

"Helina has nurtured that relationship for a long time. She hand picked Viia for Mattias, so she'll do whatever it takes to try and hide any wrongdoing. Mattias, on the other hand, has higher standards than that, and will want to end their relationship. He's not all that fond of her from what I can tell. He's willing to do his duty by her and that's about it."

"Yes, we had a little conversation about

that at lunch. He mentioned that there are few if any real love matches between Royalty and their significant others."

"He told you that?" Sander's eyes narrowed faintly.

"Yes."

"Sounds like he's pretty taken with you."

"I don't know what he is, or isn't, to be honest. I pinned him down and asked him what he wanted from me. Initially, it was to take personal, private photos of Viia when she wasn't watching. Candid shots, like that. But he said it's mostly because I don't treat him like everyone else does. I guess I'm 'safe', if that makes sense. We're worlds apart culture wise, and I don't fawn over him like half the female population of Latvala does." Chey wouldn't point out the sparks and attraction that sometimes flared up between her and Mattias. Not now, after the intimacy with Sander.

He studied her eyes, one hand flattening on the low of her back. "I'm guessing it was your looks that drew him to you at first and then your charming, blunt way of addressing the world."

Chey had never considered herself a bombshell. Hearing Sander refer to her 'looks' that way made Chey want to run to a mirror and see what she was missing. It couldn't be her slightly crooked nose, plain dark hair, and what she considered average features. At five-nine, she wasn't short, but she also wasn't a statuesque runway model with forever legs and slinky limbs.

She felt more like an aggressive little terrier than a greyhound, apt to snarl and bite when threatened.

"Maybe it was the other way around," she said, lifting her chin.

"Could have been. I'll still put money on your rack, though."

"Sander!" She swatted his shoulder. So much for worrying about her facial features and hair. "Have your eyes even made it past my chest yet?"

"A few times." He delivered his tease in a dry tone after chortling for the swat. "Your ass isn't bad, either."

"You're an absolute rake." Laughing despite her circumstances, she got on her tiptoes and kissed him.

Sander cupped the back of her head and held her there while he thoroughly explored her mouth. Breaking away, he stared down at her eyes and said, "So, you're not into him, then?"

She had a hard time refocusing her attention on the conversation. "Well, he *is* a Prince. And he's handsome, there's no denying that. I wouldn't be female—or alive at all—if I didn't realize what a catch he would make. But I also know I'm hundreds of miles out of his league, he has a girlfriend and I'm not sure his mother knows I exist even when I'm standing in the same room. Besides all *that,*

I'm kind of into someone else at the moment."

The first half of her explanation brought a funny look to Sander's features. Chey couldn't decide if he was wary, bemused or relieved. Maybe a little of all three.

"You wouldn't be the first girl to have dreams of becoming a Princess. There are women who would kill to have even five minutes of his undivided time. I'm pleased to hear of your distraction, though." Sander delivered his reply with a wan smile.

"I think Mattias finds me a novelty more than anything. He has easy access to me in the castle, a new, different brain to pick to ease his boredom. I'd be shocked if he was even a little interested," she confessed.

Before Sander could reply, a buzzing emitted from his pocket. "Just a second." He stepped away after a quick kiss to her temple and dug his phone out.

Chey stepped over to sit on the arm of the sofa while he traded texts with whom she could only imagine were the rest of his security team.

"Any news?" she asked when he was done.

"Nothing we didn't already know. We'll see if they pull off any fingerprints but I'm pretty sure the person covered their tracks." He slid the phone back into his pocket and strode past for the kitchen. On the way, he asked, "You want coffee or anything? I've informed the men that you're staying here tonight while they investigate. They'll pass it on to the other guards so no one raises an alarm when you don't return."

"What will people say?" She rose off the couch and followed him to the kitchen. Taking up a spot at the counter, she slid onto a barstool and watched while he got a pot of coffee going. As ever, he was efficient and well practiced.

"That you're staying here for protection purposes. If they wonder anything else, then let them wonder. I doubt anyone will say anything to you, because it might seem leading and suggestive. If you act like it's not a big deal, then it won't be." He glanced at the windows with sharp, assessing looks then took two mugs down from the cupboard.

She supposed he was right. If she acted suspicious and guilty, then that's what people would think. Following his glance, she stared at the windows. Past the bullet-proof panes, the night was dark. "You don't think anyone would make an attempt out here, do you?"

"Not if they've got half a brain, and it seems likely given all the other precautions they're taking."

"Let's hope so. Does this mean we can't go tomorrow night?" She glanced back to Sander just as he took the half filled pot out to pour.

"No, we're going. We'll just have to make sure we're not followed. Shouldn't be too hard." He pushed her mug across the counter and leaned his hip against the edge.

"I really hope you catch them soon, Sander.

I'm going to feel like a sitting duck every time I have to be out in the open for too long." She sipped the coffee.

"We're doing everything we can. If we get aggressive, we might scare them into hiding. Then it could be weeks before they make another move and catch us off guard." He met and held her eyes while he took a drink.

"I overheard some Prince or another at the soiree talk about rumors of an assassination attempt." Chey purposefully left out any more details in the hopes Sander would fill her in on what she was missing, and what Mattias refused to tell her.

He paused with the cup halfway to his mouth. A brow arched and his gaze sharpened on her face. "Well, wasn't that a careless mistake on the Prince's part."

"I don't think he figured anyone would over hear him."

"In a room full of people? Someone will always overhear." He grunted in displeasure.

"So you're not going to tell me, either, are you?"

"No," he replied bluntly.

"Because it's better for my own safety if I don't know details."

"That's right. And also because it's not our policy to talk about it outside certain circles."

Annoyed, she had another sip of coffee.

"What, you don't agree with that?" he asked.

"No, I understand. It's just frustrating to

have only half the picture."

"As soon as we figure it out and make some arrests, you can read about it in the paper."

"Along with everyone else." Chey quirked her lips. If that wasn't a reminder that she was one of the common folk, she didn't know what was.

"That's right," he retorted in a no nonsense tone, apparently unrepentant about putting her in her place.

Rather than get twitchy about the hierarchy and titles and whatnot, Chey set down her cup and folded her arms across the table. Her gaze started around his hips and rose inch by inch up his body until she found his eyes. If nothing else, just staring at his broad chest and strong shoulders for the next ten hours would be a delight. Maybe, if she was lucky, there would be a little more hands on contact than that.

She just had one question left for Sander.

"So. How do you suggest we while away the hours between now and dawn?"

. . .

Waking up with her cheek pressed to the sculpted plane of a masculine chest was something, Chey decided, she could get used to. Heat from Sander's skin warmed her own, the faint *thump* of his heart a soothing metronome that she'd fallen asleep to. Already there was an ache low in her belly and tenderness between her thighs. Other places paid tribute to Sander's particular brand of possession: the sting of small bites on the back of her shoulder, fingerprint bruises on her hips and the strain of muscles unused to being manipulated into *those* kinds of positions.

No less than four times had he taken her during the night. Once, after he'd come prowling back from a cursory check of the cabin, he'd been especially demanding. She knew she would wear these badges of passion for days—and couldn't find the will to care.

Lifting her head, she turned her chin to prop it on his sternum to see his face. He was staring at her, one arm cocked up behind his head. Some time during the night, the small ponytail he wore half his hair in had come down, leaving the golden mane loose and wild. She remembered dragging her fingers through the strands while he'd growled in her ear.

These were memories that would last a lifetime.

"You're looking at me like you're going to start taking bites." His voice, thick with motherland accent, was raspier than usual.

"Would you care if I did?" she asked.

"Not necessarily. Just leave all the parts attached." He put his free hand in her tousled hair, drawing the strands back away from her face.

She buried a smile in his skin. "Maybe. If you're good."

"I was already good. *Four* times, unless you lost count."

She scoffed. "Of course I haven't forgotten. You've left traces in your wake."

"None on your throat, though. That's my gentlemanly nature shining through."

Chey raised her head just enough to make eye contact easier. "And why is that?"

"Because of the stares you'd get back at the castle if you showed up with a mark or two on your neck. Unless you brought a handful of high-collar sweaters with you." He arched a brow pointedly.

She hadn't thought about that.

"See? I'm right." He gloated a little.

"Okay, okay. You did good." She nipped the skin of his chest, pleased when he rumbled a low noise of pleasure.

"Keep that up and the number will rise."

"Along with other things."

He laughed. "Exactly."

"I haven't worn you out yet?" She arched a brow.

"I should be the one asking you that."

The ache between her legs was a testament to the truth of his statement. She had the grace to blush.

"I figured," he added.

"Well, who knew you had such stamina? You can stop looking smug any time now." Chey propped her chin on his sternum again, amused at his gloating.

"What? I don't look smug." He cut her a

devilish grin and unhooked his hand from behind his head. Reaching to the nightstand, he picked up the phone he'd left sitting there the night before.

While he checked for messages, Chey yawned and stretched her spine. It was difficult to tell what time it was; weak light spilled in through the cracks of the curtains, giving her the impression it was barely twilight outside or that it was early, but overcast.

"What time is it, and is there any news?" she asked.

"Time to get up and get dressed. Your escort will be here in a half hour." He swatted her butt and set the phone down. "No new details."

"What?" She glanced up at Sander, surprised. "My escort?"

"Back to the castle. Up you go. If you want to catch a shower, you should hop in now." He sat up when she did, cupped her nape, and held her there for a quick kiss to her temple.

Chey wasn't sure what to think of being ushered off so fast after the night they just shared. She wanted to lounge and enjoy his presence for another hour or two, at least. As if he'd read her mind, Sander paused to lean closer.

"As much as I'd like to lounge around here all day, I can't. I have work to do before this evening when you come back." He tweaked her nose and threw his legs over the side of the bed.

214

Chey grumped to herself. Work. She acted like he had all the time in the world to spend in leisure and more...creative pursuits.

"I forgot. Yes, I think I'll take a quick shower." She rolled out of bed and snatched a robe, his robe, off a nearby chair.

"I'll get your clothes. Meet me out in the kitchen when you're done." He tugged on a pair of jeans and winked over his shoulder before departing the room.

"Thanks." Chey stared at the broad span of his naked back. A shudder raced down her spine when a specific memory or two assaulted her from their risque night in bed. Finally, she made her way into the bathroom, closing the door in her wake.

Chapter Twelve

The hours between leaving Sander's cabin and waiting to meet him again passed in agonizing slowness. Urmas had informed her upon her arrival back at the castle that he expected his usual morning round of pictures by four that afternoon. He hadn't asked her any questions about where she'd been, or what was going on with her bedroom. She guessed he knew. Of course he knew. He was probably heading up some of the investigation on the inside while Sander worked the outside. Or if Urmas wasn't, then Allar was, and then relaying whatever information onward.

She wondered who knew she hadn't come back to the castle the night before. Most of the guards and perhaps some of the staff. Ingel seemed to know everything that went on under the Ahtissari roof on a regular basis. Chey's absence this morning for breakfast would have been a dead giveaway.

Editing the rash of photos she'd taken on the canoe trip, Chey spent her time curled up on the bed in her room, sitting lotus style, fingers quick on the keys. Often she found her attention drifting to Sander, especially when she pulled up the photos of him inside the canoe. The smile he wore, devilish and handsome, tugged at her heartstrings. He was a fine specimen of a man, suited to the outdoors around him. These photos she would be keeping for herself. Urmas only cared about the ones she'd taken specifically for the Royal family.

At four o'clock, Urmas's assistant showed up for the flash drive. Chey delivered it with a quiet smile, relieved she wouldn't have to face Urmas just yet. A short few minutes later, before she got too involved in other activities, someone knocked at the door. It must be the assistant, back with a question. Chey, fearless now that there was so much foot traffic in the castle, swung the door open.

Elise, the pretty maid with the dark eyes and free swinging ponytail, peered at her over a tall stack of fluffy, folded towels. "Pardon, Miss Sinclair. I have your new towels. The dryer was broken this morning, so I could not exchange them on the first trip."

"Oh, hello, Elise. Come in, come in." Chey stepped back and allowed the maid to carry the towels into the bathroom. "I'm done with work for now, you're no bother."

"Thank you. How is your face? The bruises look a little better. I brought you another tube of the cover up." Elise's voice echoed from the bathroom.

"It's not as dark. That stuff you brought me really worked well." The cover up Elise delivered had almost obliterated the black and blue mark around her eye and temple.

Elise strode out of the bathroom and withdrew another small tube from the pocket of her gray pants. She wore the standard, athletic uniform instead of a traditional little skirt and apron. Once in reach, Elise extended the tube with a smile.

Chey eased it from her fingers. "Thanks. I don't think I'll need any more after this. You saved me last night."

Elise studied her face from a few angles. "Yes, it is good product. You could use a little more today," she said, gesturing to the raw places uncovered by the cover up.

Chey hadn't brought it with her when she left the castle for Sander's cabin last evening. "Yes, I certainly could."

Elise smiled, touched Chey's arm, then stepped past for the door. "We will see you in the morning, Miss Chey."

"Bye, Elise."

When the door closed, Chey went into the bathroom and liberally applied the contents of the tube to her bruises. As before, she was astounded at what a good job it did. Better yet, there was no thick, cake-like texture on her skin to give away what she'd done. Leaving the tube on the counter, she changed into a fresh pair of jeans and a long sleeved sweater of deep brown. It was heavy enough, she thought, to withstand being out in the elements this evening when Sander took her to the ruins. She made sure to put fresh batteries into her camera and a blank memory card as well. Never know what she might catch out there.

Chey left the castle just before evening was due to set in. Caught by surprise at the heavy bank of thunderclouds overhead, she glanced up at the ominous flicker of lightning as she walked across the bailey. Thunder growled distantly a handful of seconds later.

Just as she reached the bailey gate, a tingle on the nape of her neck made Chey glance back at the castle. Two guards flanked the door she'd exited a moment before, paying her little attention. Her gaze ticked up to the many windows, turrets and arches that comprised the facade of the structure. From this position, the castle towered above, seeming to punch a hole in the sky.

A flicker of movement in one of the archways drew her attention. Almost before she knew what she was doing, Chey brought the camera hanging around her neck up and snapped off three quick shots. There hadn't been any time to zoom or even focus well.

By the time she lowered the camera, that telltale flicker of motion was gone. Probably another guard walking the long halls or one of the numerous servants on their way to or from an errand for the Royals.

Uneasy, Chey turned around and broke into a jog for the gate. The first drop of rain fell just as she slid behind the wheel of the truck and started the engine.

. . .

"Are you sure it's safe to go in there in this weather?" Chey asked.

Sander glanced out the front windshield, wipers *swish-swishing* away the rain. "Sure it is. Once you get inside, the only place the rain will get to you is if you step out into an open courtyard or something."

"I'm not really worried about the rain so much as it making stairs or the flooring slick. There are probably a thousand leaks in that thing." Chey stared at the ruins through the downpour. Darkness hadn't quite swallowed the landscape, though it might as well have for how well she could see. The old castle was more silhouette and looming shape than anything else. She made out the deeper recesses of windows without panes, the top of the high wall, and a tall arch protecting a broad door that appeared to have iron hinges stretching across the surface. It didn't seem so 'small' to Chey. The castle wasn't on par size wise with the main family seat, but it was by no means a paltry dwelling.

Sitting in Sander's Jeep, she gauged the distance between the lowest floor of the castle and the tower she had to climb to get to the room Sander mentioned. It was probably five flights of stairs. At least.

"You'll be fine. Having second thoughts?" he asked with a knowing grin.

Chey swatted his arm. "No. It's just rain and an abandoned castle."

"An abandoned *haunted* castle," he corrected. "You take the first set of stairs you see up to the third floor, then follow the main hallway back to the end. There is another doorway, you can't miss it, and a second set of stairs that wind around up to the tower. Here, take the flashlight. I put new batteries in before I left the cabin." He handed the flashlight across the Jeep.

She took the flashlight and covered her camera with a plastic bag he had on hand. "I got it. Don't worry about me, I'll be fine."

"Of course you will. Remember, I'll be there shortly after you start screaming." He lounged against the seat, knees parted casually, one elbow propped against the door.

Chey snorted. "You're enjoying this, aren't you? I'm not going to start screaming, because *ghosts don't exist.*"

"Mhm." That was Sander's only reply.

Chey counted to three and got out of the Jeep. The rain pelted her at a pace that would leave her clothes drenched if she didn't hurry. Breaking into a run, she approached the stairs and trotted up with care. The stone wasn't as slick as she thought it might be.

Under the cover of the immense porch, Chey uncovered the camera and glanced back at the Jeep. Sander had cut the headlights some time before. She could barely see him past the windshield, a vague shape obscured by the rain. Nevertheless, she waved the bag and went to the heavy wooden door. As she'd thought, iron hinges spiked across the surface from one side, heavy rivets holding them in place. Sander told her the castle wasn't locked, so she had no trouble getting inside.

A large foyer opened up to a high ceiling and an enormous great hall to her right. Although gloomy, she could still make the general shape out. Stuffing the plastic bag into the pocket of her jeans, she snapped on the flashlight. Gasping at the sheer beauty of such an old structure, Chey breathed in the musty, old smell of the stone and wandered further in.

Not usually a woman prone to fantastical ideas, she could easily imagine men in armor and women in long gowns decorating these halls. The castle, she discovered, was rather well preserved. None of the walls appeared to have holes in them that weren't there by design, and thus far, she found no puddles on the floor from leaks in the ceiling.

A certain poignancy pervaded the air, as if the souls of the past were reaching across time and space, welcoming her into their home. A much more volatile time in history, she imagined the triumphs and tragedies that must have happened within these walls.

Don't let your imagination run too far away with you, she chided herself. That was all she needed. She would start seeing ghosts before she knew it and freak herself out.

Thunder growled beyond the castle, rolling instead of cracking and booming. Lightning pierced the windows, shedding yet more, if brief, illumination over the walls and interior. Fascinated by the spartan design, she followed the foyer to the set of stairs Sander mentioned. Setting the flashlight down, she angled it so that she could snap off a picture or two with interesting shadows cast across the steps. Picking the flashlight up, she ascended, mesmerized by the immense proportions and maze-like hallways.

By comparison, this castle showed its age much more than the other one. The stone looked worn, as did the stairs, though that was not to say it *felt* unsteady. Far from it. She knew she was as secure on these stairs as those at the main castle. Taking more photos along the way, she found the second door at the end of the hall and went up. These stairs spiraled around and around, winding upward through each level. The walls curved as well, the stone smoother here, less rough on her palm. Chey wondered how many times Andra had walked this route. It sent chills up her spine to know this was the exact same path the woman had taken probably thousands of times. Andra had actually stood right in this very spot. So had her murderer, if Sander was to be believed.

A rustle behind her caused Chey to spin, gasping, the flashlight beam spearing the darkness. She could only see perhaps ten feet forward or back thanks to the curving design. "Sander, is that you?"

No response.

"That's not funny. You can't cheat and scare me," she accused.

Nothing.

Thinning her lips, she listened another minute. The vague rustle didn't come again. A spate of fresh thunder encouraged her to finish her ascent. She knew when she'd come to the landing of the right room because there were no more steps to take. This was it, the end of the line in the south tower.

The door she stood in front of had been Andra's. Seizing the moment, Chey snapped off a few pictures. Caught up in the ancient history and the story Sander told her, she finally put her fingers on the iron handle and pushed the door in. The hinges whined and screeched.

Circular, the south tower room was bigger than Chey thought it would be. She could have fit ten queen sized beds in that space with room for dressers, a few armoires and a sofa or two. Several cathedral shaped windows were cut into the walls, the sills more than a foot thick. Only darkness and the storm raged beyond, obliterating whatever view Andra had from the tower. Nothing remained from that time, not even a splinter of wood from a chair or scraps of old cloth.

What *did* survive, were the beams high up along the ceiling. Chey pinpointed the center one and stared at it for an indefinite amount of time. To know that *this* was the beam Andra hung from was more than a little eerie. And she understood now why Sander had said Andra couldn't have been the one to hang herself. If there hadn't been a very tall ladder, there was no way she could have gotten the rope over the beam.

The hinge on the door whined. Startled, Chey swung her light that direction.

It's just the wind. Ghosts don't exist. True enough, there was a stiff breeze blowing in the three arched windows that could have moved the door forward or back several inches. So far, rain hadn't penetrated the pass-through.

To prove a point, she took a few pictures of the doorway, and then the beams above. The entire time, goosebumps decorated her skin under the material of her sweater. Anyone would be creeped out, she assured herself. Someone—*two* people—had been murdered in this room.

A flicker of motion out of the corner of her eye near the door caused her to whip the flashlight beam that direction again. Was she seeing things? Could the mind play such convincing tricks? *Of course it can. Sander planted a haunted story in your mind and now you're imagining a ghost around every corner.*

What felt like a touch skimmed her left arm. Chey screamed, dropped the flashlight, and struck out with a hand. She encountered nothing but air. Turning a dizzying circle, her camera thumping against her chest, she shuddered. Nothing and no one was in the room.

"Stop it, Chey. It's just the wind. It's only the wind." Talking to herself, she stooped and blindly reached for the flashlight. Thunder cracked so hard in the sky that it startled another scream from her throat. Lurching upright, she tried the button and discovered the flashlight was broken. Fantastic. That would make escaping the south tower even more dangerous as full dark descended outside.

Never mind what eerie images she might conjure thanks to a lack of light.

The hinges on the door split the air with a loud creak. Chey yelped when a definite shadow parted from the deeper shadows of the landing beyond.

"Chey?" Sander asked. A moment later, a blitz of lightning illuminated his frowning face. "I heard you scream."

She would have loved to blame Sander for the 'touch' to her arm. The fact of the matter was—she couldn't. No one had been in the room. His concern for her was real, as well, indicating he hadn't been playing tricks.

"Yeah, I don't know. Something startled me and I dropped the flashlight. Now it's broke." She didn't want to admit how good it was to see him.

He snapped on his flashlight but avoided

getting the beam in her eyes. Slanting it downward, he closed the distance and took the damaged flashlight from her.

"The lens is cracked. What startled you?" he asked.

She was loathe to admit it. "I thought I felt something touch my arm."

"Maybe it was just the wind. It's blowing pretty good through those windows." He tucked the broken flashlight into the back of his pants.

Chey glanced at the cutouts in the stone. Lightning tore through the clouds, briefly flashing more light through the room. She caught sight of Sander's expression when she looked back, expecting to see smug satisfaction there. After all, he'd accurately predicted she would wind up screaming. Instead, he only appeared as concerned as he had when he entered.

"Probably. Either way, I concede. This tower *is* creepy." She glanced once more at the high beam, then stepped closer to Sander, attempting to nudge him toward the door. Chey was more than ready to depart.

"Most ruins would be creepy this late at night with a storm like that blowing in. Come on. Hold onto my hand." He caught hers and gripped it lightly with his own.

Relieved at the contact, she stayed close as he led her back down the stairs, through the castle, and out onto the porch. Here the wind was more vicious than when they'd arrived, whipping her ponytail around her neck.

Sander locked the heavy door behind them this time. He let go of her hand and ushered her out into the rain after she'd covered her camera with the plastic bag.

Ensconced in the Jeep, he turned the engine over and cut a deviant grin her way.

"You don't even need to say I told you so," she retorted with a laugh when she saw the grin. Her mood was less volatile now that she was safe in the Jeep. If he wanted to taunt her —well. She wouldn't get too grouchy about it.

"I didn't say a thing," he replied with no small amount of amusement.

"But you were thinking it." Chey brushed rain out of her hair.

"Mm, no."

"Then what were you thinking?"

"About my next day off, and your next day off, and whether I can coax you away from the castle again."

"Speaking of work, I wonder if this weather is supposed to last. I won't be able to take the photographs tomorrow if so." She looked out the window. Rain battered the landscape. The tops of the trees swished every which way with the force of the wind. "Getting me away from the castle won't be hard."

"Yeah, actually, this storm will be here a few days if the forecasts hold. We might even see a dusting of snow with the cold front coming in over night. You'll probably have to consult with Urmas and see what changes they have in store for you." He drove with confidence and skill over the rough asphalt that wound through the countryside.

"It might still work for pictures if we have snow—just not rain. I'll ask." Chey wondered if Sander meant to invite her into the cabin when they returned. She wanted to spend the night instead of return to the castle. That could become a habit if she wasn't careful. She wasn't sure that her employers would think it a good idea for her to spend too many nights away from the family seat. On the other hand, they couldn't expect her to entirely close herself off from a personal life during her four month stay.

She had her answer after they arrived at the cabin and Sander killed the engine. Turning toward her, he grasped her around the nape and hauled her in for a devastating kiss.

Against her lips, he whispered, "Text me when you have your next day off. All right?"

Chey lingered in the kiss as long as she dared to. Shoving down disappointment, she brushed the pads of her fingers over the raspy layer of whiskers on his jaw and drew back enough to see his eyes. He stared at her with an unusual weight to his gaze. Maybe he felt the same disappointment she did at the need to observe restraint regarding their positions.

"I will. Thanks for tonight. I'd love to go back and visit the castle during the day, when I can take some better pictures. If you'll take me, that is." She covered her camera; rain still fell beyond the windows of the Jeep.

"It's a date. Drive slow and safe back to the castle, hm?" He plucked a last kiss from her mouth.

Chey breathed him in while he was close. "I'll be fine. Talk to you soon."

After another lingering look, she opened her door and got out. Thumping the door closed, she ran around the front of the Jeep to the waiting truck.

A minute later she drove out of the clearing, fingers tight on the wheel.

Sander Fisk was definitely under her skin.

Chapter Thirteen

After a restless night's sleep, Chey rose before her alarm and changed from her pajamas into jeans. Pulling a thin ribbed sweater of burgundy over her head, she forewent shoes and started editing the photos she'd taken the evening before. She was especially interested in the ones she'd taken of the main castle with the shadow in the window. No matter how much she zoomed in, or changed filters and lighting, she couldn't get any real detail to show up. There was only a vague outline of what *could* or could not be a body. It might have been anyone from a passing guard to a maid to one of the Royals en route from one part of the castle to another. There wasn't anything to indicate that she'd captured someone blatantly staring down, even if that was the sense Chey had standing in the bailey.

At eight o'clock sharp, Elise and Ingel arrived with breakfast and merry greetings. Both women examined her bruises and declared her well on the mend. The women blew through as they always did, gathering used towels and washcloths, making the bed even though Chey always made it herself, and running a duster over the furniture. One woman cleaned floors while the other did showers and sinks.

Most of the time, when Chey offered to help, she was gently turned down. The women had their routine and though they tried to clean when Chey was out of the room, they were efficient and quick when she was in residence. It always smelled fresh and new in the suite when they were done.

Once they'd departed, Chey got back to work, nibbling eggs, bacon and several pieces of fruit in between. The photos from the old castle, while beautiful and eerie, turned up nothing remotely resembling a ghost. No strange orbs, no flickers of light, no unexplained shadows within a shadow.

"I'm not sure what you were expecting, Chey," she muttered to herself. Of course there weren't any ghosts. Ghosts didn't exist.

After lunch, Chey grabbed her camera and wandered the halls of the castle. She got several great shots of the snow out a few of the large windows and more pictures of the armor lining one entire hallway. It felt good to stretch her legs and get some exercise. Moving around also took her mind off Sander.

She wondered where he was on the property and if he'd found out any news about the paper clippings. Surely he would have texted her if so.

Returning to her room an hour before dinner, she was surprised to find a box sitting outside her door.

Immediately wary, Chey approached it with caution. Although white, and glossy, with a pretty bow of red on the top, she worried it contained something less than pleasing. Like a head. Or a pair of eyes. Picking it up off the floor, she sniffed near the edge of the lid for any strange scent. All she picked up was a vague hint of something floral.

What had the world come to for her to be checking a gift box for body parts.

Not convinced it wasn't a trap, or a trick, she hesitated before taking it inside. Locking the door behind her, she walked the box to the bed and removed the camera from around her neck. Setting it aside, she pried at the box until the lid came off.

Bracing herself for all manner of horror, she put the lid down and lifted back three layers of black tissue. Folded with care was a stunning garment of blood red silk. Removing it from the box, she held it at the top and let it unfurl.

The cocktail dress sported a square shaped neckline and intricate beading on the bodice. More beading decorated the cuffs of long sleeves and when she held it up against her body, the hem landed a modest half inch above her knee. It was beautifully simple yet elegant.

A quick search of the box turned up a short note that read: *Be ready at six sharp.*

It had to be Sander. He was going to surprise her with a trip away from the castle.

Maybe to a quaint, small restaurant along the coast between here and Kalev.

Excited at the prospect, and to finally have him see her in something besides jeans and sweaters, she draped the dress over the end of the bed and headed for the shower.

She wanted to look her absolute best for their date.

. . .

Chey checked her reflection in the mirror one last time. The red silk fit her to a tee, outlining her shape with a snug bodice while the skirt flared slightly from her hips. Her eyes boasted smoky charcoal shadow and liner that accentuated the almond shape. The blue of her iris looked more vivid with her lashes coated in mascara and she'd chosen lipstick as red as the dress to paint her lips with. The wispy curls of her hair had been fashioned into a neat updo, held in place with a few cleverly placed pins. As ever, several strands slipped the fastenings and tickled the line of her throat.

Pleased overall with the effect, she daubed on a bit of feminine perfume at her wrists and throat. Transferring her wallet, ID and money into a nude purse that matched her heels, she was just snapping the clasp when a knock sounded at the door.

Grinning, anxious to see Sander in clothing a little more refined than hunting gear, she swung the door open.

"You sure know how to s--" Chey halted when she came face to face with Mattias. Austere in a black suit and red tie that matched her dress, he arched a brow.

"I sure know how to s..." Mattias repeated her and trailed, like he expected her to finish what she'd started to say.

Mattias had sent the dress? Chey stifled her disappointment and pasted on a smile. It wasn't that she wasn't happy to see the Prince —she'd just been expecting someone else.

"You sure know how to surprise a girl," she said, completing her thought. What an understatement.

He eyed her like he knew there was more she wasn't saying, then glanced at her throat. "You're not wearing the pendant?"

Chey's fingers flew to the base of her neck. "I was just about to put it on when you knocked. Give me one second."

"Do you need help?"

"I...sure. Sure." Chey stepped away from the door, leaving it ajar for Mattias to follow. The necklace was back in its box in her dresser. She fished it out and handed it back, then scooped the escaped strands of her hair out of the way.

Mattias accepted it, undid the clasp, and draped the chain around her neck.

Acutely aware of his presence behind her, of his masculine cologne, she cautioned herself to tamp down her surprise and just go

235

with it. She twitched faintly when his fingertips brushed her nape.

"There. Ready?" he asked, turning to offer his elbow.

Chey released the wisps of hair and glanced at his arm before lifting her gaze to his eyes. "Yes, sure. *Where* are we going, anyway? I wasn't expecting this."

"It's a surprise. You look ravishing, by the way. Red suits you." He led her to her door and waited patiently while she locked it behind them.

"Thanks. You look very nice yourself," she said. But then, Mattias always did. Clean shaven, hair combed back, he was the epitome of polished masculinity. She wanted to ask him what he was doing gifting her with diamonds and expensive dresses, but decided that he would give her an answer along the lines of the one he had at lunch the other day. Maybe he was testing her to see how she performed under pressure. To what end, she couldn't guess.

"Thank you. I've noticed your absence around the castle the last couple of days. Everything all right with you?" He escorted her down the hallway and around the corner for the other set of stairs. The ones leading to the third floor.

Places off limits for people like her.

"I was taking pictures of the Latvala wilds." Which was true. The canoe trip definitely fell into that category.

"And did you like what you saw?" Mattias slowed his pace leading her up the stairs.

"It's beautiful country. I hope to explore more of it during my stay. Closer to the mountains, perhaps."

"Better hurry then. By the middle of November, the days will be much shorter and the snow deep enough to be a hinderance." Mattias guided her toward a tall archway on the Royal's personal floor.

"Thanks for the warning. I'll make it a priority in the next couple of weeks."

"Excellent. If you need escort, or a more rugged vehicle, let me know and I'll arrange something." He didn't pause before sweeping her into the vast, formal dining hall.

Whatever Chey might have said evaporated when she spied the long, elaborately set table and the people either seated or standing around it. The entire Royal family appeared to be present. The King and Queen, Paavo and Aurora, Natalia and another man and woman Chey hadn't met. It was either the eldest brother, Dare, or the youngest, Gunnar. He was as striking as the other men, though not quite as tall, with blonde hair and green eyes.

Chey didn't have time to decide who was who before her gaze landed smack on Viia.

She was going to kill Mattias. Kill him dead.

Mattias halted their progress halfway to the end of the table. Chey guessed Viia had everything to do with the sudden, cold expression that crossed his face. The two must have had a falling out, or an argument, or some other point of contention between them. Either that, or Mattias was just that disgruntled to see her there.

Silence descended on the entire group.

Wishing a great black hole would open up in the floor and swallow her, Chey glanced from Mattias's murderous look to the others. Paavo and his wife seemed genuinely surprised. The King stared with displeasure clear on his features while the Queen leveled a rather direct look on Chey.

It was Natalia, of course, who broke the awkward pause. Her chair scraped back over the floor when she stood up.

"What is *she* doing here?" Natalia demanded.

"Quiet your mouth," Mattias hissed. "Miss Sinclair is my *invited* guest to dinner. I want to know which one of you extended another to Viia without my knowledge or approval."

Had Chey been on the receiving end of Mattias's dark tone and predatory stare, she would have withered and disappeared under the table. Pronto.

"I did not realize an invitation was needed," the Queen said after a long sip of her wine. "After all, Viia *is* your intended. This woman is not."

This woman. The Queen could not have sounded more disdainful if she'd tried. Chey bristled inwardly but took care not to let it show where everyone else could see. Although if she was honest, the Queen was only being truthful. Chey had no business attending a private, Royal family function.

"She is not my intended and each one of you know it. Now, who invited her?" Mattias's quiet fury could not be contained. A muscle twitched along his jaw.

"*I* invited her, brother. Your behavior lately is inexcusable," Natalia spat, before turning a venomous stare on Chey. "And *you*. I have had about enough of this. I want her fired--"

"Enough!" Mattias's voice boomed through the elaborate, richly decorated dining hall.

Chey twitched in surprise. She'd never heard him raise his voice that way before. Real fear gripped her gut. Natalia would push to have her fired after this. Or maybe she would get her way before Chey could even escape the dining hall.

Oh *no.* This was a disaster.

"Mattias--" The King got no further before Mattias cut him off.

"No. This ridiculousness ends tonight. Viia, take your leave." He snapped the order her way. When she didn't move fast enough for him, Mattias cracked another command. "*Now.*"

Openly flustered and upset, Viia set her wine glass down and stalked from the room.

Chey knew better than to make eye contact with her. Just then, she wanted to be at Sander's cabin, far from the tension and strife of being involved with the Royal family. His life was so much simpler.

Mattias had never done her wrong, however, so she stood resolutely at his side while he sent one girl from the room and faced down the rest.

Natalia burst into their native tongue, using a finger to point at Mattias with obvious accusation. Mattias, with steel control, replied in a way that convinced Chey he had the upper hand in the conversation.

A moment later, Natalia's face went white and she fled the hall in Viia's wake.

The Queen's lips pressed together, but she said no more.

"If anyone else intends to be rude to my guest, kindly take your leave," Mattias said. He guided Chey to the table and pulled out a chair.

The last thing she wanted to do was sit down. If he expected her to eat after this, he was sadly mistaken. Still, she eased into the chair, waiting to see who else was going to get up and depart.

Paavo and Aurora sat down across from them.

There were four place settings between their seats and the King and Queen and Chey thanked her lucky stars that Mattias had the wherewithal to give everyone some distance.

"Nothing much has changed in our absence, I see," the unnamed man said. He escorted his companion to a chair next to

Aurora and sat down himself.

"Miss Sinclair, my youngest brother Prince Gunnar and his wife, Princess Krislin." Mattias took his chair while making terse introductions.

"Pleasure to make your acquaintance," Chey said. She didn't offer her hand across the gilded table, accustomed already to the Ahtissari tradition as far as that was concerned.

Krislin, with her tawny hair and blue eyes, assessed Chey without the judgement so common with everyone else. And she smiled, nearly catching Chey off guard.

"Miss Sinclair," Krislin said, inclining her head.

"Miss," Gunnar added.

Paavo and Aurora tacked on quiet greetings and took their seat closer to the King and Queen.

Much to Chey's surprise, neither Aksel nor Helina retreated from the table. She soon learned it would have been much better if they had.

Over a first course of fine bullion and black rye bread, Helina asked, "What of your family line, Miss Sinclair? Where do they hail from?"

"My parents were both born in Washington. They met in college and got married after they graduated. Beyond that, I have more distant relatives that came from France, Italy, and Ireland, among others." Chey struggled to sip spoonfuls of the broth without choking. She was sitting here talking to the Queen of Latvala like it was an every day occurrence.

"What of their occupations?" she asked next.

Chey squirmed in her seat. She didn't miss the look Mattias shot his mother.

"My father owned a small business in Seattle and my mother was a teacher."

"And your grandparents?"

"Stone mason, automobile factory employee, seamstress and my other grandmother stayed at home to raise her child." Thankful for the wine Mattias poured, she picked up her glass and had a much needed sip.

"A family of laborers, then," Helina surmised.

"Yes." Chey refused to show shame. More than half the people in the world were laborers of one sort or another. Not everyone could be Royalty.

"And how many--"

Mattias cut the Queen off with a quiet word in their native language.

"...how many brothers and sisters do you have?" Helina, apparently unintimidated by Mattias's interruption, finished asking her question.

The second course arrived. Platters of broiled pork, fish and salads were set near each person. Sliced potatoes in some sort of cheese sauce followed, along with slices of a different kind of bread Chey couldn't place.

"None, your Majesty. I'm an only child." Chey remembered Mattias explaining how Viia had been chosen because of her extensive family line.

"What of your parents?"

"All but one had a brother or sister. My mother was an only child as well. My grandmother miscarried two before her."

Silence fell over the table. The only sound for five minutes was the gentle clink of silver against china.

If you'd been petitioning for a place as one of the Prince's wives, Chey ol' girl, you just shot yourself in the foot. Dry commentary ran through Chey's mind as she picked up one of three forks set on a separate napkin. She couldn't help that her grandmother had difficult pregnancies.

Mattias muttered something under his breath. After that, the rest of the meal passed in relative peace and quiet. Everyone concentrated on eating, which absolved the need to converse.

The food turned out to be well seasoned and excellently prepared. Chey hardly noticed. It was a distant appreciation in the effort to finish so that Mattias would escort her back to her room. If this was what it was like to be an intimate part of the Royal family, Chey wanted no part of it.

She felt sorry for them all, unable to even enjoy a meal without Natalia making mountains out of molehills.

Finally, after a course of dessert, the torture was over. Mattias excused them at the same time Paavo and Aurora pushed back their chairs. Chey bade them all good evening and breathed a sigh of relief once she and Mattias were in the hallway.

He said nothing. One hand low on her back, he guided her off the private floor to the stairs and down to a more suitable level. Chey wasn't sure what to say to all that and her urge to kill Mattias a little had passed. He couldn't have known that would happen.

Could he?

At her door, Mattias released her and maintained eye contact. "Open it."

"...what?" Startled, Chey frowned. He wanted to come in? Did Mattias have the entirely wrong idea about what was going to happen tonight?

"Your door. Open it," he repeated.

"Mattias, now look here--"

"I want to check and make sure no one is hanging around that shouldn't be."

Of course he would have heard what happened by now. Feeling ridiculous that she'd suspected he wanted something else from her, Chey fished her key out and opened the door. He stepped in before her, stalking through the space with a critical examination of the most obvious hiding places.

"Is it always like that? Dinner?" she asked, setting her purse and keys on her dresser. While he stepped into the bathroom, Chey pulled the pins out of her hair and set them down. Running her fingers through the curls, she let them settle around her shoulders and toed off her heels.

He returned, hands clasped behind his back. Mattias swept a look over her, head to toe. "Not always. Sometimes it's worse, sometimes more tolerable."

"Why did you bring me?"

"I wanted you to meet my brother and his wife, for one. And because you're a guest in this house. Guests should be treated like they matter, shouldn't they? The King and Queen entertain only those they have to or the ones who can do something for them."

"So they do it when they can't get around it, you do it to soothe your conscious." That was the conclusion Chey came to after hearing his reasons and watching his stern expression.

"I think it's a little more involved than soothing my conscious."

"Is it?" she challenged.

Mattias stopped in front of her and stared down into her eyes. Without her shoes on, she had to lift her chin another inch to maintain easy contact.

"With you, it's more than just soothing my conscious," he repeated.

"Why? Oh, because I don't fawn over you like other women? I'm not afraid to speak my mind?"

"Viia and Aurora will speak their mind,

have no doubt. As you've seen already. You wear your cynicism like a badge; Viia uses it as a shield. There's a difference. Not to mention that you're generally more pleasant to be around on the whole." He arched a brow and stepped away to the door without warning. Grasping the handle, he paused to add, "The photo session has been moved indoors tomorrow. We're expecting the snow to continue and increase overnight, making an outdoor shoot difficult at best. The entire family will be present this time, so make whatever adjustments you need to."

Chey wasn't sure what to think about her cynical side. He cast a new light on it, however, leaving her puzzled and bemused. Only half paying attention to the details about work, she inclined her head.

"Okay. Where am I supposed to go?"

"The south solar. Urmas will show you if you can't find it on your own." Mattias paused half in and half out of the room. "I would apologize for tonight, except this is who we really are. It's unfair to pretend otherwise."

Chey opened her mouth but he was already gone. Crossing to the door, she closed and locked it in his wake.

What a complicated situation. What a complicated *family.*

Chapter Fourteen

The south solar turned out to be an elaborate solarium with fully one whole wall and half the ceiling nothing but windows. Encompassing a view of the east woods, it was furnished with expensive leather and mahogany furniture, beautiful potted plants and collectible vases along with statues in marble wrought from the finest sculpting hands. Lacking the gilded décor of the King and Queen's private sitting room, the solarium made up for it with its tall backed tapestry chairs, tiki carved tables and large alabaster columns with complex designs engraved into the flaring top and bottom.

While members of the staff moved the furniture to her liking, she stared out the windows at the woods. Off limits to her by Sander's command, she wondered what made them different than the woods to the west. The longer she stared, the more she noticed smaller detail. That was how she came to see the thin wisp rising from the tops of the trees. Squinting against the gentle fall of snow, she tried to bring the sight into better focus.

"Miss Sinclair."

The sharp snap of her name whipped Chey's head around. Urmas stood six feet behind her wearing a frown.

"Oh, I'm sorry. I was looking at the landscape and the snow." She smiled and brushed a strand of hair away from her temple. For the session, she'd chosen another strict suit, this time with pants instead of a skirt, in black and white. It was austere and businesslike without being staid.

"Come away from the windows, please, and tell me if your arrangement suits." Urmas gestured to the collection of chairs and divans Chey rearranged to accommodate the entire Royal family.

The quick look Urmas sent past her head to the window nearly caused her to turn and glance again. What was he looking at? Had he seen the wisp, too?

"It looks perfect, yes. Except maybe move that potted plant a little to the right. I don't want it looking like the fronds are sticking up out of the back of someone's head." She guided an aid to move the pot. Despite the solarium setting, there was still an elegant, regal appearance to the room. One expected Royalty to reside here.

"Excellent. The family will be arriving shortly. You have your placements ready?" Urmas asked with a crisp tone.

"I'm ready when they are," Chey assured him. She glanced at the liaison, curious at his abruptness.

He stepped away to double check everything was as need be.

248

In the interim, Chey pulled out her cell phone to check for messages. She was hoping for one from Sander. Stifling disappointment when there were none, she contemplated leaving one for him. Was that too forward? Maybe he was just that busy with work and hadn't had time to send her anything.

A flurry near the doors brought Chey's attention up. She slipped her phone into the pocket of her jacket as Paavo, Aurora, Gunnar and Krislin arrived. Much to Chey's surprise, the men wore military uniforms of royal blue and silver. The blue, deep and rich, was offset by silver buttons and a splash of red and gold medallions marking their rank on the chest. Silver tassels hung off shoulder boards and a belt at the waist supported a sheath with a sword nestled inside.

Chey understood enough to realize that the darker color of the uniforms indicated their Royal status as well as rank; the other military members wore dove gray and silver, with just the medals denoting their standing.

The women wore understated, beautiful dresses in lighter colors to offset the dark blue of the uniforms. Aurora had chosen pale blue while Krislin wore peach.

Entering in a stream, security arrived as the King and Queen made their appearance. Aksel's uniform was more elaborate, with a band around his chest, a wider belt and insignias ranging from stars to stripes to bars over his heart. Helina's ankle length gown of cream had dark blue piping around the collar and cuffs that exactly matched the blue of the uniforms.

Chey transferred her placements to Urmas, who then guided the Royals into their positions on the divans and chairs.

Natalia arrived a few seconds ahead of Mattias. Her beaded dress was a variation of her mother's. Mattias in uniform was a sight to behold. He wore it proudly, elegantly, exuding a capable air of command and intelligence.

Fiddling with the camera equipment, she made a point not to stare at any of them. It shocked her to realize Viia would not take part in this session. Mattias must have put his proverbial foot down.

"Prince Dare," someone said near the door in greeting.

Chey straightened and glanced over. Finally, the final member of the immediate Royal family.

Sander strode through the archway, blonde hair neatly pulled into a low tail at his nape, jaw smooth and clean shaven. Broad shoulders filled out his uniform, lean hips encased by a sword belt. Regal and authoritative, Sander looked every inch a Prince. His height set him apart from everyone else, even the King, and the sharp glint of his blue eyes missed no detail. His presence was almost too much for the solarium, overflowing with charisma and palpable confidence.

He met her eyes as he stalked by, not shying away from the utter deception he'd perpetrated upon her the whole time.

"You'll catch a fly." His voice didn't carry, the murmur for her ears alone. He glanced at her mouth, indicating she should close it before someone noticed. Then he was beyond the range of the equipment, sheath hanging at his side.

Chey snapped her mouth closed. Shock held her immobile and fury threatened to immolate her where she stood.

Sander freaking-Fisk was none other than the elusive Dare Ahtissari.

. . .

If her position in the household had not been so precarious, Chey would have read that bastard the riot act up one side and down the other.

Liar. How could he have looked her in the eye all that time and deceived her to such a degree? She paused when the realization hit that she'd *slept* with the heir to the throne.

Dear God.

What would Mama Queen have to say about that. Her precious boy bedding the help.

A thousand sarcastic, scathing quips burned the end of her tongue, begging for release.

Just that fast, many things that had niggled at the back of her mind made perfect sense. Why he hadn't needed to be in an office as 'head' of security, the freedom to do what he wanted, when he wanted. How all he had to do was make a call and someone jumped to do his bidding. Like leaving the truck at the end of the canoe trail and gathering the horses from the river.

Fisk wasn't his last name and his mother was *far* from the chef he'd portrayed.

"Miss Sinclair?"

Someone was saying her name. Chey snapped her gaze over her shoulder. Urmas stood there, frowning.

"Yes?"

"Where would you like Dare?"

Oh, *oh* what a loaded question. A muscle twitched in her jaw. Forced to look back at the array of Royals, she studiously refused to meet anyone's eyes and gestured to a spot behind the Queen's chair next to Mattias.

"That'll do."

"Are you all right, Miss Sinclair?" Urmas asked.

"I'm fine." She wasn't fine, she was pissed. Angry as she hadn't been in a long time. Gathering the remote, she transferred further pose instructions to Urmas and waited for everyone to face forward. She could feel the weight of Sander's—Dare's—gaze. Mattias's, too. Just how much did *he* know about his brother's shenanigans? Had Mattias been in on it?

Unthinkable.

252

Pressing her lips together, she clicked the shutter twice. Three times.

"Tell them to smile," she said to Urmas.

He frowned again, then strode forward to request the members smile for the camera.

And so it went. Chey had Urmas arrange the family into a slew of different poses. All the men together. Then all the women. Couples, the King and Queen. Individuals. By the time Chey was through, Natalia was openly complaining and bitching. The Queen required a staff member to fan her while the King finished off his third stiff drink.

Her fury had abated to something cold and unforgiving, movements stiff, gaze anywhere but on Sander. She took only the camera and left everything else for the staff to break down. Sliding it into the case, Chey slung the strap over her shoulder and strode from the room.

"Miss Sinclair." Sander's voice rose through the solarium.

She kept walking.

Someone gasped.

"*Miss* Sinclair," Sander repeated, this time with an edge to his voice.

Chey marched out into the hall without looking back.

. . .

All hell was breaking loose behind her. Chey could hear Natalia demanding Chey be fired for her impudence. The Queen wanted to know *exactly* what was going on, and SanderDareWhatever-his-name-was left the solarium with her name on his lips. Urmas kept a quick pace just off Sander's flank, failing to rein Chey in with a reprimand sharp on his tongue.

Let them all burn.

Was the money worth this? Not hardly. She would rather sleep homeless in a dumpster than be used at this rate. How she would pay back the money she had already spent, she didn't know. At least a month's rent had been worked off. There was some solace in that.

She made it all the way to the end of the private hall before a hand caught her elbow and spun her around. Not a grab or snatch, but a firm grip that wouldn't be denied.

Chey let him. She used the momentum Sander obtained to bring her hand up for a ringing slap. This was becoming customary between them.

He pulled her to him, daring to bring her even closer.

"Don't," she hissed. *"Don't."*

In the hallway, people were gasping again. Murmuring. Shock rippled through the Royals and staff alike.

"You're going to listen to me whether you like it or not," he said, scowling. The blue of his eyes glimmered with determination.

"No, actually, I'm not. Arrange whatever with whoever—I'm going home. Make it happen by tomorrow." Chey tugged her elbow out of his hand. He was intimidating looming over her like that, with his towering height and commanding presence. She turned her chin up, however, defiant in the face of his orders. A part of her was sick, just sick, at the turn of events. What she hated most of all was the ache around her heart. She'd allowed herself to get too close, to trust him and begin to believe in him.

"I don't think so. Not until you listen to what I have to say." Gruff and abrupt, Sander stared at her as if he might bend her to his will by the sheer force of his gaze.

"I'm not your prisoner here. I'm an employee and I just quit." Chey spun on a heel and headed for the stairs. She wanted off the private floor, wanted to put as much distance between herself and Sander—Dare—as she could. Panic over the money was a secondary concern.

Somehow, she would figure the whole sordid thing out.

. . .

Twenty minutes into packing her first suitcase, a knock came at her bedroom door. Changed into jeans and a sweater to make the task of preparing to go home easier, Chey at first refused to acknowledge the visitor. It was Sander, she was sure, ready to defend his reasons for lying.

The knock came again.

She ignored it.

Five minutes after that, another trio of knocks.

Exhaling her frustration, she tossed down the folded shirts and went to the door. Swinging it open, she found herself face to face with Mattias.

"I don't want to talk to you or anyone else. I'm leaving tomorrow," she said, turning away from the door but leaving it open. She knew he would just come in anyway.

Mattias entered and closed the door behind him. Like her, he had changed out of his uniform into something more suitable for every day business. Black slacks, white shirt with the buttons open at the throat.

"Unfortunately, you won't be leaving tomorrow. The weather will not permit it. This storm is growing and becoming dangerous. You will have to stay until it passes."

Chey put her hands on her hips and stared at the wall rather than Mattias. When her anger got the better of her, she turned a hot look his way.

"Were you in on it, too? Did you know the whole time?"

"I knew after the shooting in the woods. The day he took you to the cabin for the first time." Mattias observed her with shrewd, dark eyes.

"Why didn't you tell me? Why didn't *someone* tell me who he was?"

"Because he preferred that we didn't,"

Mattias said in a matter-of-fact tone.

"And what about what *I* prefer?"

"It wasn't your choice at the time. It was Dare's."

"What is his name, anyway?" She loathed that she would always think of him as Sander rather than Dare. Which only added fuel to her ire.

"Sander Darrion Ahtissari, is his full name. Those of us closest to him call him Dare."

Small relief. His real name *was* Sander. "And you're wrong, Mattias. Someone should have told me."

"It would have changed things--"

"Of course it would have changed things!" She slapped her hands on her thighs in exasperation. "He's the heir to the throne!"

Mattias thinned his lips. "Precisely. Did you ever stop to think that maybe he wanted to just be himself without all the trappings of his position? If you would consider something besides yourself a moment, you would understand why he did what he did."

Bristling at his insinuation, Chey paced from the bed to the window. Snow fell faster than it had earlier beyond the panes.

"What I know is that he lied."

"He delayed the truth," Mattias argued.

Chey scoffed. "Please, Mattias."

"Do you really think he thought he could hide it forever? Ask yourself why he wanted a head start when he got to know you. Why would he have reason to wait?"

An answer popped into her mind immediately. She didn't want to admit the reasoning behind it. Mattias however, proved to be as quick witted as ever.

"Because he sensed something between you. He was *interested* and instinctually knew that if he told you who he was, it might have been impossible for you to bond the way you did."

Chey rubbed her forehead with her fingertips. "Yes, and fat lot of good it'll do me. I remember, most clearly, the talk we had about your broodmares. And without repeating your Mother last night, I am as far from a prime choice for dating as there could possibly be. Sander knew this, yet he proceeded to play with my heart, my affections—and it was wrong."

"I disagree. Perhaps because I live this life, and I know how impossible it is to find someone who will like you for you and not the title attached to your name. There are no guarantees anything will work out between you, but the two of you have a head start that none of us ever get. He saw a rare opportunity and took it. What is so wrong with that?" Mattias leaned a shoulder against the door frame.

"He lied to achieve his goals, that's what's wrong with it."

"That is a matter of perspective. He told you his real name, that wasn't a lie."

"Yes, and also told me he was the head of

security, which he is not." Chey arched a brow at Mattias, daring him to deny it.

"A small consequence." He brushed it off as nothing.

"Why did you take me to the city? Invite me to the gala? For the reasons you said, about liking my company, even though you knew about Sander and I?"

"That and I was keeping an eye on you for him."

Chey stopped pacing to stare at Mattias. "What?"

"I said, I was keeping an eye on you. From the day of the shooting, we suspected something was wrong. We never did find the shooter, you see."

"But you said--"

"To put less strain and stress on you. Dare was worried, especially after the attack in your room. So I took it upon myself to enjoy your company while making it a lot more difficult for the culprit to get their hands on you. At least for the time you were with me." Mattias delivered the facts with a straight face and honesty in every word. "In the very beginning, we had to make sure it wasn't an attack directed at Dare. He ruled that out pretty quickly."

Processing the details, Chey stared alternately at the floor and at Mattias.

"Why didn't he just come back to the castle? Why does he live down there in the cabin?" None of that made sense to Chey.

"He arrived back early from his...trip...abroad, and decided to delay confronting the Queen about the woman she intends to be his bride. He stays there often, as a matter of fact. There is, unless you are blind and deaf, dissension in the ranks around here."

"Mm, yes. The woman he was supposed to court or something. What happened?"

"I think you should let him explain." Mattias straightened away from the wall. "And I think you should not hasten away from Latvala so cavalierly. Take a moment to breathe, to assess. Try to put yourself in his shoes."

Mattias had a point. It did not lessen her ire, exactly, but she could see that Sander deserved a chance to explain himself.

"All right." Truth be told, Chey didn't *want* to leave. Dysfunctional family aside, Chey was fascinated by the inner workings of the castle and its occupants. It did not give her hope for she and Sander, however. Chey understood that whatever they shared, it was temporary. The Queen—and probably the King—would never allow them to date on a serious level. Even Mattias bringing her to family functions as a guest caused unbelievable turmoil. Knowing they were doomed before they ever got off the ground put that familiar ache back in her heart. How depressing. And how infuriating that he wasn't the simple man she believed him to be.

"I'll see you tomorrow, if not sooner." Mattias exited without another word.

Rubbing the back of her neck, Chey stood near the window and watched the snow swirl down from the sky. Her emotions were a wreck. It might take her a day or two before she was able to face Sander with any kind of control.

With the weather worsening by the hour, time was a commodity she had plenty of.

Chapter Fifteen

For a full day and a half, Chey kept to herself. The only visitors she had were Ingel and Elise when they brought breakfast and dinner. Lunch was a meal Chey went to the kitchen for herself. She knew Mattias had something to do with Urmas and Allar laying low after the explosive session in the solarium, and for that she was grateful. She didn't know what she would say to any of them.

Returning the second day from the kitchens, where she'd filched a simple sandwich and a piece of fruit, Chey opened her door and was just about to step across the threshold when a folded note on the floor grabbed her attention.

Bending down, she picked it up and opened it.

Meet me at the old castle at five.

This was the first she'd heard from Sander, too, since that fateful day. She wasn't sure how she felt about seeing him again. A part of her was still quite angry. Another part wanted to have it out, to hash the details away from the castle and prying eyes and ears.

Smoothing her thumb across the slanting script, she folded the paper and pushed it into the pocket of her jeans.

The clock on the fireplace mantel told her she had three hours to wait. In the meantime, she took a shower and chose a fresh pair of jeans to pull on. Because the weather was so frigid, she donned an ivory sweater with a thick collar and sleeves to her wrist. Taking a long coat from the closet, she laid it over the bed. She dried her hair until every ounce of dampness was gone then added a few curls, a light layer of make up, and a dab of perfume on her throat.

Checking the window, she noted the sky was still the color of iron, overcast though the snow had finally stopped falling. She wondered if the road to the old castle would be impassable. Collecting a flashlight and a few tissues for her nose, she stuffed those into the pocket of her coat. Her phone went along with them.

At four-thirty, she headed down to the truck parked just outside the bailey walls. It took her five minutes to scrape snow and ice off the hood and another five to defrost the windows.

Climbing inside, she turned up the heat and drove toward the road. Pleased to find it already plowed, she rumbled along at a sedate pace, music set low, thoughts on the meeting ahead. Now was the time to decide what she was going to say. What she was going to do.

What *was* she going to do?

Sander had played her. Maybe not for a fool, but he'd played her nevertheless. The lies stacked up against his favor and omitting that he was next in line to the throne was as bad as lying about it.

On the subject of thrones—the King and Queen would never allow them to date if they knew. Which might also have been a reason why Sander kept their tryst hidden. The best she could hope for long term with Sander was to be his some-time mistress. As his duties stacked up and he took over ruling the country, he would have less and less time. Not that she would willingly be some married man's mistress anyway.

The more she thought about the position she was in, the angrier she became.

All of this could have been avoided. Sander wasn't the only one to blame. She should have —done something. Asked more questions. Checked his background. Chey barked a little laugh at the thought.

"Hello, you've just tackled me onto the ground, and you're kind of hot, and we might some day have sex, so will you submit to a background check so I can make sure you're not really the heir to the throne? That would be terrible if I fell for you--" Chey stomped the brakes when that last sarcastic sentence came out. The truck fishtailed and came to a stop sideways in the road. She sat forward, hands gripping the wheel. She hadn't fallen for Sander—had she? Was it possible in a week? Had it only been a week?

Sitting back, stunned at the thought she

might be falling for him, Chey took a moment to just *breathe.* That would be a disaster, especially considering all the cons she'd listed in her mind. Too many cons, not enough pros.

No, whatever glimmer this was had to be stifled. Before she really did fall in love and wound up with a shattered heart. The heir apparent was not a man she had the luxury of loving.

Putting the truck in gear, she eased back onto the road and started for the old castle. At least now she knew what kind of conversation she was going to have when she got there.

. . .

The headlights cut through the growing gloom, illuminating the facade of the old castle. Chey chided herself for feeling like she was letting go of something special, of wondering what might have been. Some day, Sander would rule all this. The history of the events in the ruins before her was part of Sander's ancestry, had shaped the generations leading to his birth. It was awe inspiring, intimidating and fascinating all at the same time.

Cutting the lights and the engine, she zipped her coat up higher toward her throat, pulled the keys from the ignition and climbed out. Although the snow had stopped, she could feel tiny needles of sleet pelting her cheeks. A light spray that could very well grow thicker and heavier before midnight. Sander's Jeep wasn't here yet, but she decided to wait inside out of the immediate cold. The door might be locked, but the arching shape of windows with no panes allowed her access anyway. Sliding over the stone sill, she straightened and glanced around the great hall. Digging the flashlight out of her pocket, she snapped it on and shined it over the ceiling and the walls.

She still couldn't believe she'd slept with the heir to the throne. The man who would inherit the highest seat of power in the land. She'd canoed with him, laughed with him, played games with him. Sander had allowed her to glimpse pieces of himself he probably wasn't able to show many people. She hated the sorrowful pang that lanced through her for the talk to come.

Meandering into the tall foyer, she was about to lean against the archway and wait when the flashlight beam passed over a piece of paper on the floor. Walking to it, certain it hadn't been there on her last visit, she bent to pick it up.

South tower.

Sander must have been dropped off, thinking he would catch a ride back to the cabin with her. And wasn't that arrogant of him, to just assume she would forgive and forget and hop right back into bed with him?

"I really don't think this is funny," she muttered to herself. Stuffing the note away, she climbed the stairs to the second level and from there hit the other stairs that would take her to the South tower. A gust of chill wind blew through one of the windows on her way up, making her shiver.

Good grief it was cold.

Arriving at the door to Andra's old room, she pushed it open and stepped in.

"I don't know why you're making this all dramatic and poignant by bringing me up here." The spear of light landed on a masculine silhouette standing at the window. Looking out, like he was contemplating things.

For whatever reason, the posture struck Chey as solemn, maudlin. It tugged at her heartstrings. The beam cut across a few strands of golden hair before she snapped the light off. Tucking the flashlight in her pocket, she approached and stood directly behind him.

"Sander, look..." Trailing, she set her hands on his waist over the thick coat he wore. She shouldn't be touching him, shouldn't allow her heart to ache over the treachery *he* had wrought. This could have been avoided, she repeated to herself. Just then, as Sander turned his chin toward his shoulder to peer at her with one eye, Chey realized what her subconscious had been trying to tell her ever since she entered the tower.

Something was *off*. It was the shape of him under the coat, his height, even the breadth of his shoulders. Now that she was almost pressed up against his back, Chey discovered that he was too short, too stocky, and the eye that peered at her over his shoulder wasn't blue, but black. Or so dark brown the shadow made it look black.

Either way, she let go all of a sudden and stumbled backward. He turned, proving as his features were briefly illuminated in the faint overcast glow from the window, that he wasn't Sander at all.

"We *did* try to warn you," the man said, his accent heavy and rolling.

Oh, this couldn't be happening.

Pivoting on a heel, Chey bolted for the open door. Just as she surged out onto the landing, a large hand clamped down on her shoulder and spun her around. She swung a fist as she went, a scream tearing up her throat.

The fist connected with a strong jaw but had little effect.

Trapping one arm against her side, the brute bulled her back into the tower room. Chey kicked at his knee, hard, causing the man to grunt in pain. He did not release her, though his grip slackened a little. Putting both feet down, she dug the tread of her winter shoes into the floor, making it twice as hard for him to move her forward. Another scream bounced off the stone walls, deafening in the confined space.

"Shut up," he growled near her ear, picking her up to move her three feet fast toward the window.

Chey tipped her head forward and slung it back as hard as she could, legs kicking out in front of her to catch against the window sill or the wall—*anything* to stop her from being thrown out.

That was his intent. To dump her out and make it seem as if she'd jumped or fallen.

The bastard.

A crack of bone was her reward. The brute released her all at once and staggered to the right.

Chey stumbled forward, catching a hand on the wall. Spinning, she didn't run for the door but for *him,* using the momentum of his stagger to send him sprawling into the wall with a shove. With any luck, he would hit his head and go unconscious.

No luck. He crashed against it, blood dripping from his nose, but didn't go down.

Then she ran. Ran like the devil himself was breathing down her neck. To the door, onto the landing. Down one step, two. Panting, heart racing, unable to see as well as she needed to.

A grunt and rustle behind her told Chey the man was already in pursuit.

Oh God.

One hand shot out to the wall to help steady her descent, to maybe help catch her if she suddenly stumbled and fell. Or was pushed.

What she didn't expect was to run into a body coming *up* the stairs as fast as she was going down them. The collision bounced her back a half step and she screamed again, throwing an elbow forward to try and connect with a chin or a nose.

An arm wrapped her shoulders and rolled her past to the stairs below. Putting himself between her and the brute just before impact. Chey caught the distinct scent of Sander's cologne, knew by feel and by the shape of his body it was him.

She glanced back in time to see Sander engage the brute; the men battled on the stairs, fists flying. Chey saw the whole thing in strobe-like glimpses rather than as a whole. There wasn't enough light spilling in a skinny window to cover the entire staircase.

Backing down another three steps, one hand braced on the wall, Chey watched in horror as one man threw the other onto the stairs and battered at his face with a fist. Just then, she couldn't tell who was who. Both had blonde hair, both wore thick coats.

A *boom* blew through the stairwell, so loud that Chey temporarily went deaf.

One man slumped onto the stairs.

"*Sander!*" Regardless of the danger to herself, she rushed back up the stairs, ready to gouge the eyes out of the brute. The thought of Sander dying sent a spike of fear straight through her.

"I'm all right, I'm all right," Sander said, pushing himself off the step. The gleam of a gun shone in his hand.

Chey, overwhelmed with relief that Sander hadn't been shot, hugged him tight.

He caught her and held her with one arm, the other lowering the gun to his side.

"What happened? Who was that? Is he dead?" Chey asked, twisting a look down.

"I don't know who it is yet, too hard to see in here. But he's dead unless he's talented enough to survive a gunshot to the head." Sander sounded disgusted.

"I thought he was you up in the tower. He pretended to be you to lure me here," she whispered, turning her head away from the fallen man.

"I knew something was up when I saw you heading out to the truck. Come on, the cavalry should be here shortly." Sander guided her around the dead man and down the rest of the stairs.

Chapter Sixteen

The interrogation took place in a formal office Chey had never seen. Located on the first level at the far back of the castle, the room sported a long, square table, endless chairs and a television screen attached to the wall at one end.

Coffee came at regular intervals as Chey precisely and accurately detailed all the events that had happened since her arrival at the castle. Allar was there, as well as Hendrik with his scar and his scowl. Urmas paced at one end while an array of security took notes and asked questions. The King and Queen's personal guard, decked out in military uniforms, flanked the hall outside the doors.

Sander and Mattias sat at the other end of the table, alternately answering questions and asking them, as well as studying her with astute, keen glances. They couldn't look more different, one with dark hair, dark eyes, the other blonde and blue. Mattias had the slimmer build of the two, though he was still built and honed.

"Are you positive, Miss Sinclair, that there is nothing else you recall that might lead you to believe this man did not act alone?" Allar asked.

Chey rubbed her temple with her fingers. She considered the question, a repeat of one before, so that they knew she was cooperating fully.

"No. I—well. Once, Sander asked me--"

"Prince Dare, please," Allar said, politely interrupting her.

Chey cleared her throat. "Prince Dare asked me once about the person who attacked me in bed. I told him that I didn't have the sense that the person was large, as in as big as the man in the tower. I can definitely say it was not him that pinned me down that night."

"Things can seem different in the dark, when you're woken by surprise. Are you certain, one hundred percent, Miss Sinclair, that it was not the man?" Allar asked.

"Yes."

"That statement means the man acted with another, leaving no room for doubt," Allar clarified. "Which also means that not just one, but *two* people wanted you dead almost as soon as you arrived here."

Chey, not one for shrugging, lifted a shoulder helplessly. What could she say? She had no more clues why someone would want her dead barring her job.

"I checked and double checked every photo I've taken since arriving. I can't find anything in any of them that seem compromising to someone else. Then again, maybe I just don't know what I'm looking at. That's the only thing I can think of. He and whoever he's working with thought I caught something on camera, or thought I *might*." That was the best Chey could do.

The men in the room fell to silence.

"In the tower, he used the term 'we', you said," Allar mentioned.

"Yes. I heard that distinctly," Chey replied.

"I think we should have her stay on castle grounds here until we have more information," Sander said.

"I agree, Your Highness." Allar set down the pen he'd been holding and glanced from Sander to Chey. "Within sight of the guards when you're outside at all times, yes Miss Sinclair?"

"Of course." Chey wouldn't bring up quitting again right now. Not after all this. Sander and Mattias, as far as she knew, were the only ones who knew she intended to leave. And she still did, once the investigation was over. Nothing had changed about that.

"All right. Let's convene for now. Thank you for your time, Miss Sinclair." Allar stood from his chair. Sander and Mattias followed suit.

Chey rose and inclined her head to the group. Her gaze touched on Sander's for a split second before she exited the office.

What a tangled mess she was in.

. . .

"We need to talk." Sander grasped her elbow and guided her into a darker parlor before Chey ever reached the stairs.

"I suppose we do." Rounding into the room, with the cold fireplace and vague light spilling in three tall windows from lamps outside, Chey walked across to a lush sofa and leaned the back of her hips against it. Folding her arms over her chest, she watched Sander close the door, dousing them into gloom. Dressed in sleek black slacks and a snowy white button down, he looked less like the rugged Sander she was used to and more like first in line to the throne.

Coming to a stop ten feet from where she leaned, he mimicked her stance and crossed his arms over his chest.

"Tell me what's on your mind," he said, inviting her to begin.

Chey didn't say anything at first. She stared, taking in the smooth line of his strong jaw, the gleam of his blue eyes. He'd left his hair tied back into a low tail, which only enhanced the handsome angles of his face. The cut just above his eye from the fight had stopped bleeding some time ago. A faint bruise was forming on one cheek as well, sure to be darker by morning. Finally, the pent up rush of emotion couldn't be stayed any longer.

"You. You're on my mind. I'm pissed off at you for negating to tell me who you were, and while I get it, that changes nothing. Why, you ask? Why does it change nothing? Because you're playing with my heart. It's not like we met, had a one night stand, and never saw each other again. You *knew* I would be here for the next four months and yet you engaged me anyway. We both know that nothing can ever come of this except a few good nights in bed. And while that might have been all right at some point in my life, it's not all right now. It's not all right for you to assume that's *all* it would be to me." She never raised her voice, but the words started coming faster halfway through. At one point, that was exactly what Chey thought Sander would be to her. A winter fling to be forgotten once she went home. Funny how things changed.

He regarded her with an unreadable expression. Finally, he looked away to the window, dropping his arms to bring a hand to his jaw. He rubbed his fingers along the defined edge. Thoughtful.

"No, it probably wasn't right to withhold my status from you. But I did, and I still stand by my reasons," Sander said. He paced toward the window and away, making a slow circuit in front of her. "You have to understand that this doesn't happen every other day. It hasn't happened once in my lifetime until you. Every meeting, every date, every idea of romance is arranged. I know in advance who I'll be taking to dinner, who I'll be escorting to a party, who I'll be expected to kiss goodnight. Then along comes your haughty self, with your face slaps and your indignation. You didn't treat me different because you didn't know—and I enjoyed it. I liked goading you and pushing your buttons. You're not like the women I'm expected to court. And I'll freely admit—I wasn't looking further than a one time shot with you. Not at first. But you have this way about you. It grows on a person who appreciates a little rebellion along with beauty." Sander glanced at her.

Expecting a diatribe something along these lines and hearing it outright were two different things. Enraptured by the stalking half circles he made, by the way his clothes fit and the sheer command of his presence, Chey could only stare and swallow down the sensation of sawdust in her throat. A full minute went by in silence. She sorted through how she felt compared to what he said. At the end of all things, however, the outcome never changed.

"All right. So you wanted to flirt and be flirted with outside the usual parameters. I can't blame you for that, not after what I've seen and heard. Mattias told me what it was like for you and at the time, it seemed so loveless. So...futile. I don't envy your titles, money and position when you can't even choose to be with someone you love. Or even like. Despite all this, Sander, it doesn't change the outcome. Sure, we can flirt and go canoeing and have our fling—but what then? Why risk heartache when we both know it's going nowhere?"

"You didn't strike me as the type of woman who gave up easily, or allowed someone else to run roughshod over you without a fight, that's why."

"What does that mean?" She narrowed her eyes.

Sander swerved out of his languid cycle of figure eights and walked right up to her. He stared down, searching her eyes.

Chey had to crane her chin up another notch because he was so tall. Being this close to him made her heart pick up speed. It shortened the breath in her throat. She waited him out, almost afraid of what he might say.

"It means I want you to stay and fight. Stay and risk it. Throw caution to the wind because you think I might be worth the time and effort to get to know me better. It means, Chey, that I'm willing to take the system on if you're willing to honor your agreement to finish the four month contract my family signed you to. We need time to figure out if we're right, if *this* is right, and we have a perfect shot to do it if you'll change your mind about leaving." He didn't touch her, just stared into her eyes like he might discern her answers before they left her mouth.

She knew what he was asking her to do. Sander thought they might have a chance, wanted to give them a shot at making it together and to hell with the odds. To hell with the rules and regulations and what his parents wanted. But he was right—they did need time. Time for more canoe trips and dinners and talks about the future. They had to have a chance to date, to learn each other, to see if the spark would catch flame or if it would wither and die. It meant risking her heart, risking falling in love and then being rejected if he didn't feel the same.

It also meant allowing her a better look at what it took to be involved in the Royal family. Already she had her doubts. Chey wasn't bred for this. Maybe it would have been different if he was second or third in line to the throne—but this meant that one day, if it all worked out, she would be Queen.

Queen. She couldn't wrap her mind around it. Couldn't picture herself in Helina's role. Did she even want that kind of life? Did she want the stress, the spotlight, feeling like she was a bug under a pin? And what of the system? Would she and Sander even be allowed to marry? Chey suspected it would be a lot harder than just deciding to tie the knot.

"Will you give me a day or two to think it over?" she finally asked.

"Of course. I'll hold off telling anyone else that you're quitting until I hear what you're going to do. I'll also make sure there are no shoots scheduled so you have time to recover."

"Thanks." She unfolded her arms and straightened from her lean. There was a lot to consider between now and the next two days.

"You have my number. Text me if you need anything. And remember not to leave the sight of the guards," he reminded her.

"I won't." She tried on a small smile that didn't quite reach her eyes, then stepped past him for the door. Chey didn't want to touch him because she fretted she might wind up in his bed for the night and that would cloud her judgement.

She exited without looking back.

Chapter Seventeen

When Chey walked into her bedroom, the first thing she smelled was food. Elise hovered over the cart, pulling off lids to platters of roast chicken, salad and steaming vegetables.

"Elise, you're a Godsend. That smells heavenly." Closing the door, Chey toed off her shoes and approached the small table near the window.

"Mister Mattias had your dinner delayed until you were ready and said you might appreciate a hot bath. So I ran you one." Elise transferred the plates to the table. "Wine, water or coffee, Miss Chey?"

"Wine, please. A whole glass." She thought drinking straight from the bottle sounded fantastic, but didn't want to scar the staff with her heathen habits. She fell into a chair and slouched, rubbing her head with her fingers.

Elise uncorked the bottle and poured, then set the glass on the table. She peered down at Chey like a hen at a newborn chick. "If you would like the bath first, I can recover all this and wait."

"Thanks. No, I'm all right. Just a lot on my mind." She picked up the glass, still feeling odd about people waiting on her in a private setting. At a restaurant, one expected it. Here,

Chey felt conspicuous and strange.

"I'll just put the clean towels out and then I'll go," Elise said.

"That would be great." Chey picked at her food while Elise disappeared into the bathroom.

"It is terrible what happened to you at the ruins. I am so glad you are okay." Elise's voice echoed off the tile.

"So am I. What a nightmare." Chey set down her fork and picked up the wine again. She had several long sips.

"Do you have any injuries? Should I bring more ointment?"

"No thanks, Elise. I'm fine. Just a few minor scrapes. The scare was the worst part."

"I've been to the tower room. Just once. I never wanted to go back. It is scary by itself, is it not?"

"It's not pleasant, I'll say that." Chey set down the wine and propped her elbow on the table. She knew she needed to eat, but her appetite was waning quickly.

"There, everything is set out. Just ring if there is anything else, Miss Chey." Elise paused at the door to smile.

"I will. See you in the morning." Chey returned Elise's smile, though hers felt more hollow than she meant it to.

Elise departed with a quiet click of the latch.

Once she was gone, Chey picked at her food for another fifteen minutes. She managed to get enough down to stave off hunger pains over night and covered the rest with lids.

Lighting a few candles in the bathroom, she sank into the jacuzzi tub, flipped on the jets, and soaked for a while. Her mind raced with questions and suppositions, discarding one idea for another. It was maddening and disconcerting, the constant buzz of activity. She couldn't shut her thoughts down at all.

By the time she crawled out of the tub, she was wrinkled and her skin was pink. Still, her mind revolved around Sander and his request that she at least think about staying and giving them a shot to work it out.

Too restless to sleep, she pulled on jeans and a simple zip up, velveteen shirt in pink. After sliding on socks and shoes, she departed her room for a walk. Glad to see the hallway empty, she decided to head downstairs to the gallery and the portraits lining the walls. Passing several guards, she returned polite nods and wondered at something vague that kept niggling her mind. It was one of those things she couldn't pinpoint for the life of her yet persisted enough to pose a distinct distraction.

At least until she reached the gallery. It was a long hallway on the main floor with paintings of Ahtissari ancestors dating back centuries. All the Kings were on the left, the Queens and children on the right. Crossing her arms over her chest, she began meandering along the corridor, taking her time with her study of each one. The archways leading into parlors and libraries and other formal rooms were dark at this time of night, the guests of the party long departed.

Several feet from a dark sitting room, she heard the low thrum of voices. Pausing, she cocked her head to see if she heard it again. Maybe she was imagining it. A moment later, the voices resumed. Taking a few steps closer to the doorway, she tried to make out the words. They were male voices, no doubt about that.

"So just *how* well did you look after her, anyway?" Sander asked with a note of curious caution.

Chey caught a gasp before it could slip free.

"Does it matter?" Mattias answered.

"It does if there are feelings involved."

"She's a unique woman. I'm not sure she realizes her own appeal," Mattias said.

"Did you kiss her?" A harder edge entered Sander's voice.

"Not once. But I thought about it a time or two."

Shocked, Chey covered her lips with her fingers. Mattias wasn't hiding the spark that had flared between them. She would have preferred to brush it under the carpet and forget it ever happened.

"And Chey? Is she interested in you that way?"

"There was a mutual attraction—*is*—a mutual attraction, but it was never more than that. You needn't worry, brother. I'm not going to attempt to win her from you."

Chey had half a mind to interrupt them. She wanted to tell Sander that yes, there had been a mutual attraction, and yes, she had wondered what Mattias wanted from her. More than anything, she wanted to tell him that after the canoe trip, she'd consciously put a block up between her and Mattias. Not just that...Sander had become the focus of her attention and interest. She wanted to confess that in the tower, on the stairs, for those few terrifying seconds after the gunshot, she'd been stricken with fear that Sander had gone down instead of the attacker.

"A wise choice. We have a chance, her and I, and I mean to put us both to the test. I'll crush anyone who stands in my way."

"Spoken like the true heir to the throne," Mattias said. Wryness could be detected in his reply.

"Don't act like you wouldn't do the same. We all know your 'relationship' with Viia is, and has been, a complete farce." Sander scoffed. The clink of ice in a glass followed.

"It has kept mother off my tail for an entire year. We can't say the same about you, can we?" Mattias laughed a devilish kind of laugh. "Speaking of which—good luck with *that*."

"Mm." Sander hummed agreement. "What's worse, is her father and mother want the match, too. I believe he is going to petition father for an official marriage decree."

The woman Sander had gone to see. Whoever she was, she must belong to a powerful family. Chey frowned. Her assessment that things would be difficult for her and Sander was truer than she knew.

"If that's true, Dare, you might as well send the little photographer home and forget about any designs of courtship."

"No. This time, Mattias, I *will* at least give myself a shot to see if I can have something close to normal with Chey."

Chey straightened and took two steps back from the edge of the doorway. She'd heard all she needed to hear. More than she ever meant to hear, too. It was time to escape back to her room and think hard about her decision to stay or go. The obstacles in her path were many and great, and there was every indication she would wind up the one with a broken heart.

Pivoting on a heel, she came face to face with Natalia.

. . .

"Do you make it a habit to eavesdrop on *private* conversations, *Miss* Sinclair?" Natalia asked, raising the volume to be heard half way down the hall in both directions.

Chey gasped first, then cringed. There was no way Mattias and Sander could miss Natalia's announcement. How, exactly, would she defend herself this time? To say she hadn't been doing what Natalia accused her of doing would be an outright lie.

A shuffle and shift of muscle under material indicated Mattias and Sander had entered the hallway.

Natalia, tumbler in hand, swirled the amber liquid in the glass before taking a drink. "Brothers, look what I've discovered lurking outside your door. And you actually entertained the idea of *courting* this bitch, Dare? You can't be serious."

"Watch your mouth, Natalia," Sander warned.

Chey turned to face Mattias and Sander. "She's right. I was listening."

Mattias wore a vague frown. Sander's expression was curiously neutral. Chey knew better than to think he was unmoved by her eavesdropping.

"I don't have to watch my mouth, Dare. This is blasphemy. She's unfit to even consider dating, much less anything else. An *American?* Really?" Natalia broke into a shrill, disbelieving laugh.

Chey twitched with anger. Natalia's condescending glance made her want to cold cock the woman.

"Mattias." Sander said his brother's name in a way that sounded like another warning.

Mattias thinned his lips and looked from Chey to his sister. Stepping across the short distance, he grasped Natalia's elbow and firmly guided her away from Sander and Chey.

"Hey, *hey!* I wasn't done. Doesn't Dare want to hear that I plan to tell mother everything?" Natalia called back.

Mattias muttered threateningly under his voice in their own language.

Natalia had no other choice than to go with Mattias. She threw more threats out as she went, some in her native tongue, others in English.

Stricken by the entire ordeal, Chey looked away from the pair to the floor at her feet, then aside and up to Sander. He was watching her with the same unreadable look he'd had when he came out of the sitting room.

"I didn't know anyone was in the room. I was just looking at all the portraits," she said in her own defense, gesturing to the long line of paintings down the hall. It didn't explain why she'd lingered to listen, and she knew it.

Sander raised his glass and drained what liquor remained. At first, he said nothing. Finally, he asked, "Do you have feelings for him? Now is not the time to lie."

"*No.* I care about his well being, yes, and I think we're friends. We get along well and he did not lie that there has been an attraction between us. But it was never what you and I have. At first, I didn't like you at all," she confessed in her typical blunt way. "But after you fixed lunch that day, and then with the canoe trip—I got to see a different side of you than the man who tackled me off the mare."

His lids lowered to cover half his eyes. The

corner of his mouth ticked like he briefly fought off a smile. "And?"

Chey brushed away an errant strand of hair from her cheek. She maintained eye contact with him. "And then I looked forward to seeing you. Thought of ways to visit the cabin and spend more time there. And if I'm being really honest, I thought the dress Mattias sent for that disastrous dinner with your family had been sent by you and expected to see you standing there when I opened the door. He caught me off guard and I didn't know how to say no after all that. I would have much rather spent the evening with you."

Sander laughed and took two steps closer. "See, that's what I like about you. Most women would never admit that my brother sent you a dress and that the dinner with my family was a disaster. But not Chey Sinclair."

Distracted by the glimpse of his chest past the few undone buttons of his white shirt, Chey lifted her gaze to his when he came to stand right in front of her. He exuded casual sexuality coupled with a regal mantle that had been missing at the cabin. Or had it? Perception was a funny thing. Maybe he'd worn it all along and she'd been too distracted by his sheer sense of presence to notice. In a giant hall full of staring portraits and gilded accents, Sander seemed larger than life. He dwarfed the space with his predatory charisma and incisive stare.

"It was. A disaster, I mean. The King all but ignored me, The Queen interrogated me and if looks could kill, I would have been dead on the floor thanks to Natalia. Maybe Viia, too." Now that she thought about it, half the room had been upset at her presence.

"Interrogated you about your lineage?" Sander guessed.

"Yes. I made the gross mistake of mentioning miscarriages in my ancestral past." She quirked her mouth and eyed Sander closely. Would that matter to him, too? It was his job, of a sort, to carry on the family line.

Sander's expression waned, then turned wry. "I can imagine how well that went over." Leaning into her, he stretched an arm and set his glass on a small half table against the wall.

Chey resisted putting her hands on his hips, or his sides, but she gave in to the desire to take a deeper breath while he was close. The masculine scent of his skin and cologne tantalized the senses. Looking at him from under the veil of her lashes, she expected him to steal a kiss.

He didn't. Sander, though watching her like a hawk, leaned back to his original position and kept his hands to himself.

"She's never going to approve of this," Chey whispered.

"No, she's not," he replied honestly. "You have a lot to think about. What you've been exposed to so far is only a fraction of the machinations and turmoil that go on around here. I won't lie—sometimes, this will not be easy. Even if we manage to get past the obvious obstacles, you'll be expected to gain citizenship here, learn the language and customs, live here at least ninety percent of the year and take on all the responsibilities of your position."

Chey hadn't considered citizenship or living arrangements or any of that. It was overwhelming.

"To start with," she guessed.

"To start with, yes. There is a lot more."

"I never did thank you," she said out of the blue.

"For what?" He cocked his head.

"Earlier. In the tower. Thank you for showing up when you did."

"I saw you leave, like I mentioned, and decided to follow. I knew you wouldn't be going out at that time of the evening, in this weather, unless something happened."

"It occurs to me that they must have been watching us the whole time. That day we visited the castle...they knew." Once again, Chey had a niggling feeling that she was overlooking something. Her brow furrowed in thought.

"I'm sure. The tale that goes along with the tower is infamous around here, so it probably wasn't difficult to guess that's why we went." He paused, then asked, "What is it?"

She glanced at his eyes. "I don't know. I keep getting the sensation that there's something I'm overlooking. A little niggling feeling that I can't get rid of."

"And you can't pinpoint it?"

"Not really. I guess I'll remember when I'm supposed to remember."

"Maybe." He sounded thoughtful. "Do you want me to walk you to your room?"

"No. I'm going to finish my perusal of your ancestors then head up." There were so many guards around that Chey wasn't worried of an attack in the castle.

"I'll see you tomorrow, then. Good night." Sander hovered close, then, after a quick smile, headed the opposite direction.

Chey wondered if he was withholding his attention to make her want it more. And it was working, the bastard. She was sorry she hadn't reached out. To touch, to kiss, to...something. Any kind of contact was better than none.

After he was gone, Chey turned to the hallway. Many pairs of painted eyes seemed to follow her every move. If she'd been of a superstitious nature, she would have thought the ghosts of Sander's ancestors were weighing and judging her, deciding if she would do justice to the man himself and the Ahtissari family name. But she wasn't, and they weren't. They were just images in oil on canvas, preserved for posterity, reminders of those who had come before.

It was up to Chey to figure out if she wanted to engage in a courtship that might become something more.

Chapter Eighteen

The following day, after a restless night's sleep, Chey showered and changed into clothes geared for cold weather. Drawing on a coat that landed a few inches past her knees, she gathered her camera, departed the castle and headed outdoors. Ankle deep snow didn't inhibit her trek into the bailey, where she paused several times to take pictures of the castle. It was stunning with a dusting of white on the turrets and spires.

From this vantage, a surreal quality surrounded the entirety of the Ahtissari family seat. The daunting structure sprawled over several acres of land, protected by gates and guards, the Royal flag flying high from a tall mast. There was so much history, so much prestige.

If she was truthful, Chey didn't feel qualified to even consider dating a Royal heir. She was a small town girl, from a small family, with no worldly experience behind her. The Ambassadors, Liaisons, Princes and other Royalty of the world would likely eat her alive.

There were no guarantees that she and Sander would even make it beyond the courting stage. The question became whether she thought it was worth the risk to try.

Snapping another picture, she let the camera hang around her neck and gave her situation the grave consideration it deserved. She had to make a decision soon.

In her quest to find new angles to capture the castle, she made her way through the bailey, into a covered corridor and out into the front courtyard where the cars parked to drop off Royals and guests alike. Just before she could step out of the shadows, a flurry of movement from the doors drew her attention. Pausing near the wall, she watched as a security detail emerged and fanned out near a sleek black car parked before the stairs.

A moment later, Sander strode out, dapper in a suit of black. The shirt beneath was crisp and white, his tie a pale blue that probably accentuated his eyes to perfection. Wearing shades to cut the glare of the sun, he had his golden hair tied back at his nape.

Her heart flipped over at the masculine authority he projected, at how her initial instinct was to drop everything and run to him.

Bringing up the camera, she snapped several shots of him on his way to the car and getting inside. It was almost inconceivable to her that this was the same man who had taunted and goaded her on the canoe trip. The one who had expertly cooked her fajitas and tackled her to the ground at the first sound of gunfire. He wore many hats, could step into any guise and pull it off effortlessly.

Outdoorsman, canoe expert, chef, businessman, heir to the throne. Fighter. Lover.

After the car pulled away, Chey spent the next hour photographing the castle from the courtyard and the flag that flew high overhead. Engaging in something she loved so much helped her sort through the problems with Sander.

Finally, with enough pictures to suit, she made her way inside. Taking the stairs to the second level, she headed to her bedroom and closed herself behind a locked door. Removing the camera from around her neck, she set it on the dresser and popped the latch to pull the little image card out.

It was then that the thing that had been niggling at her bloomed into a distinct thought that made her stifle a gasp with her fingers.

Setting the card down, she hastily pulled her cell phone from her pocket and shot off a quick text to Sander. She hoped he didn't have his turned off for whatever errand he'd left on.

"Put the phone down, Chey."

Closing her eyes, Chey exhaled a quiet breath of frustration. And fear. Turning around, she faced Elise.

The maid had a gun with a long silencer pointed at her head.

"I should have realized last night that no one would have told you about the south tower," Chey said. That's what had been bothering her. Elise had known details no one would have given her. Why hadn't she thought about it sooner?

You've been distracted with everything else. It wasn't any consolation, her distraction with Sander and his offer.

"I wondered when you were going to put the pieces together," Elise said. She wore the usual gray athletic wear with white stripes down the sides.

"I just don't understand *why,* Elise. Why?" Chey hadn't put the phone down yet. She held it cradled in her laced fingers.

The muzzle of the gun trembled. Elise stared at her down the barrel, dark eyes gleaming and intent. "You should have taken the early warnings we gave you and left after the shooting. Come to the table and drink from the water."

Chey wasn't so shocked to hear that those shots in the early morning by the lake had been a warning. An attempt to scare her off before she really got in deep with her job. She glanced at the table and the bottle of innocuous looking water. Something insidious must be inside. Poison? An undetectable substance that would stop her breathing or her heart? She'd heard of such things.

Perhaps if she screamed, a guard would get here not long after Elise pulled the trigger. Chey might have a chance to recover from a bullet wound as long as it wasn't to the head or a major organ.

As if reading her thoughts, Elise shook her head. "Do not think it. I am an excellent shot and you will not have a chance to summon a guard before I kill you. Now come over here."

In Chey's hands, the phone chimed a text alert.

Elise narrowed her eyes. "Put the phone down. *Now.*"

Chey couldn't text Sander back without risking her life. She tossed the phone onto the bed.

"You still didn't tell me why. Or who. Who put you up to this, Elise?" Chey stalled approaching the table. She wasn't drinking whatever was in the bottle. Certain death lurked there. At least she had a slim chance of surviving a bullet wound.

"You ask many questions. *Move.*" Elise gestured with the gun.

"I deserve to know. I'm carrying it to my grave anyway. What does it matter?" Annoyance flared to temporarily smother the fear. She wanted to know whether it was Natalia or Viia that ordered the attacks. It had to be one or the other. Elise, as far as Chey could discern, had no reason to hurt her.

"Viia sends her regards. You should not have meddled." Elise gestured again, this time more impatiently, toward the water.

Chey had expected Viia or Natalia but hearing a name put to the madness still shocked her. Viia. The woman probably paid the staff for inside information. It wouldn't have been difficult for her to find out about the meetings with Mattias. There were eyes everywhere, as the attacker the night in her room had suggested.

Taking a few steps closer to the table, Chey glanced across the surface for a weapon. A basket of fruit sat in the middle, useless.

"You don't want to take the fall for this, Elise. If you shoot me, then you'll be prosecuted for murder."

"I think not. It will be covered up like all the other dark secrets of the Ahtissari's."

"What dark secrets?" Chey frowned. Did Viia have enough pull to create that kind of cover up?

"On the count of three, Miss Sinclair, I am going to pull the trigger whether you have taken the water or not," Elise said. "One--"

"Okay, okay." Chey flashed her palms and closed the final few steps to the table. Picking up the bottle, she twisted off the cap. Elise stopped counting. Chey bought herself another second in the guise of lifting the water. At the last second, she gripped the base and shook water out of the bottle at Elise. Right at her face. A hard splash that landed exactly where Chey intended.

Startled, Elise jerked. The gun wavered.

It was now or never. Chey lunged for Elise's wrist, swinging her arm wide. A bullet thwipped from the silencer, penetrating the ceiling.

Elise clenched her teeth and shot her other

hand out for Chey's throat.

Struggling to keep the gun trained away, Chey was about to shout for help when Elise clamped her jugular and squeezed. All that came out was a low garble of noise that wouldn't gain the attention of anyone.

The door to the bedroom burst open as the women tilted precariously, wrestling for control of the gun. Chey saw motion in periphery and the next thing she knew, blood bloomed bright in the center of Elise's forehead. The maid slumped to the ground.

Chey whipped a look to the door, fear lodged thick in her throat, sure that whoever had just entered meant to take them both out.

Allar stood there, gun still drawn, frowning first at the dead maid, then at Chey. "Are you all right, Miss Sinclair?" he asked, lowering the weapon.

"Oh thank God. Yes, yes, I'm all right." Shaking, Chey backed away from the body on the floor while Allar, followed by Hendrik, rushed inside. They went straight to Elise and knelt down to feel for a pulse.

Allar pulled his fingers away from Elise's throat. "She's dead."

. . .

Interrogation, round two, went much as Chey expected. Allar led the inquiry, with Mattias present along with Urmas and several other prominent members of security.

Sander, to her dismay, had not yet arrived back from his trip.

She recited the events exactly as they happened, leaving out no detail. Each question put to her she answered with precision and patience, though her mind was a hundred miles away.

What dark secrets had Elise meant? Things from the past? Murders, like Andra? Just how far would an elite family go to keep those kinds of secrets?

All the way.

She had no doubt that Elise's death would be explained away as something other than what it had been. The Royals and their advisers wouldn't want it getting out that staff members were following through with threats and murder for others.

And something else bothered Chey. Something no one touched on during the investigation. Would Elise have risked her life for someone not yet a part of the Royal family? Viia wasn't even Mattias's fiance. Yet that had been the name on Elise's lips, not Natalia. It would have made little sense for Elise to lie when she thought Chey was as good as dead.

The deceased told no tales.

Then again, perhaps the money had been too good for Elise and the attacker in the tower to pass up. He'd been a stablehand, Allar informed her, somehow coerced into doing murderous deeds for someone else. Money was excellent motivation.

Departing the office, tired in ways she hadn't been since her parents death, Chey headed for the stairs to the second floor. By now, Elise's body should be removed from her room. It gave her the creeps, just a little, to think of sleeping there after Elise's death.

"Chey."

She paused in the upper hallway at the sound of Sander's voice. Turning, she saw him striding toward her in the same clothes he'd had on a few short hours ago. He even still had his sunglasses on.

"Hi." She murmured a greeting, arms crossed over her chest.

Sander didn't hesitate. He enfolded her into a bear hug, pulling her against him. "Are you all right?"

She unwound her arms and slid them around his middle. He smelled divine. A combination of masculine cologne and the scent that was uniquely his.

"Yeah. I should have known when Elise mentioned the tower that you or the other security wouldn't have told her about it."

"I knew the moment you asked me in the text. We were in Kalev by then and I had to see my meeting through."

"Allar got there quickly. It's a good thing. I'm not sure I could have overpowered her."

Sander leaned away and cupped her face in his warm hands after pushing up his sunglasses. "I'm sorry you were ever subjected to that kind of danger. Viia will be arrested and sentenced."

"I guess she really felt threatened. It's a shame. If she only knew." Chey met and held Sander's eyes. Her fingers stroked over the back of the fine suit, feeling the lay of muscle beneath. He felt strong and competent under her palms.

"She has been a social climber from day one. I never expected her capable of this, however." Sander stroked the pads of his thumbs over her cheeks.

"I have to say—even with all the dirty looks and warning glances, I didn't expect it, either." Chey paused, then asked, "Is it always like this? I mean with the danger?"

Sander pressed his lips together and looked past her down the hall. Toward some distant, irrelevant point. Then met her eyes again. "I will not lie. It can be. We receive threats weekly. Most are disgruntled musings from a disturbed mind, but others...others are real and tangible. Rarely do we have this sort of situation, though."

"But you *do* have them."

"Yes."

Chey dropped her gaze to the knot of his tie. "She spoke of dark secrets. Was she being melodramatic, or is there more to it?"

When he hissed in annoyance, Chey glanced up. Sander wore a complicated expression, as if being forced to chose between lying and telling half truths. Chey didn't deceive herself into thinking she would be trusted with anything more.

"I'm not at liberty to disclose those kinds of things at this time. I'm sorry," he said.

"I understand." And she did. Chey had not been a part of his life nearly long enough to earn the right to whatever secrets they were hiding.

"I've had your things moved to another room. I'll show you there." He looked like he might kiss her, then shifted out of the tilt and dropped his hands.

"You read my mind. I wasn't looking forward to going back to the other one." Chey slid her hands off him as well and followed Sander down the hall.

"I don't think many people would be comfortable. If this new room does not please you, we'll find one that does." He went all the way to the end of the hall to a pair of double doors on the left. One of these he opened with a key and entered, holding it for her to follow.

It wasn't just a suite, like her other had been, but an entire apartment. A separate living room, kitchenette and two bedrooms, along with an expansive bath, took up the whole corner of this floor. Windows overlooked the woods to the east and multi-paned doors led onto a broad balcony already furnished with a table, four chairs and an umbrella. The overhang prevented snow from reaching half the balcony; the rest was covered in several inches of the white stuff.

Chey investigated it all. The décor was as

stunning as every other room in the castle, done in tones of cream, sage green and faded purple. Gold trim accentuated the walls, the ceiling and the furniture.

"This more than suits. Thank you for thinking of it," she finally said, meeting up with Sander at a dining table near the windows. She ran her hands over the intricate carving around the edges.

"It will remain your room should you decide to stay on."

Chey glanced at his eyes. He stood resolute behind a chair, hands resting over the back. She couldn't read his expression any better than earlier. The comment in itself was a reminder, though, one she did not miss.

"I'll keep that in mind."

He inclined his head. Reaching up, he slid the sunglasses off, folded the arms, and slid them into the front pocket of his coat. "How about I bring you dinner tonight? I'll make it myself. Say, six?"

Chey almost asked him if they could go to the cabin, but refrained. She needed to stay here and learn to accept things the way they were—or not.

"That sounds fine. Six it is."

He smiled and stepped away from the chair. "I have a few things to do before then. I'll see you at dinner."

"I'll see you then, Sander." He would always be Sander instead of Dare.

Chey followed him to the door, said a last

goodbye, and closed it behind him. She engaged both dead bolts.

By the time they were finished with dinner, she intended to give him an answer.

Chapter Nineteen

Chey dressed for the occasion as if they were attending a formal ball. She wore black, with a snug bodice embroidered in matching black thread and a skirt that floated around her calves. She secured the half up-half down style of her hair with a beaded clip and added a heavier layer of make up that accented her eyes, cheeks and lips.

No matter how many ways or angles she studied her reflection in the mirror, she still couldn't see a Princess or a Queen. She just saw Chey, American rebel, with rather plain features and a sassy pout.

Sander arrived at precisely five minutes to six.

She opened the door to find him standing behind a cart, resplendent in a suit of navy pin stripes, white shirt and polished shoes. It seemed they both had the same idea regarding attire.

Struck by his magnificence, she didn't immediately think to move out of the way so he could push the cart in.

He cleared his throat and arched a brow.

"Oh, sorry. Hello." She stepped out of the way.

Sander pushed the cart in like he did it

every day, as if he wasn't heir to the throne, used to other people doing it for him.

"You look fantastic." He passed an appreciative glance at her as he went by.

"So do you. Who needs fancy, noisy restaurants?" She closed the door and locked it in his wake.

Sander set up the table with impressive speed and agility. He laid out china, silver platters laden with bias-sliced peppered beef, steamed vegetables on skewers and individual caesar salads. Wine followed, red as blood, with the bottle left to chill in a bucket.

He held her chair and then took his own after removing his coat.

"You miss no detail," she pointed out, deferring to a sip of wine before anything else.

"Do you?" he asked with an arched brow.

"I'd probably forget two or three things if I tried to do this." Chey smiled a lopsided smile.

He laughed. A warm, resonant laugh that left tingles on Chey's spine.

"We're brought up learning this. It's second nature to us all, boys and girls alike." Without preamble or fuss, he started on his meal.

"Well, when you have to deal with Royalty and others of your ranking, then I suppose it's necessary. I know the basics, at least." She liked that he didn't stand on ceremony just to eat, even if they were dressed so elegantly.

"It's sort of expected, yes." His eyes met hers across the table.

Chey spent the next few minutes

alternating between bites of food and staring at Sander. He was such a presence in the suite, and for more than the way his shoulders stretched broad under his shirt. He was the same man she'd consumed fajitas with in a cabin, and not the same man at all.

"What's on your mind?" he asked.

"How you seem so different than when we're at the cabin. Yet not different at all. It's weird."

He laughed. "It's just the clothes and the castle. Changes perception."

"Maybe it's the man instead." She arched a brow.

"I'm the same Sander, trust me. You just didn't know then what you know now. It changes things."

Chey considered it. "Could be. It's fascinating, though."

"You don't look like the same woman, yet there's no escaping the blunt tongue and the gleam of cat-like curiosity in your eyes." He looked amused.

She meowed.

Sander must not have been expecting it. He guffawed.

"I can't help that I'm curious." Grinning, she straightened the lid on the platter of meat that had been sitting askew. "Or that I'm blunt."

"No, I don't believe you can." He had a drink of wine, blue eyes gleaming. Then, "Tell me five things I don't know about you yet."

Chey took a bite, chewed, and considered his question.

"I suffer on-again, off-again OCD. It seems to get worse when I'm nervous." She sat back in the chair, turning her wine glass around in circles by the stem.

His brows arched hearing that, but he said nothing.

"I'm fascinated by history, I love green olives, and I've always wanted to visit Holland."

"Why Holland?"

"I saw pictures when I was a girl, and it's been an obsession ever since." She had another drink of wine, watching Sander absorb her idiosyncrasies.

"Interesting. That's four," he said.

Chey set down the wine glass and dabbed her mouth with the napkin. Done with her meal, she set the cloth aside and rested her hands in her lap. She'd saved the best for last.

"And I've decided to stay in Latvala and be courted by a Prince."

Sander paused with his glass halfway to his mouth. Lowering it to the table, he stared. Then, he smiled. A devilish, pleased kind of smile.

"You're just full of surprises," he said.

"I try. Now, tell me five things about you I don't know."

He drew in a slow breath and regarded her across the table.

"I play the violin, I love Divinity candy, I've

never been to Disneyland but always wanted to go--" He paused and gave her the stink eye, like he thought she might make fun of him. "I absolutely *loathe* figs and I planned to dance with you tonight after dinner."

Chey echoed his guffaw from earlier and clapped her hands together in amusement. "Disneyland? That was random."

"I know. I'm still a kid at heart or something." He winked across the table.

"With all your money and position, I can't believe your parents never took you."

"We were busy with other things. Mostly, the desire to go was from when I was about ten, but I'd still go now."

"I've been twice. It's as fun as it seems," she confessed. "Even when you get older."

"Then we'll make plans to visit. Maybe when we go back to—what was it? Seattle?" He pushed his chair back and stood. Rounding the table, he walked over to the entertainment center and flipped on the stereo.

"Wait, when 'we' go back?" She covered the rest of the dishes, then left her chair. "You want to come to Seattle?"

"Why not? I'd like to see where you're from. Where you grew up." Something dramatic and orchestral poured from the speakers. He turned back and advanced on her.

"I think that's an excellent idea, actually. I live in a small apartment. You won't be impressed," she warned him. Meeting in the

311

middle of the room, Chey set a hand in his and another on his biceps when he swept her into a slow sway.

He laughed. "You don't have to prepare me. I already know you don't hail from Royalty."

Goosebumps rained down Chey's arms at the expert way he guided her through the easy steps of a dance. He was proficient, skilled. She skipped a glance from his mouth to his eyes, and smiled.

"It's going to be an interesting four months," she whispered.

He held her gaze, then lowered his head until his lips were next to her ear.

"You can count on it."

. . .

About the Author

Born and raised in Corona California, Danielle now resides in Texas with her husband and two sons. She has been writing for as long as she can remember, penning works in a number of genres. To date, she has published fourteen novels and nine short stories. Her interests vary wildly: reading, traveling, photography, graphic art and baking, among others.

There is a black cat named Sheba involved who thinks Danielle's laptop is her personal grooming station.

Check her website for trading card offers, giveaways and announcements!
www.daniellebourdon.com

More books by Danielle Bourdon:

Romance:
Heir Untamed (Royals Series 1)
King and Kingdom (Royals Series 2)
Heir in Exile (Coming March, 2013)

Fantasy/Romantic Suspense:
Sin and Sacrifice (Daughters of Eve 1)
Templar's Creed (Daughters of Eve 2)
The Seven Seals (Daughters of Eve 3)

Thriller/Romantic Suspense:
The Society of the Nines (Society Series 1)
Violin Song (Society Series 2)
Vengeance for the Dead (Society Series 3)

Young Adult/Fantasy:

The Fate of Destiny (Fates 1)
The Fate of Chaos (Fates 2)
The Reign of Mayhem (Fates 3)
A Crisis of Fate (Fates 4)

Paranormal Romance:
Bound by Blood

Fantasy:
Dreoteth

Made in the USA
Lexington, KY
13 May 2014